The American Candidate

A Jayne Sinclair
Genealogical Mystery

M. J. Lee

ABOUT M. J. LEE

Martin Lee is the author of two series of historical crime novels; The *Jayne Sinclair Genealogical Mysteries* and the *Inspector Danilov* series set in 1930s Shanghai. *The American Candidate* is the third book featuring the genealogical investigator, Jayne Sinclair.

ALSO BY M. J. LEE

Jayne Sinclair Series

The Irish Inheritance

The Somme Legacy

Inspector Danilov Series

Death in Shanghai

City of Shadows

The Murder Game

Fiction

Samuel Pepys and the Stolen Diary

Writing as Martin Lee

The Fall

This book is dedicated to all those who suffered during World War Two. May we never see such terrible strife ever occur again.

Contents

Chapter One

July 23, 1942
Wielodz, Krakow, Poland

For some reason, she stopped in the middle of the wooden bridge and clutched her wicker basket closer to her chest.

The wind rustled through the leaves, whispering its secrets carried from far away. The early morning sun peeped through the canopy, throwing long shafts of mote-laden light across the clearing. Beneath her feet, the stream trickled louder, weaving its gentle way down to the Vistula.

She cocked her head to one side. The birds in the forest had gone quiet. *Why had they stopped singing?*

The bridge wasn't constructed from stone or anything remotely permanent – only two long planks of wood, placed side by side across the stream to help the villagers get to their fields without tramping through the muddy ground.

She could feel the planks bend and flex beneath her bare feet, the wood warm to the touch despite it being early in the morning.

Why had the birds stopped singing? she thought again.

For a moment, she considered running back to the village to wake her mother and her brothers, but what would they eat for breakfast? It was her job to come to the forest early each morning to look for mushrooms hidden in the mulch and leaves of the undergrowth.

She was adept at spotting the Kania, Kurka, Mask and Pieczarka hiding in the damp loam of the leaf litter. Early morning was the best time to gather the harvest; before the sun had shrivelled their caps in the harsh glare of its rays.

1

She loved the forest at this time, when the chaffinches were singing their joy at seeing the world and the robins flitted from tree to tree, their red breasts puffed out and important like old-fashioned soldiers on parade. The squirrels raced up the trunks and across the branches, looking for nuts and fruit to last them through the long, cold winter, the young ones more intent on playing than finding food to store.

It was her time. The time when she was alone and there were no other chores to be done. No chickens to feed. No washing to hang on the line. No cotton to be strung into the long fibres her mother would later use to weave cloth.

She no longer went to school. There was no point, they had all been closed down. But she would have left at thirteen anyway. As her father said, 'Girl no use at school, can't do the housework if thy nose is buried in book.'

She missed the books, though. Their stories of far-off lands, of princes and princesses, of clever animals that could walk and talk, and tales of wooden boys whose noses grew with every lie they told.

But she had her own stories to keep her company during the day. She made them up as she washed her brother's clothes or stole eggs from the chickens, barging them off their nests with a knock of her hand. They were her stories, not to be told to anybody else, for her and her children when they arrived.

The birds were still quiet.

Had they not woken this morning?

Why were the birds not singing?

And then she saw the men, at the edge of the tree line, just beyond the stream.

Were they the ghosts of the forest?

They stood still, one kneeling down and pointing a long stick at her.

She stared at them, too shocked to move. Or shout. Or run.

The one with the long stick lowered it. He had blond hair and a round face with stubble on his chin as thick as her father's. He brought one long dirty finger up to his mouth and laid it across his lips. She heard a long shushing sound, like the wind rustling through a thatched roof.

She knew this game. It was often played by her mother when her father was asleep in bed, after he had come home from a night drinking vodka with Mr Resnick. It was a sound that meant 'don't say a word, don't make a noise, don't wake the angry bear'.

But that was before he had left them to fight in the war. So long ago now.

She stood still.

On either side of her, men in grey with metal hats ran across the open glade and splashed through the rocks and mud of the stream. None of them looked at her.

The man in front smiled. Not a happy smile, but one filled with sadness.

She took her basket, turned and jumped off the bridge, racing back to the village along the well-worn path. She had to tell her mother about the strange men in the forest before it was too late.

Chapter Two

July 23, 1942
Wielodz, Krakow, Poland

The Unterscharführer watched as the small girl ran back to the village, still carrying her wicker basket. She would shout a warning to the others, but it was too late. By now, Leutnant Gerber would have brought the rest of the squad round to the rear, blocking any chance of escape.

His men were fanning out through the forest, running as quickly as they could, but still covering each other and using the infantry tactics they had spent many long and painful hours learning in the training camp at the Lichtefelde Barracks.

Move. Stop. Cover. Look. Move again.

So simple but so effective.

He walked across the small wooden bridge where the girl had been standing. The planks bent and flexed with his weight. His men were at the edge of the tree line now. One open field lay between them and the village, a single cow standing in the centre of it.

He walked forward, no longer seeking cover. The girl's shouts came to him, caught by the breeze and carried across the open field: 'Mamusia, mamusia.'

He didn't mind the noise now. It didn't matter. Nothing mattered any more.

He raised his arm and waved his men on.

They stood up and began walking towards the village across the open field, not bothering to conceal themselves. If they were going to be attacked, now was the time.

The Unterscharführer expected to hear the staccato zip of a machine gun any second. Or the soft pop of a mortar escaping from its metal tube. Or the harsh crack of a rifle.

But he heard nothing.

All was silent in the village. Smoke reached out from some of the chimneys, thin tendrils of grey-flecked ash stretching for the sky. Off to the left, a cock crowed his ownership of a flock of mangy hens. A solitary dog barked. Even the girl's shouts could no longer be heard.

His men pressed on, advancing steadily across the open field. He came level with the cow. A pair of mournful eyes stared at him, the mouth still moving from side to side, chewing its morning feed.

He removed the Luger P08 from its holster, took careful aim and shot the animal between the eyes.

It dropped to its knees on the spot and slowly rolled over, one hind leg kicking out at an imaginary taunting devil.

The men would have beef tonight. It was so long since they had eaten beef.

The shot galvanised both his men and their prey. They began hurrying towards the rush-roofed houses. From the village itself, he heard shouts.

But it was too late.

It was always too late.

With practised efficiency, his men worked their way through the village, kicking in doors and herding the shell-shocked people into a grassy field in front of a wooden hall. There were a few ancient, un-shaven men, fewer boys, and many women and young girls.

One of the old men advanced towards him, shouting something in Polish or Yiddish, he didn't know which.

He brought his Luger up and across the shouting face, feeling the metal barrel bite into the man's nose.

A scream came from the girls and the man collapsed at his feet.

'Really, Unterscharführer, you will have to control your temper.' Leutnant Gerber stepped forward and helped the old man to his feet, carefully avoiding the blood dripping from his face.

'Yes, sir. I will, sir.'

'We mustn't startle our little flock, must we?'

He pointed to the herd of villagers now gathered together, each clinging to the other like frightened sheep.

'It will only make our work more difficult. And we wouldn't want that, would we?'

'No, sir.'

Leutnant Gerber looked down at a spot of blood that had landed on the toe of his newly shined boots. He took out a handkerchief and wiped it quickly. 'What is the name of this place, anyway?'

'Wielodz, sir. Sixty-two inhabitants. Mostly Jews.'

The Leutnant looked over the village, taking in its ramshackle houses with their rush-covered roofs, the hastily planted kitchen gardens, the washing lines hanging from battered posts, the chickens scrambling for food in the rubbish, unconcerned by anything else that was happening.

Then he sighed and in a bored voice announced, 'You may as well begin, Unterscharführer.'

'Yes, sir.'

His men didn't need any further orders. Two of them lit their torches and began to set fire to the roofs. A collective moan rose from the throats of the villagers as the black smoke billowed from their houses, to be followed by the first crackle of flames.

The moans were silenced when four members of the squad separated the first group of twenty men, women and children, herding them against the white-washed wall of the village hall. The soldiers were shouting all the time in pidgin Polish, *'Pospiesz się, pospiesz się.'*

The firing squad was already in position; they were a well-drilled team, adept at their work. The villagers huddled together as the shots rang out. A loud, well-disciplined volley.

As if all the strength had been removed from their bodies by an invisible wind, the villagers collapsed in front of the white wall, now pockmarked with holes from stray bullets.

The Unterscharführer stepped forward, carefully placing his feet in the gaps between the corpses. He was looking for those small signs of life; the flicker of an eye, the groan from an open mouth, the last attempt to crawl away.

He shot those villagers who were still alive in the head, as a last act of mercy.

The second set of victims was hurried forward by the soldiers and made to stand in front of their dead neighbours. One woman refused to go, sobbing, pulling at her hair and pushing a small boy toward one of the soldiers. He shoved the boy back to her, kicking him in the arse.

She shouted at the soldier in Yiddish, and threw herself at him, clinging to his uniform and his boots, begging him to save her son.

He took out his pistol and shot her through the head. The boy stared at the limp body of his dead mother, not saying a word, his hand touching the edge of his lips.

The shots rang out again.

And once again the villagers fell down like puppets with their strings cut by a sharp knife.

The last group of villagers were hurried forward. One elderly man stumbled and was helped to his feet by a young woman, his daughter perhaps. He mumbled his thanks and carried on walking. Next to him an aged woman was chanting her prayers, staring up to the sky where the cotton candy clouds hid the face of her god.

The Unterscharführer noticed the girl from the bridge in this group, holding on to the skirts of an older woman. She walked past him, staring all the time.

For a moment, he was tempted to reach out and grab her, pull her out of the crowd to his side.

But he didn't, and she continued to walk past him, handing on to the skirts of the woman he presumed to be her mother.

The moment was gone.

The villagers lined up in front of the dead bodies of their neighbours and the shots echoed off the white walls. In the distance, a murder of crows rose from the forest, cawing and croaking at the disturbance.

Once again, the villagers fell to the ground.

The haze of gun smoke drifted off to join the black clouds pouring from the thatch of the village houses, rising together up to the sky in a thick murky plume.

The Unterscharführer checked his pistol was loaded and moved among the villagers lying at his feet for the last time.

Chapter Three

July 23, 1942
Wielodz, Krakow, Poland

She wasn't afraid.

Around her some people were moaning, others praying. A few more struggled with the soldiers who forced them forward or shot them dead on the spot.

Her cat ran through her feet and off towards the woods. One of the soldiers took aim as if to shoot it, but then smiled and shouted something to his comrades. The cat ran on, saving one of its nine lives.

A soldier was pushing her mother forward now towards the white wall, the pile of neighbours lying in front of it. She saw one of her friends, Sabcha, lying on the ground, her hand still holding the yellow ribbon she used to tie her hair. She mustn't have had time to fix her hair that morning. How she loved her long, flowing hair, held in place with its bright yellow ribbon.

She saw the soldier from the forest. A thin blue line of smoke was escaping from the barrel of the pistol he held in his hand. His eyes were a deep shade of green. She hadn't noticed his eyes before. How cold they were. No emotion, no feeling, just a pair of eyes like emeralds in a marble statue.

Perhaps she could write a story about a man with eyes like emeralds?

She wanted to run now, back into the forest where the mushrooms grew, but her mother held her close. She knew she could hide there. They would never find her in the circle of beeches where the best mushrooms grew. Nobody knew about the place except her. It was the place where she spoke her stories out loud to the listening trees.

9

A soldier pushed her mother and her towards the wall of the village hall, with its mound of people lying in front.

She walked past the man with the green eyes, holding on to her mother's skirts. They pushed her into a group and, for the first time, she noticed the men with the long sticks kneeling down ten yards away.

She stumbled over a hand. It held Sabcha's yellow ribbon. She bent down to pick it up. It mustn't get dirty. Sabcha wouldn't like her ribbon to get dirty. As she did, there was a loud noise and her mother fell across her.

She struggled to get up. But her mother's lifeless body pinned her down. Other bodies were on top of her too now, covering her, not letting her breathe.

She wanted to scream, but she didn't, knowing it was the wrong thing to do. Another body fell on top of her. The smell of damp overcoat filled her nostrils and something hot and wet began to drip on her face. She felt it run down the edge of her cheek and off her chin on to her dress.

Please don't dirty my dress, I don't want to wash it again.

A loud moan came from her mother. She snuggled tightly into the still-warm body.

And then another bang from a gun, closer now, the pungent smell stinging her nose. The body lying above her was being moved. She could see the sunlight and the man silhouetted against the sky.

She watched as he bent closer to her. On his collar, the two lightning flashes of the SS twinkled brightly in the sun.

The long metal barrel appeared in front of her eyes. Its end was a perfectly round circle with a wisp of blue smoke escaping at one side.

And then it pointed away from her. The man's dirty fingers took the yellow ribbon from her hand.

The barrel was pointing at her face again.

She looked past the metal, and the hand holding it, to the lapel of the grey jacket the soldier was wearing. A badge with two flags side by side. On the left, the flag of death; the swastika. And next to it another flag, a pretty flag, one she had seen when she was in school. The flag of Britain – the Union Jack, she remembered it was called.

Why was it called the Union Jack?

Then the end of the metal barrel erupted in flame.

Chapter Four

Monday, April 17, 2017
London

Jayne Sinclair spotted the two men immediately. They sat in the left-hand corner of the small restaurant with their backs to the wall. As soon as she entered, they both stood up in a gesture of old-fashioned politeness.

Jayne crossed the empty restaurant, avoiding the chairs and tables heavy with cutlery and wine glasses. A single waiter stood leaning against the door to the kitchen. He was staring at his cuticles, paying no attention to her.

'Mrs Sinclair, I presume.' The elder of the two stuck out his hand. The accent was American; Boston or somewhere nearby, Jayne thought. He was stockily built, wearing the classic Brooks Brothers shirt and tie combination with an instantly forgettable dark blue suit.

'Mr Wayne?' Jayne placed her bag on the back of the chair and took the offered hand. The shake was firm but the hand itself was slightly clammy, like it was wearing a medical glove.

'Please, call me Jack. Before you say anything, my real Christian name *is* John. And yes, I've heard most of the jokes about saving the Alamo. In my parents' defence, he was an extremely popular actor at the time. Luckily, they always called me Jack and I like to continue the tradition.' He gestured for Jayne to sit opposite him. 'Unfortunately, as far as we know, there is no connection in my family to the great actor.'

The other man leant over and shook Jayne's hand without saying anything.

'This is my assistant, David Mercer,' Jack Wayne added.

The man was young and preppy, the product of one of the better New England schools, Jayne thought. He was handsome in a fresh, young way, with the body of somebody who enjoyed the ritual of morning exercise.

'Happy to meet you, Mr Mercer. You sent me the email?'

'I did, Mrs Sinclair.'

Jack Wayne interrupted their conversation. 'Can I get you anything? How was the journey?'

Jayne glanced back towards the empty restaurant and the single waiter standing as far away as possible.

'Oh, I arranged that we shouldn't be disturbed. I hate to talk in restaurants full of people, don't you?'

Looking at all the unoccupied tables, Jayne shook her head. 'I'm fine, Mr Wayne.'

She had left Manchester early that morning, taking the train to London Euston and a taxi to the restaurant, arriving punctually at 1.00 p.m. It was a beautiful English spring morning with a bite of coolness in the air to add freshness to the day. The journey itself had been smooth and easy, with the beauty of England zipping past outside her first-class window like a series of tourist postcards.

Jack Wayne checked at his watch. 'You're on time, Mrs Sinclair, I like that in a woman. Shall we get down to business?'

Jayne nodded her head. Finally, she would find out what this was about. The email had been cryptic; a promise of a week's work as a genealogical investigator at $1000 a day plus expenses. Jayne's father was getting remarried ten days from now, and the money would come in handy to give him and his new wife, Vera, a wonderful honeymoon cruising Alaska. Plus, she could pick up something special for the wedding at Harrods. A gift she couldn't get anywhere else.

She had come to London, for better or for worse, not knowing what to expect. It wasn't like her to be so undisciplined, but since the split from her husband a few months ago, life no longer held any terrors for her. 'Seize the day' was her new motto, so here she was seizing it fiercely.

Jack Wayne brought his hands up to his mouth as if in prayer, touching his fingertips to his lips. 'We have a family history problem we would like you to investigate.'

Jayne stayed silent, waiting for him to continue.

Instead, David Mercer produced a sheet of paper, passing it across the table.

Jack Wayne spoke as she reached for it. 'Before we describe the mission, Mrs Sinclair, I'm afraid there is the small matter of a non-disclosure agreement.'

He smiled like a crocodile who had seen a young calf fall into the river. 'Please take your time to read it but the gist is that you are unable to divulge anything to outside parties about what we tell you. Or anything you may discover in the future.'

Again, that unsettling smile.

Jayne glanced through the document. It was the usual confidentiality agreement, not normal but also not unusual in her profession. A pen appeared in front of her face, held by David Mercer. She took it and signed the paper at the bottom, dating the signature.

Jack Wayne removed the sheet of paper, stared briefly at the signature and passed it back to David Mercer.

'What's this all about, Mr Wayne?'

'Straight down to business, Mrs Sinclair, I do like a woman who gets down to business.'

Jayne resented being patronised by this man. She had taken an instant dislike to him. Perhaps it was his clammy handshake or the smug, self-satisfied smile. Or even the military language. She investigated people's family histories, she didn't embark on missions. Whatever it was, she was tempted to get up and walk out. He could stuff his job and his money in a place where the sun didn't shine.

He continued speaking. 'I can now tell you the nature of your mission.' Once again the hands came together in prayer.

'I'm all ears, Mr Wayne.'

'We would like you to investigate the next President of the United States.'

Chapter Five

Jack Wayne stared at her for ten seconds, expecting a reaction.

No emotion crossed Jayne's face. She had worked out years ago that, in situations like this, the best strategy was not to do anything. Let silence do all the work for you. It had been particularly successful in her previous life as a police detective. Within the force she was famous for being able to extract confessions from even the most hardened criminals; silence, as many a priest knew so well, was a great precursor to confession.

Jack Wayne coughed once. 'Did you hear what I said, Mrs Sinclair?'

'I heard you perfectly. I was waiting for an explanation.'

It was David Mercer who coughed this time. 'Mrs Sinclair, I...'

His boss stopped him by holding up a hand. Instantly, the young man was silenced.

Again the crocodile smile. 'I will attempt to explain it myself.'

David Mercer opened a briefcase and handed across a folder with a large crest on the cover. Jack Wayne took it without looking at or thanking his assistant. 'As you are aware, the next Presidential election in America is in 2020. Obviously, we are checking into possible candidates now in preparation for that election.'

Jayne noticed a glossy sheen covering the man's forehead and cheeks as he spoke. 'Who is "we", Mr Wayne?'

The man smiled again, his fleshy lips coming together like two inner tubes. 'I'm sorry, I should have explained earlier.' He handed over a small white card, embossed with the same crest as the folder. Jayne read it quickly: *Jack Wayne. Vice President, Democratic Solutions.* Beneath was an address in Washington.

'Are you affiliated to any of the major parties?'

'We are not. And I will explain why later, if that is okay with you?'

Jayne nodded.

He smiled his crocodile smile and brought his hands up in front of his face. 'How much do you know of recent political developments in America?'

'Only what I read in the papers.'

'Well, you probably don't know much.' He laughed. 'The newspapers; those institutions so beloved of President Trump and his followers. Ninety per cent of them and most of the mainstream media supported Hillary Clinton, and still she lost. Why?'

Jayne shrugged her shoulders. She wasn't going to play this man's game.

'Because she was a politician. And Americans hate politicians almost as much as they hate taxes. The Democrats made a huge mistake in nominating a career Washington insider as the candidate. They should have known better. Their previous choice, Barack Obama, was a young senator from Chicago, not seen as a part of the political elite. His rallying cry for change touched a large segment of the American population fed up with politics as usual. In 2016, Donald Trump campaigned as an outsider, not as a politician.'

'Wasn't "Drain the Swamp" one of the rallying cries at many of the Trump election meetings?'

'That's correct, Mrs Sinclair. He struck a chord with those voters tired of the shenanigans of Congress and the Senate. They wanted change, and what

17

did the Democrats give them? Another politician. As President Trump would say, "A huge mistake, a *huuuuuge* mistake".'

A deep intake of breath and a quick glance across to his assistant. David Mercer laughed even though he had probably heard the joke many times before. It was a well-rehearsed moment, Jayne thought. Jack Wayne had made this speech many times.

'So, the last two Presidential election winners have been political outsiders. Both Barack Obama and Donald Trump defeated far more experienced and better qualified opponents, John McCain and Hillary Clinton.' Jack Wayne shrugged. 'There is a deep distrust among American voters of Washington and all it stands for. That's why myself and my colleagues believe that in 2020, an independent candidate affiliated to neither political party will have a wonderful chance of winning. Perhaps the best chance since America was founded in 1776.'

'A true candidate for change, affiliated to neither party,' David Mercer interrupted, receiving a withering stare from his boss.

'And where do I fit in with all this? I'm an English genealogical investigator. I don't even have a vote in the elections.'

The hands steepled together once again. 'As we are all aware, the family background of a potential Presidential candidate is crucial to getting out the vote. Jack Kennedy played on his Irish heritage to ensure he was elected. President Bush pointed to his ancestors' long history to show his connection with the traditions of America. President Obama managed to appeal to two different ethnic votes; Black and Irish, in support of his presidency. And of course, the present incumbent, President Trump, highlighted the immigrant background of his own German grandfather to show he was a product of the American dream; a grandfather who came to America and built an exceptional business.'

'And there is a negative side, too.' David Mercer spoke again, to the obvious irritation of his boss. 'President Obama was hindered by the Birther Movement for most of his first term, having to go so far as to release his own birth certificate, unprecedented for an American President.'

Jack Wayne held up his hand to stop his assistant from speaking. 'So you can see, Mrs Sinclair, the family background of any potential candidate is key. Not only for getting out the vote but also to ensure there are no skeletons in the closet.'

'So you want me to investigate the family history of one of the candidates, Mr Wayne?'

'Not one of the candidates – our favoured candidate. A wonderful man; a non-politician who runs a successful internet investment company. He had the ability to pick winners such as Facebook, Instagram, Google and YouTube when they were just gleams in their founders' eyes. Charismatic and articulate, yet a man of the people, as at ease in the corridors of power as he is in the corridors of his kids' elementary school.'

To Jayne this sounded like a party political broadcast. 'Who is this paragon of virtue?'

'Rather than listen to me singing his praises, why don't you meet him in person? The next President of the United States of America, Daniel Jackson.'

As if on cue, a tall, handsome man with salt-and-pepper hair and a winning smile walked through the door, accompanied by an elegantly dressed woman. He advanced toward Jayne with his hand held out. The handshake was firm and warm. 'It is a pleasure to meet you. Jack here has been singing your praises.'

He turned towards the woman at his side. 'Let me introduce my wife, Catherine.' As the two women

19

shook hands, he continued speaking. 'Actually, I call her my wife, but she's far more important to me than that. She's my partner, my consigliere, my brains, my accountant, the mother of my children, my humanity and my soul all wrapped in one rather neat package.'

'Dan, you flatter me too much,' Catherine protested. 'I haven't been your accountant for years.'

'See what I mean. And she makes a mean lasagne.' He waited while his wife and Jayne sat down at the table. 'Now, I believe you are going to help me discover my family background, Mrs Sinclair.'

Jayne liked this man. He had charm in spades, yet was surprisingly gentle. He looked exactly how she imagined an American president should look; square chin, broad shoulders, a brilliant smile and eyes that seemed to focus on her and her alone. 'I hope I can help, Mr Jackson.'

'Call me Dan, please. Mr Jackson sounds so old.' Again the charm was heaped at Jayne's door.

'Well, Dan, what do you know about your family? You must have been told something as a child.'

Dan Jackson instantly went into work mode. 'I was told all my family were killed in the Second World War. My grandfather, Thomas Jackson, was the only one who survived and came to America in 1946. He was a quiet, taciturn man who never said much, even to my father. He died when I was seven years old, so I'm afraid I don't remember a lot about him. When my father passed away in 1997, the only picture I found of my grandfather in his effects was this one.'

From the inside of his jacket, he pulled out a tattered black-and-white photograph of a young man wearing a boy scout's uniform; shirt, badges, short trousers and knee-length socks. He turned it over and written on the back in pencil was, 'H.J. August 1939'.

'Just before the Second World War broke out,' said Jayne. 'But I thought you said his Christian name was Thomas? Why are the initials H.J.?'

Dan Jackson shrugged his powerful shoulders. 'Beats me.'

'Did your grandfather fight in the war, Mr Jackson? It would make him easier to find if he did. Britain has extensive military records for the time.'

'Honestly, I don't know. Until I was six, the family lived with my grandfather but I think he and my father had an argument and we moved away from his house. The two men weren't close. Even at a young age, I sensed they didn't like each other much.' He paused for a moment and his eyes became unfocused as if he were reliving a moment buried deep in his past. 'I do remember one day, though,' he eventually said. 'My grandfather was sitting in his living room watching a war movie, some Audie Murphy film, I think. I asked him then if he'd fought in the war. His eyebrows knitted together and he frowned at me and my father. "Don't ask questions, boy. I was proud of what I did, proud of what I had to do." Then he stood up and walked out of the room, leaving my father and me to finish the movie. Even though I was only a kid, I thought it was strange. He died not long afterwards.'

Dan Jackson's wife interrupted him. 'I think many people were proud of their war service, even if they didn't fight. My daddy was always pleased with what he did during the war, even though he never left America.' She laughed and was joined by the others.

Jayne stayed silent, staring at the photograph. 'Can I keep this?' she finally asked.

'Yes, but please take care of it. It's the only one I have.'

'And this is your grandfather?'

'I'm pretty certain it is. Of course, when I knew him he was much older.'

'Your father never talked about your grandfather?'

'Never. My dad wasn't the talkative type. He was too busy making money.'

'Do you remember anything else?'

Dan Jackson shook his head. 'The only other thing I remember is my father saying that Thomas was born in Hereford in England around 1920, if it's any help. That's all, I'm afraid.'

'It's a starting point but you haven't given me much to go on. Have you checked the BMD records?'

Jack Wayne raised his hand. 'BMD, Mrs Sinclair?'

'Births, Marriages and Deaths. Every event has to be registered in the U.K.'

'No birth record for that name and that age in Hereford,' answered David Mercer, leaning forward.

'Did you check a couple of years either side? Sometimes people forget their date or want to make themselves appear younger.'

'Or older,' interrupted Catherine Jackson.

'I checked five years on either side of 1920.'

'Still nothing?'

'Nada. Zilch. Not a birth, death or marriage with that name.'

'Strange…'

'You see our problem, Mrs Sinclair.' Dan Jackson focused his eggshell blue eyes directly on her.

'But we do have the grandfather's naturalisation certificate here for you.' Jack Wayne tapped the folder in front of him, opened it and handed her the certificate. It looked like currency with an elaborate border and those easily recognised block letters for 'The United States of America'. The certificate was numbered 7556743 and stamped with the words

'Duplicate'. A classic passport picture of a man stared out at her.

'Your grandfather?' she asked.

Dan Jackson nodded.

She compared both photographs; the young boy in the Boy Scout's uniform and the head shot of the man in the certificate. 'Probably the same man, but it's hard to tell. And he looks nothing like you, Mr Jackson.'

'I always say Daniel takes his looks from his mother, may she rest in peace,' Catherine interrupted again.

'I'll keep both of these.'

Daniel Jackson nodded.

Jayne thought for a moment. 'As a recent immigrant to America, it should be relatively easy to find out his background.'

Jack Wayne shrugged. 'We thought so too. But...nothing. It's like Dan's grandfather materialised from nowhere and stepped on to dry land in New York to begin a new life.'

'But that's not possible. When did he arrive in America?'

Jack Wayne checked his file. 'February, 1946.'

'And he was naturalised before 1956?'

The man nodded. 'That's correct.'

'When he arrived in the States, he will have needed a visa. An Alien file will have been created. This Alien file, or A-file, will have been consolidated with his C-file in 1956. There should be A-file documentation with his naturalisation certificate.'

Jack looked across at the future President of the United States and smiled. 'Looks like we've chosen the right woman, Dan.' He turned to David Mercer. 'You should have found this out.'

The young man stared down at the table.

'Get on to our contact at Homeland Security straight away. We need those files.'

'Yes, Mr Wayne.' David was already tapping out a message on his mobile phone.

'Will the visa application give us more information, Mrs Sinclair?' asked Catherine.

'It should do. Date and place of birth, last residence in the U.K. – even a copy of the birth certificate, if we're lucky.'

Dan Jackson nodded at Jack Wayne. 'It looks like we're making progress already. But you see our problem, Mrs Sinclair.' He placed his hand on her wrist.

Jack Wayne carried on talking. 'We have a brilliant candidate to be the next President of the United States but neither himself nor his family have any history.'

Dan Jackson removed his hand.

'I could see that may present a few difficulties to your acceptance, Mr Jackson.'

Jack Wayne laughed out loud. 'Difficulties? Is that an example of British understatement, Mrs Sinclair? A President without any family history has about as much chance of being elected as this wine glass.'

Jayne ran her fingers through her hair, pushing a stray strand behind her ear. 'That's why you want me to investigate?'

'No, that's why we *need* you to investigate,' answered Jack Wayne.

'You will help, won't you, Mrs Sinclair?' Again, the hand touched Jayne's wrist lightly.

'But there must be thousands of American genealogists who could do this work.'

The dazzling smile with its perfect teeth was flashed towards Jayne. 'You underestimate your credentials. An ex-police officer with a tradition of solving difficult cases. One of your previous clients, John

Hughes, is a major donor to our cause. He recommended you and your services wholeheartedly.'

'Mr Hughes is too kind.'

Jack Wayne leant forward. 'There is one other thing. Including today, you have only five days to report back. On April 21, we will have an important meeting with our backers to confirm Mr Jackson as the independent candidate to face President Trump, if he runs, in 2020.'

Jayne put the papers back on the table. 'It's not enough time, Mr Wayne. How can I be expected to conduct a proper investigation in only five days?'

Dan Jackson held his arms open wide. 'I'm afraid that's all the time there is. Myself and Catherine will return to London on Friday.' He ran his fingers through his salt-and-pepper hair. 'An election costs millions, sometimes billions of dollars.' A self-deprecating smile crossed his face. 'Even though I'm rich, I'm not that rich, Mrs Sinclair. I need backing from other people, wealthy people, who support the sort of change I want to introduce into America. We meet with these people in five days' time. After this meeting, we decide whether I am going to stand as an independent candidate. If the answer is yes, we'll announce the candidacy right away, in time for a splash in the Sunday papers here and in America.'

Catherine interrupted him. 'We need to dominate the news cycle for at least the next two weeks, Mrs Sinclair. It's the only way we can make Dan's candidacy an event. If we don't announce on Friday, we lose them for another week. And as one of your prime ministers once said, a week is a long time in politics. I'm sure you understand, this *is* the only time that is right for us.'

Jayne thought for a moment. 'There's one more thing worrying me.'

Once more Dan Jackson's hand appeared on her arm. 'Please tell us what's troubling you.'

Jayne looked into his eyes. If this man was faking sincerity, he was outstanding at it. He was going to be a great candidate. She decided to be brutally honest with him. 'I have an aversion to all politics, and especially the politics of a country of which I am not a citizen.'

'Is that all? Then let me make it clear. You are not involving yourself in our politics, you are simply checking my family history. I want to know who I am, whether I stand as a candidate or not. Isn't that what you do? Help people to find out who they are and where they came from?'

Jack Wayne produced a cheque from his pocket. 'We will be paying in advance for the work.'

Jayne immediately thought of her father's marriage. The cheque would cover all the costs of the cruise, leaving a tidy sum left over for her to buy another present for the couple. 'And if I find nothing?'

Jack Wayne smiled again. 'Then nobody else will either, Mrs Sinclair. And we can proceed with the nomination.'

'You have such confidence in my abilities?'

'We only work with the best. We've done our homework on you and, in England, you are the best there is.' Jack Wayne slid the cheque across the table.

'If nothing else, my husband will find out about his family. At the moment, he knows nothing,' said Catherine.

Jayne stared at the cheque and then looked up at Dan and Catherine Jackson. They were both sitting at the edge of their seats, waiting for her decision. There was something that didn't feel quite right about this case. What was it? Why did her guts scream to her to get up and walk away? Why did she feel so uncertain?

But wasn't her job to help people find their long-lost family? And what better challenge than to research the family of a potential President of the United States? It was a wonderful opportunity to do something she had never done before.

And then the image of her father and Vera enjoying their honeymoon in one of the state cabins of the *Crystal Serenity* popped into her mind. A lovely image.

Jack Wayne leaned forward. 'Well, Mrs Sinclair, what's your decision?'

Jayne looked at the cheque lying against the white tablecloth. She could clearly see the figure of $5,000 printed in black against the light blue of the paper. She reached for the cheque, held it up for a moment, before pushing it back across the table towards Jack Wayne.

'I'll happily take the job, but you will only pay me when I produce my report. If I don't find anything, there will be no charge, except for expenses. Is that fair?'

Jack Wayne pocketed the cheque. 'More than fair, Mrs Sinclair.'

'Thank you, you don't know how much this means to me.' Once again, Dan Jackson touched her hand.

'We should be going, dear, the flight for Washington leaves in ninety minutes. We don't want to miss it.'

'Yes, darling. Goodbye and good luck with the research, Mrs Sinclair.'

They both stood up.

'How can I contact either of you? In case I have questions...'

'Through Jack or David here. They will be my eyes and ears. After myself and Catherine leave for the airport, they will also finish the briefing.'

The charm had vanished and the man was all business once more. 'I look forward to seeing your report on Friday. We've booked a suite at the Hilton, you can present what you find there.'

Just as quickly as they had arrived, the Jacksons departed, a car meeting them at the kerb and whisking them off to the airport.

Chapter Six

September 27, 1936
Manchester, England

It was his birthday. Seventeen years old today. A day to rejoice and be happy, a day to share with friends and family, and even loved ones.

Instead, Thomas Green was poring over a tightly packed page of figures, written in the small, cramped handwriting of Mr Bronstein, the Chief Accountant.

Outside, through the glass of the window in front of him, the birds were singing, the trees were still laden with their summer leaves, tinged with a touch of gold, and the sun was shining. Inside, the large clock on the rear wall ticked on remorselessly.

He glanced behind him. 3.45 p.m. Just two hours and fifteen minutes left before he would be released from his misery.

The figures spun and jostled in front of his eyes like some whirling dervishes. He let his head nod forward for a second, before stabbing his leg with the sharpened pencil.

Got to stay awake.

His charcoal grey trousers were full of tiny holes on his thighs. Evidence of the regularity with which he used the array of pencils on his desk to keep himself alert. He had wanted to clean his suit yesterday, but his mother had admonished him. 'Thomas, suits don't grow on trees, you know,' she had said in her strong German accent, despite having lived in England since marrying his father in 1919.

It had been one of those marriages that happen between soldiers and the local population. His father had been a corporal with the Royal Artillery, part of the occupying forces sent into the Ruhr after the armistice. She had been one of six daughters to Wolfgang and Trudy Schnaubl. They had two sons as well, but both had been killed in the last year of the war. Anyway, one thing led to another and his mother found herself pregnant with him. His father had done the right thing – ever the dutiful man, his father – and married her, bringing her back to England when he was demobbed.

The marriage hadn't lasted; such liaisons never did. His mother remained in England, though, never returning to her native land, content to admire it from afar, like one would appreciate the beauty of a landscape from the hand of a skilled artist.

'Are you dreaming again, boy?' Mr Bronstein was leaning over him, tapping the ledger with his ink-stained finger. 'I've warned you about daydreaming on the job. Perhaps I should speak to your Mutti again. She wouldn't like to hear you were wasting your time daydreaming.'

Bastard. One day, we will sort out you and your kind. But he didn't say these words. Instead, he mumbled, 'Sorry, Mr Bronstein, won't happen again, Mr Bronstein.'

The chief accountant snorted and walked on to check the work of one of the other young clerks aligned in a single row down one side of the Accounting Office.

Thomas stared at the man's retreating back. What would Bronstein think if he knew where Thomas was going after work? Who he was going to share his birthday with? He probably would have wagged his ink-stained finger and said, 'It will lead to no good, Mr Green, you mark my words. No good at all.'

He had been able to get the position at Hawley and Son through the auspices of his mother, who was the Bronsteins' cleaner. One day, she had come home as he was relaxing in the kitchen and announced she had found him a job as a trainee clerk at the princely wage of 23 shillings and five pence a week.

Such riches.

Even his younger sister was happy for him, singing in that joyous way only ten-year-olds can sing: 'Tom has got a jo…ob. Tom has got a jo…ob.' She was the product of a liaison with Uncle Frank in 1926. That man had fled the marital nest too, never to be seen again. There had been so many over the years, but none had stayed long, tiring of his mother as soon as their passion was spent.

He was going to work whether he wanted to or not. He would have much preferred to stay at home, reading his books and going to meetings in the evening, but his mother wouldn't hear of it.

'It's an excellent job. Look at Mr Bronstein, he is the Chief Accountant and him a Jew. Who would have thought it?'

'But you work for them, Mutti, cleaning their floors, washing their clothes, scrubbing their toilets.'

She had mussed his hair. 'Beggars can't be choosers, Thomas. Beggars can't be choosers.'

But he was no beggar.

Not now. Not ever.

He glanced behind him again to the clock on the rear wall. It must be nearly five p.m. now.

3.48.

Would this day never end?

It did, of course, eventually. But not before Mr Bronstein had administered two more admonitions to Thomas on the quality of his work, finding a mistake in an addition of tuppence halfpenny.

'I think I will talk to your mother, Thomas. Your work is not satisfactory, something must be done.'

Thomas was putting on his jacket, desperate to leave. But the old fool was still lecturing him, the ink-stained index finger stabbing the table like Jack the Ripper working on a prostitute.

Hadn't the Ripper warned London all those years ago? What had he written on the wall? 'The Juwes are the men that will not be blamed for nothing.' Johnnie had told him about the message at the last meeting.

Johnnie was Johnnie Hawley, son of the owner of the sock factory where Thomas worked as a clerk. It was Johnnie who had started their branch, and who would be leading the meeting this evening. He rarely, if ever, set foot in the factory, despite having his name on the door.

'Such an awful place, Thomas, I don't know how you can stand working there.'

These words came to Thomas as he stood in front of Mr Bronstein's desk, the lecture still continuing.

'I can't let this continue much longer, Thomas.'

'No, Mr Bronstein.'

'You will have to pull your socks up and put your nose to the grindstone.'

Thomas chuckled to himself. Bronstein was always using these strange idioms he picked up from the books of Dickens he devoured in the evenings after work.

'It's our duty to Mr Hawley and his son to perform to the best of our abilities. A mistake of tuppence halfpenny in the receivables is simply not good enough, is it, Thomas?'

'No, Mr Bronstein.' Thomas glanced at the clock on the wall. He wished the bugger would finish so he could get off to his meeting. They were planning the march on Sunday, and he wanted to be involved.

Bronstein caught him looking at the clock, but instead of the sharp rebuke, Thomas heard a softer, gentler voice. 'This is not the best of times for you, Thomas, is it?'

'I don't know what you mean, Mr Bronstein.'

'Your mother, her illness. It must be trying for you.'

'My mother? What illness?'

'But we mustn't let it affect our work, must we? Otherwise, what would Mr Hawley and his son think? And even worse, what if they had found the mistake in the receivables rather than me?'

It was Mr Bronstein's turn to glance at the clock. The voice was kindly when it came. 'I realise this is your birthday, and you may be a little distracted. My wife tells me your mother has prepared a cake for you. Please go now and share it with her. You can come in fifteen minutes early tomorrow and we will go over the receivables once more. There must be no more mistakes.' Again, the wagging finger pointed directly at his face.

As he was leaving the office, the chief accountant called to him once more. 'Wish your mother all the best, Thomas. She has had a hard life but we have tried to help her as best we can.'

Help her? Help her? The voice in Thomas's head screamed. *You've had her on her knees for the last twenty years, scrubbing your floors and cleaning your shit and you think this is helping her?*

Despite the voice shouting in his head, he simply answered, 'I'll let her know, Mr Bronstein.'

* * *

The meeting had already started when Thomas arrived. They were upstairs at the Red Lion, in a small room painted a dirty custard yellow with rows of spindly chairs facing a tiny stage.

The speaker was standing on the stage as Thomas entered. For a second he stopped speaking, eyed the new arrival with apparent distaste, and then carried on with what he was saying.

'The current uprising by the peasantry of Spain against their Comintern rulers is an inevitable expression of the Will of the People to retain their rightful place in society and not to be press-ganged into a state of equals and lionised "workers".'

Thomas saw Johnnie Hawley in the front row. He wasn't difficult to spot, his teal blue scarf shining out against the dull greys, beiges and blacks of the people seated around him.

The topic of this evening's speech was imaginatively titled, 'The People of Spain versus the Comintern'. The speaker was not very well known and so the turnout had not been expected to be high.

It wasn't. There were only twenty-four people in a room that could easily accommodate 150. Twenty-five now, when Thomas added himself.

As he slid into a seat beside Johnnie, the speaker seemed to warm to his subject.

'The murder of priests, the raping of nuns' – here he paused and licked his lips, obviously imagining the prospect – 'and the wholesale destruction of churches has awakened the peasants of Spain from their slumber. Generalissimo Franco has galvanised this motley crew of illiterate farm workers into a force, changing Spain forever. A force that, as Herr Hitler has shown in Germany, can tame the rapacity of the Jewish bankers and the forces of International Capitalism.'

A man in the second row put his hand up. The speaker acknowledged the raised hand by nodding his head.

'Isn't it true that it wasn't the peasants that rose up at all, but the army in Morocco?'

The speaker laughed. 'And what is an army but the people of Spain in a uniform? No, sir, it wasn't the army uprising against the Second Republic and its Comintern masters, but the people of Spain themselves.'

The man persisted. 'Is it also not true that Germany and Italy, in the shape of the Condor Legion, have supported the rebel army units?'

The speaker's eyes darted towards Johnnie Hawley. 'A response to the malicious influence of the Comintern in the internal politics of Spain, providing technical and emotional support only. I have enjoyed your questions, sir, but would ask which organisation you represent.'

The man adjusted his hat. 'I'm a reporter for the *Daily Herald*.'

'Oh, the left-leaning newspaper supporting the murderous activities of the Soviet regime?'

'We report things as we see them, not as Mr Stalin, Herr Hitler or Mr Mussolini would like us to see them. We report the truth.'

'The truth?' The speaker threw his arms up in the air dramatically. 'You wouldn't know the truth if it came and kicked you up the bum.' The retort produced a titter from the audience. The speaker took advantage of this to continue. 'You wouldn't know the truth if it was driving a 112 bus to Stretford, waving a green and white flag and hammering "God save the King" in Morse code with the bloody hooter.'

Thomas watched as Johnnie nodded to two burly men standing at the back of the hall.

'You wouldn't know the truth because your newspapers are owned by a vicious cabal of Jewish financiers, international businessmen and fellow hangers-on, determined to feed the British worker a diet of untruths, exaggerations and downright lies in order to maintain its control over the fruits of the sweat of their brow. To oppress the British worker, keeping him in a state of perpetual hunger, debt and poverty, whilst they enjoy lives of elegance, riches and opulence. I spit on you, sir, and on your newspaper.'

The audience, or what there was of it, erupted in cheers and clapping as the speaker dramatically spat on the wooden stage.

The two burly men stood behind the reporter. One whispered something in his ear, whilst the other lifted him up by the elbow and pushed him towards the exit. The reporter adjusted his jacket, placed his hat back on his head and left, followed by the two thugs.

'Good riddance to bad rubbish,' the speaker shouted to the departing reporter, producing another round of applause from the audience.

Thomas leant closer to Johnnie. 'How did he get in?'

A small smile appeared at the edge of Johnnie's lips. 'Through the door like everyone else. He will, however, be departing through a window.' The cut-glass accent and playful tone hid a menace in the words. 'Harry and Bill will make sure he doesn't come back again.'

The speaker continued in the same vein for the following thirty minutes, blaming the world's woes on an unholy alliance of Jewish money, Russian communists, French bankers and American capitalists. The only people he did not blame were the Royal Family.

After the meeting, the branch retired downstairs to the pub to discuss the upcoming march through the East End of London. Thomas hung in the background as the beers were ordered in case the barman challenged his right to drink at such a young age. But eventually the beer was delivered and he drank a large mouthful, pretending to enjoy the warm yeasty flavour.

Johnnie Hawley led the discussion as chairman. Manchester would be sending a contingent, of course. Should the branch charter a bus or go by train?

A bus was decided, as long as there were enough members who could pay the five-shilling fare. They would travel overnight, arriving in London early the following morning in time to join the march.

'Is there gonna be trouble?' asked a burly man on the other side of the table.

'I doubt it,' answered Johnnie. 'Sir Oswald will make sure the Reds and their followers stay away.'

Thomas took another long swallow of the beer. He didn't like the taste but he loved the way it made him look and feel.

'No,' the man continued, 'I meant, are we supposed to make trouble?'

Johnnie played with the glass of whisky in front of him, inhaling the aroma. 'We're marching through the East End, what do you think?'

The other men seated around the table all laughed and picked up their pints.

'Are you coming, Tom?' asked Johnnie, staring straight at him.

'I'll... try...' Thomas stammered, putting his glass noisily down on the table.

'If your mother will let you...' Johnnie laughed at his joke.

All the men were staring at Thomas.

'It's not that, it's...'

'It's what?' persisted Johnnie.

Thomas's eyes darted left and right, searching for an excuse. 'It's... It's taking time off work.'

'It's only a Saturday morning. I'll clear it with my father. I'm sure he will be happy for you to go.'

The cultured, lazy voice again. Thomas felt everybody at the table staring at him. 'But... But... I haven't got the fare.'

'Is that all? As it's your birthday, it will be my treat. A free trip to London to see the king and beat up some Jews. Who could ask for a better present? Well, Tom?'

Thomas raised his glass, spilling a little down the side as he did so. He remembered the words of a speaker from three weeks ago. 'Here's to the wreck of London and all who live in her.'

The rest of them raised their glasses and toasted with him. Now all he had to do was convince his mother.

*   *   *

She was waiting up for him when he arrived home.

'You've been drinking.'

'Too right, had two pints.'

'I wish you wouldn't drink, *liebling*, your father drank and look what it did to him.' She mussed his hair. 'Anyway, happy birthday. Seventeen today. I made you a cake.'

'Old Bronstein told me you had.'

'They gave me the flour and sugar, but I had to provide the eggs myself.' She removed the tea cloth in the manner of a magician in the Vaudeville. Beneath it, a small Victoria sponge lay with a single candle in the centre. 'No cream, *liebling*, but I managed to find strawberry jam. Just for you. Let me light the candle.'

'*Mutti*, don't bother.'

'But we must light the candle and you can make a wish, just like when you were a child. You always told

38

me your wishes when you were a child. One year, it was to fly to the moon. Such strange ideas you had.'

She lit the solitary candle and then stood back, admiring her handiwork. 'Make your wish, *liebling*.'

Thomas Green bent over and an image flashed in his mind of a journalist being thrown through a plate-glass window, the shards of glass penetrating his thigh and blood pouring from a long gash in his arm.

He made a wish.

'Don't tell me this time, *liebling*, I don't want to know now. At seventeen, your wishes must be kept secret.'

'*Mutti*, I have one request for my birthday.'

She mussed his hair again. 'See, my boy has become a man.' She puffed out her chest and imitating his voice said, 'I have one request for my birthday.'

Thomas's face went bright red. 'I want to go to London on Saturday. There's a big march through the East End. Scare the Reds back into the dirty holes they crawled out of.'

His mother went silent. 'How much does it cost?'

'Five shillings.'

'You know we can't afford it. The rent alone on this place...'

'Johnnie Hawley says he will give me the money.'

'You should not be taking money, even if it is from nice Mr Hawley.' She tucked a strand of dyed blonde hair behind her ear. 'Will he be going with you?' she asked tentatively.

'Of course he will.'

'Then...'

Thomas threw his arms around her. 'Thank you, *Mutti*.'

'What are you going to tell Mr Bronstein?'

Thomas looked at her as if he didn't understand.

'You will miss work on Saturday.'

'Mr Hawley's given me time off. He supports the work we're doing.' He looked at the cake. 'Or you could tell him I was feeling ill. Something I ate.'

'We should cut the cake now. Only one piece for me.' She ran her hands down her body. 'I have to look after my figure. A man likes something to get hold of, but not too much.'

Thomas hated it when she talked about men. Her whole life after his father left had been one long quest to find a new man. There had been some who had stayed. One – Uncle Frank, his sister Ellie's father – had even lasted three months, but they all eventually drifted away like flotsam on an ebbing tide. It didn't stop his mother in her quest, though. The older she became, the more obvious her need.

It sickened him. Where was the elegance of an Aryan woman? Where was the pride in one's race?

He watched as she bit into the cake. Despite her protestations, it would be the first of many pieces. She licked the sugar off her fingers. 'Try some, delicious.' She spoke with an open mouth. For a moment, he could see the yellow of the cake, interspersed with gobs of red jam on her pink tongue.

The sight disgusted him.

'I'm not hungry,' he announced, walking out and up the stairs.

'But, *liebling*, I made it specially for you. It can't all go to waste, there's three eggs in it.'

He stomped up the stairs and threw himself on his bed fully clothed. He closed his eyes and images of her face, covered in blood, her eyes black and closed, her dyed blonde hair sticky and red, leapt into his mind.

He couldn't take any more of this. He had to get away. At least with the party there was the sense of belonging, of unity, of a shared mission. Johnnie Hawley was going to lead them down to London where they would show the Yids and the rest of their kind what real men could do.

He'd never been to London before. Perhaps they would see the king or the trooping of the colour. After they had smashed the Yids, of course.

Chapter Seven

Monday, April 17, 2017
London

'I told you he was a great guy, Mrs Sinclair, and he's going to be a great candidate; young, successful, charismatic, a Washington outsider. A successful businessman, philanthropist, internet entrepreneur and all-round mensch.'

'He certainly knows how to turn on the charm does Dan Jackson.'

'He could charm the angels out of heaven. And he's going to charm the American voter into electing him President.'

'As long as I find nothing untoward.'

'To help start your research, here is a short biography of the family since they arrived in America.' David Mercer tapped another folder he had placed on the table. 'Plus, we compiled a series of articles about Dan Jackson from *Wired*, *Time*, the *Wall Street Journal* and the *Economist* for you to read.'

Jayne glanced at the folder. 'You seem to have prepared well, Mr Wayne. But what exactly do you want me to do? You've only given me five days.'

'Put quite simply, we want you to find out where his grandfather came from. Who were his family in England? What did they do? Any black sheep? Any family secrets? Anything that could be used by the opposition to blacken his name? Mr Jackson is as anxious as we are to find out the truth. Do what you're good at, Mrs Sinclair – discover who his ancestors were.' He paused for a moment to scratch his nose.

Another piece of paper was handed to her by David Mercer.

'Here is a letter from Mr Jackson, authorising you to research his family.'

She read the printed type quickly.

I, Daniel Jackson, authorise Mrs Jayne Sinclair to research and investigate my family and antecedents, reporting the findings to myself and Mr John Wayne by 21 April, 2017.

The signature was written with an elaborate flourish and dated yesterday.

'He was so certain I would say yes?'

'Mr Jackson can be extremely persuasive.'

David Mercer sat forward. 'I've looked as best I could, but I could find nothing. And Jackson is such a common name in Britain, I wouldn't even know where to start.'

Jack Wayne smiled broadly and pushed back his chair to stand up. 'Glad to have you on board, Mrs Sinclair. If you need anything, just contact David. Our number is on the card I gave you.'

David Mercer collected all the sheets of paper and placed them together in one folder, before handing it to her.

These people do not waste time in idle chit-chat, thought Jayne. *Once they have an agreement, it's on to the next item of business.*

'We'd like you to get started straight away. Where will you begin?'

Jayne also stood up. She put the folder in her bag, feeling Mr Wayne's hand in the small of her back, encouraging her to leave. He was in a hurry.

David ran out from behind the table and opened the door of the restaurant. As she stepped out on to the pavement, Jayne caught sight of the waiter vanishing into the kitchen, his service over.

They both stood on the quiet street with its narrow pavement. Had Jack Wayne arranged for no pedestrians too? She wouldn't put it past him.

She heard a cough. 'I asked where you were going to start, Mrs Sinclair.'

'Two places. I'll look at the births, marriages and deaths in the area first; maybe David missed something. Perhaps we can find a Jackson death, which could lead us to an address. After that, I'm going to check the 1939 census, find out if there were any people with the surname Jackson living in Hereford at the time. From there, we'll work out a plan of attack.'

'Can we give you a lift anywhere? We booked you into the Marriott for two nights, just in case.'

Jack Wayne smiled at her again. God, he was a smug bastard. They had even booked a hotel for her, so confident she would take the case.

'A lift to the hotel would be fine, Mr Wayne.'

As she spoke, her phone rang in her bag. She reached in and took it out. The caller's name was in capital letters on her screen: FATHER. 'If you'll excuse me for a few seconds, I have to take this. My father is expecting me to return this evening and visit him tomorrow.'

Jayne moved away further down the street to get some privacy. David Mercer and Jack Wayne remained waiting at the edge of the kerb.

She pressed the answer button. There was a fumbling noise before her father's voice was loud in her ear.

'Damn these bloody buttons. Hello, who is it?'

'It's Jayne, Dad, you called me?' She spoke softly, trying to ensure her conversation wasn't overheard.

'What's that? You'll have to speak up, Jayne, you sound far away.'

'I'm still in London.'

'That explains it then. You are a long way away. Vera asked me to call. She wants to know if you could go shopping with her tomorrow when you come round, she's starting to panic over the design of the dress.'

'Listen, Dad, I won't be able to make it tomorrow.'

'Oh, what a shame. Vera was so looking forward to shopping with you.'

Jayne noticed a motorbike driving slowly down the street, the soft roar of its engine echoing off the high buildings. A rider and a pillion passenger, both dressed in black leather and wearing full helmets, were looking directly at her. 'Please tell her I'm sorry. I'll be back...'

The motorbike was level with her two clients now, the black helmets turning to stare at them on the edge of the pavement.

Jayne watched as, in slow motion, the pillion passenger's right arm stretched out.

Something was in the man's hand. Something dark and metallic and threatening.

A Glock.

Jayne ran back to the man nearest to her, David Mercer, pushing him backwards towards the plate-glass window of the restaurant.

A shot rang out, striking the stone just above Jack Wayne's head. Instantly the man ducked, bringing his briefcase up in a vain attempt to protect his body.

For a second, the sharp crack of the shot thrust her back to that day four long years ago. Her partner, Detective Sergeant Dave Gilmour, lying on the concrete floor of the apartment block, blood seeping from a wound in his chest.

He had died in her arms and she had left the police, unable to trust herself any more.

She threw herself at Jack Wayne, dragging him down to the pavement, away from the men, trying to crawl back towards the restaurant.

The bike stopped for a split second. A black helmet, its visor reflecting the street, looked down at them lying on the pavement.

Jayne stared up into the black mass of a face.

The gun lowered towards her, its small black snout pointing directly at her body. She could see the tension on the man's finger as it bent against the trigger. The black hole of the Glock's barrel moved towards her head.

She waited for the noise, the impact of the bullet, her blood splattering across the street, her last breaths. How would it feel? How would death feel?

Instinctively, she threw her bag at the men. It struck the driver flush on the helmet, knocking him sideways.

Suddenly, there was a loud roar and a blast of blue exhaust from the rear of the bike. It reared up on its back wheel and the passenger was thrown off balance, barely hanging on to the driver in front.

For a second, the bike hung suspended like the freeze frame of a film, then the tires began to grip and it surged forward down the street in a plume of steel-blue exhaust, the passenger turning and firing two more shots in rapid succession.

Jayne heard the bullets whine past her head before burying themselves in the wood of the door. She crawled over to where Jack Wayne was lying on the ground, his hand clutching at his chest.

She pulled the arm away to reveal a small red mark that grew bigger as she stared at it.

He grunted, trying to lift his head off the pavement to look at the spreading pool of blood across his white shirt. 'Someone shot me?' he said in a voice laced with surprise.

Far away, Jayne could hear the sound of a police siren approaching at speed, the rising and falling modulation of the noise cutting through the air.

'What happened?' David Mercer spluttered. 'Did someone just try to kill...' He stopped speaking as he saw his boss lying on the floor, the pool of bright red blood spreading over his white shirt.

Jack Wayne's lips moved and his head slumped to the left. Out of the corner of her eye, Jayne could see David Mercer turn to the gutter and vomit his breakfast into the drain.

Jack Wayne's lips moved again and his hand gripped her arm tightly.

'What's that?' She lowered her head, so her ear was close to the man's mouth.

'Keep on...'

Before the sentence was finished, Jack Wayne's face slumped away from her and lay there unmoving, a small ribbon of blood dripping from the corner of the mouth and running over the chin.

She sensed a presence at her side. David Mercer was back, but he wasn't helping. He was standing there, staring at his dead boss. 'We've got to get away. They might come back.'

Jayne cradled Jack Wayne's head in her arms. Again, images of Dave Gilmour flashed through her brain. The same scene four years ago. This wasn't supposed to happen, not here, not now, not again.

The siren was getting louder now, the noise seeming to come from everywhere as it echoed off the surrounding buildings.

'We have to go, they might be coming back.' David Mercer's voice was high, on the edge of panic. He was turning his head quickly, checking both sides of the street, fear in his eyes.

'We're staying. Police and ambulance are on their way. We have to stay.'

47

David Mercer ran to the edge of the pavement. 'We have to get out of here.'

'Give me my bag. Now.'

David Mercer was stopped for a moment by her command. He ran to pick up the bag, passing it back to Jayne.

She rummaged through it, looking for something, anything to clean the blood from the dead man's face.

'We've got to get out of here.' David Mercer shouted again.

His shout was interrupted by the scream of tyres as a police car turned the corner at speed. The siren, loud now, was behind her. A long slide across asphalt as the brakes were applied and the car slid sideways. A crunch of hinges as doors were flung open.

Jayne turned to look at the police car and knew instantly that she was in danger.

Chapter Eight

Monday, April 17, 2017
London

The first policeman was walking towards them, a cold smile etched into his mouth, and a livid scar cutting vertically across the eye on the right side of his face. His large hands were screwing a silencer onto the end of his pistol.

'Move, now!' Jayne shouted. She grabbed the bag with her bloodstained hands and pushed David Mercer down an alley leading off the main road.

He fought against her, trying to go back. 'But you said the police...'

As he struggled with her, a bullet struck the wall above their heads, sending sharp shards of brick cascading down on them.

'What the...?'

Jayne pushed David Mercer further into a narrow gap between two tall buildings. Hanging Sword Alley. 'Get away... Quick, down there.'

They ran down the dark alley. Jayne glanced behind her, expecting to see the policeman standing silhouetted in the opening, his gun levelled at her.

Nothing.

On either side, high walls towered above them as they rushed down the narrow defile, banging into the sides.

A bullet zipped past Jayne's ear, just missing David's head and exploding into the wall.

'Faster, this way.' She directed him towards the right, down another narrow alley which widened into an open courtyard.

Behind them, she could hear the noise of heavy boots on the flagstones.

How many people?

She had seen two coppers getting out of the police car, but there could have been more. Her heart was thumping, ready to explode from her chest.

Who were they?

Jayne knew something was wrong when she saw the leading policeman fitting a silencer to the end of his pistol.

No warning. No call to check. No identification. And no real policeman ever used a silencer.

Who were they?

David tripped over a box lying in the middle of the alley, and went sprawling along the ground. Jayne stopped and turned to help him up.

The sound of boots was getting closer now, the slap of leather against stone echoing off the brick walls. Jayne glanced over her shoulder. A shout, not far away.

We have to get out of here.

The alley opened out into a round courtyard, with a stone obelisk in the centre of a tiny garden.

She slung David's arm over her shoulder and helped him limp past the obelisk and into another passageway on the left.

St Brides Avenue.

'My ankle... it's hurting.' David grimaced and gritted his teeth.

'We've got to keep going.'

There was a shout behind them. A gruff male voice. Not English. Russian, or something similar.

Why would a group of Russians be dressed as English policemen?

She banished the question from her mind and concentrated on helping David down the passage. It opened out to another courtyard. On the left, a white church tower rose in layers to the sky. At the end, a red-brick building and a bright blue plaque.

Behind her more shouts, but further away now.

She ran down to the other end of the courtyard, David limping heavily beside her.

A steep flight of stairs led past one of London's ubiquitous wine bars and out on to a small street. Jayne stopped to gain her breath. David was leaning against her now, unable to support the weight on his left foot.

Jayne looked down the avenue, deciding which way to go. The Bridewell Theatre was on the right. Straight ahead past the church, the busy roads of Fleet Street and Ludgate Hill.

Behind her, the pursuers had found their trail again. Harsh Slavic shouts echoed down the narrow alley.

'We've got to keep moving.' She grabbed David around the shoulders and hurried on, his weight slowing her down, his face contorting in pain with every step.

The voices were getting louder, clearer – she could hear them shouting to each other. More than two voices now, others must have arrived.

On the left, she spotted a black door set into a wall. It was their only chance. She pushed David into the alcove.

She checked the lock; a Yale. She took a credit card out from her wallet, sliding the plastic in between the jamb and the lock.

She pushed on the door.

Nothing.

The shouts were louder now. The heavy sound of footsteps on the stairs where they had been just a few moments ago.

The alcove would keep them hidden from view until their chasers drew level with them. After that, they would be sitting targets with nowhere left to run or hide.

She slid the credit card between the door and the jamb once more. Feeling for the lock, hoping it would spring back.

Nothing again.

The voices were even closer now, with footsteps running down the narrow street towards them. She slid the credit card down the jamb once more.

A slight give in the lock. She pushed the door open and jumped in, dragging David after her. As she closed the door, she caught a glimpse of dark blue trousers and brogues.

No policeman wore brogues.

Who the hell were these people?

'What's happening? What's...?'

Before David could finish his sentence, Jayne had pushed him down to the floor and clamped her hand over his mouth. 'Shhhhh... They might hear us,' she whispered.

David nodded and she released her grip.

They were kneeling in a small room with no windows. Heavy oak furniture stood out against the white-painted walls. A white porcelain sink sat in the corner with a small mirror above it. In the opposite corner, a cassock and a chasuble were draped across a coat stand. The only source of light came from a slender crack in a door in the far wall.

'Where the hell are we?' David whispered.

'At a rough guess, we're in one of the crypts beneath St. Bride's Church.'

The door where they had entered suddenly rattled on its hinges. For a moment, it stopped and then rattled again.

'Locked, didn't go in here,' a heavily accented voice shouted to somebody.

'They must be in the theatre.'

Jayne and David held their breath. The door rattled again as someone shook it. The shadow of a bulky figure blocked the light coming through the gap in the door.

'I've tried that, it's locked. Come with me.' A commanding voice, used to issuing orders. An English voice.

Once more the door shook on its hinges. The sound of footsteps hurrying away. More shouts, distant now.

Jayne finally exhaled, and the tension flooded out of her body.

It was David who spoke first.

'What the hell do we do now?' he asked.

Chapter Nine

Monday, April 17, 2017
Somewhere beneath the streets of London

'Sir, Blake reports both targets have escaped.'
'Find them.'

The operator stared at his bank of consoles whilst speaking into the microphone covering his face. 'He is requesting back-up, sir.'

The man scratched the back of his hand before removing the cover from his porcelain cup. The delightful aroma of freshly cut grass rose from the green tea. He took a tiny sip of the warm drink. 'Hack into CCTV. Track them.'

'Yes, sir.' The operator's fingers danced along the keyboard as he wormed his way into the central computer controlling London's closed-circuit cameras. The city was the most watched place on earth, with over 5,000 cameras covering virtually every footstep of every person who walked its streets.

'In now, sir, bringing up the area cameras right away.'

Above his head, the bank of screens gradually illuminated to reveal the streets of London. People hurried along, intent on shopping, or making money, or even worrying about what they were going to do that evening, unaware they were being watched from a small room hidden in the bowels of a building in the city.

'Shall I use facial tracking, sir?'

For a moment the man lifted his hooded eyes from his own screen and nodded his head.

The operator's fingers again rattled over the keyboard. On two small screens to the left, the faces of Jayne Sinclair and David Mercer appeared. At the same time, the outline of a white square began to form across the unknowing pedestrians of London's streets. It focused on one woman for a second, then jumped to another target, the recipients of this attention totally oblivious to the fact they had just been rejected by a computer.

'They must be hiding in the area. Order Blake to begin a building search. Flush them out.'

'Yes, sir.' Once again the operator spoke softly into his mouthpiece. 'He's requesting more resources, sir.'

Blake was becoming tiresome: even the simplest mission turned into a drama.

'What shall I tell Blake, Mr Ostransky?'

'No additional resources... yet. Carry on the search.' He picked up his tea once more as the operator whispered into his microphone. The disappearance of these two was an unfortunate blip in the accomplishment of his goal. But that's all it was - a blip. He was sure the computers would soon find them again. After all, hadn't he designed and configured them himself?

He sipped his tea and relaxed back into the padded comfort of his chair. London was such an interesting city to observe. The behaviour of its citizens, ant-like in their obsession with making money, making time or making love. What had Eliot written about them? He didn't know 'death had undone so many'?

Jack Wayne had known he was going to die, it just happened to be today.

No matter.

Jayne Sinclair and David Mercer would also die eventually, it was just a matter of time.

There were only five days to go before their man would be chosen as the next presidential candidate. Nothing must get in the way of that choice.

Nothing.

He looked up at the stylised head of a wolf hovering above the bank of screens. The Organisation had been working towards this day for the last 75 years. Nobody was going to get in their way now.

Chapter Ten

Monday, April 17, 2017
St. Bride's Church, London

'What the hell's going on? Why were those police shooting at us?' David was standing at the door, trying to peer through the gap.

In the half-light of the crypt, Jayne could see the agitation on his face. She put her hand on his arm, trying to calm him even though she felt the shivers of fear running through her own body. 'Keep your voice down. Nobody must hear us.'

'You're telling me to keep my voice down? I've just watched my boss being shot dead. And then I was chased through the streets by British policemen intent on killing me. And you're asking me to keep my voice down?' David's voice had risen throughout this speech until he was almost shouting by the end of it.

Jayne clamped her hand over his mouth. She used her weight to force him backwards over her outstretched foot. His body crashed to the floor against the leg of a heavy oak table.

She went down with him, staying in control all the way. 'No, I'm *telling* you to keep your voice down.'

She leant into him, pressing the point of her right elbow against his chest and increasing the pressure of her left hand against his mouth.

He struggled for a few moments to escape her grip, his legs lashing out to kick one of the oak cupboards.

Jayne pressed down harder with her elbow, feeling the ribs bend beneath her weight. 'If you don't get control of yourself, you will get us both killed.

Do I make myself clear, Mr Mercer?' she whispered in his ear.

A pair of eyes nodded assent.

Jayne released the pressure over his mouth slightly.

'But...'

Her left hand clamped his mouth again, her right hand coming over his forehead to force the head downwards. 'I won't tell you again. Get control of yourself,' she hissed through gritted teeth.

Above their heads a chair was scraped across a wooden floor.

Both went quiet, staring up at the dark, kippered ceiling of the crypt.

Silence.

Jayne spoke first. 'Those people weren't police. I don't know who they were but they weren't coppers.'

She stared at David Mercer's face. The eyes had lost some of their wildness. His breathing was slower, calmer now. She released the pressure.

David slowly sat up, rubbing his jaw as he did. 'You have a strong grip, Mrs Sinclair.'

'I was trying to be gentle.'

He rubbed his jaw once more. 'If that's gentle, I'd hate to see you trying to hurt me.'

Another scrape of a chair across the ceiling. Both of them stared up at it. 'What are we going to do?' David finally asked.

'Do you have a mobile?'

'Back on the street. What about yours?'

'I dropped it when we were attacked.' Then she thought about her father. Had he heard the shots? What would he do? She pushed the image of her father from her mind. She needed to focus now on getting them out of there alive. 'We need to call the police.'

'Perhaps the church has a phone?'

Jayne checked the room, opening the doors to the cupboards. A few glasses, some tattered church magazines, a stack of well-thumbed bibles and a black fedora, but no phone. 'What time is it?'

David Mercer checked his watch. 'One fifty-five.'

She sat down beside him, leaning back against the whitewashed wall. 'We'll give it a few hours, then we'll look upstairs. I think St Bride's closes at five.' She pointed to a door in the corner of the crypt. 'We'll go up to the church. Hopefully, our pursuers will be gone by then.'

'And if they aren't?'

'Then we're in trouble. For some reason, those people want to kill us. Why did they shoot your boss?'

David Mercer shrugged his shoulders. 'I've no idea. After briefing you, he was going to return to Washington whilst I stayed in London in case you needed me.'

Again, the noise of scraping chairs above their head, followed by footsteps across a wooden floor.

They both stopped talking, staring at the ceiling, holding their breath.

It went quiet again. As silent as a crypt.

Jayne spoke softly. 'Somebody wanted him dead. What else was he working on?'

'Nothing. There's nothing more important than this. We're talking about the next President of the United States, for Christ's sake. Nothing is more important.'

'Then somebody didn't want him or us to invest-igate Daniel Jackson. Why?'

David shook his head. 'I dunno.'

Jayne noticed she still had Jack Wayne's blood on her hands. It was sticky, very sticky, and had begun to form globules in the creases of her palms. She stepped across to the sink to wash it off, the water turning a purple colour as it vanished into the plug-hole.

David had smears of blood across his face where she had pushed him to the floor. She took a paper towel, dampened it and reached up to wipe it away.

'What are we going to do?'

She finished wiping his face and threw the damp towel into the sink. 'The only thing we can.'

'Which is?'

'Wait.'

Chapter Eleven

Monday, April 17, 2017
Somewhere beneath the streets of London

'Blake has finished searching the buildings in the area, sir. He reports nothing found.'

So our tiny mice have gone to ground, hiding in a hole. They will soon get bored and pop their heads out, and when they do, we will be ready to pounce. 'Tell him to stand down.'

'Yes, sir.'

Now it was a waiting game. And he was used to waiting. His business was all about patience - waiting for the right moment, not acting too quickly, sitting back and letting the opponent think they were in control by forcing the game. And then, when the time was right, he struck hard. He didn't think of himself as a particularly patient man, but when he truly wanted something, he could have the patience of St Cuthbert.

The Organisation had worked long and hard for this day. He wasn't going to spoil it now by rushing into unplanned action.

He looked up at the logo of the wolf's head above the bank of screens again. It always amused him to see it openly displayed after so many years of being hidden.

Now, the same logo was found in millions of homes across the world but most people never saw it. It was in their fridges, powering their lights, answering their calls, driving their cars, protecting their streets. A small transistor that had made him, and the Organisation, millions, and would make them millions more as other uses were found. The Internet of Things was a wonderful idea to enable tech companies to sell more stuff to even more gullible consumers. But it made virtually every home, office or government department vulnerable to people like him, especially when most people never change the default passwords of their glitzy new machines. He laughed to himself. He was a modern-day Ali Baba with a magic 'Open Sesame' to most of the world's connected devices. And the more connected they became, the more he could control them.

With that ability, they finally had the power to realise their ambitions. Dreams discussed and created a long time ago, in a dank castle on the Austrian border in 1943.

When the Organisation had been formed.

He had always been attracted to the images of the National Socialists as they marched through Europe; organised and committed men, who would let nothing get in their way. The cream of the genetic pool.

It was no surprise that he was approached by the *Hilfsgemeinschaft auf Gegenseitigkeit der Angehörigen der ehemaligen Waffen-SS*, the mutual aid organisation for former SS members, when he was at university. He was immediately employed in his speciality – computer programming. Even in the dark days of the 1980s, the Organisation understood where the future lay.

But it was only as he rose through the ranks of the Organisation that he understood the aid society was just a front for something far more exciting. Something that even Adolf Hitler in his wildest dreams could not have imagined.

He had a meeting with the Organisation and the Führer later to report on today's events. He didn't have to tell them every minute detail, just outline the progress of this operation.

He removed the painted cover from his Japanese cup and sipped his green tea. They were only interested in the big picture, not the tiny details; that was his job.

Now the only thing was to wait. The mice would show themselves again. When they did, he would not let them out of his sight this time.

Chapter Twelve

Monday, April 17, 2017
St. Bride's Church, London

There were two sharp raps on the door, followed by a shout. 'I can hear voices. Is anybody in there?'

Jayne immediately sat upright. For more than two hours they had talked, going over the events of earlier, replaying the death of Jack Wayne over and over again.

Two more raps on the door. 'I know you're in there. Come out now.' A woman's voice – an old woman's voice.

She looked across at David Mercer. He was holding his breath and staring at the door.

Should she answer the woman? What if the killers were with her? What if it was a trick?

'I'm going to open the door now. So you'd better come out.' The voice was becoming querulous.

A key rattled in a lock. The handle began to turn. The crack of light widened as the door opened.

Jayne reached over and kissed David Mercer hard on the lips, pressing her body into his.

The light clicked on. A middle-aged lady stood framed in the doorway, wearing a light violet twinset topped by a thin rope of pearls. She looked down at them, holding each other tightly, David's arms wrapped around Jayne's body. 'You can't do that sort of thing here. This is a church.'

Jayne pushed herself off a startled David Mercer and pretended to smooth down her clothes, tucking her blouse into her skirt. 'Sorry, didn't know it was a church.'

The woman stared at the cassock and chasuble hanging from the coat rack in the corner.

'Hmm, well you can't be in here. It's not allowed. Only the vicar is allowed in here.' She folded her arms across her chest. 'It's a good job I checked. I'm just closing up for the day. You could have been locked in here all night and then what would you have done, tell me that?'

Jayne smiled, helping David to his feet. 'I'm sure we would have thought of something...'

The woman grunted. 'You'd better leave now. And don't come back. Young people today...'

'We are sorry, Mrs...?'

'Mrs Hobbs. And let me tell you, I've raised six children without resorting to these sorts of shenanigans.' She stopped speaking for a moment as a thought struck her. 'How did you get in here?'

Jayne pointed to the door leading out on to the street. 'We thought it was the entrance.'

'I'll kill the vicar, I will. I'm always telling him to close the doors properly when he goes out, but will he listen? Will he never.' She strode over to the door and pushed down the snib on the lock, checking it was closed. 'You can leave through the church.' She pointed to the door on the opposite wall and the steps leading up to the apse.

'Can I ask you one thing before we leave? Is there anybody else up there?'

'You mean more like you? I hope not. I got rid of everybody five minutes ago.'

'Thank you, Mrs Hobbs. We are sorry we disturbed you.'

'And I'm sorry I disturbed you too. But this is a church and if you want to get up to that sort of thing I suggest you get a room.'

'We will... next time.' Jayne coughed. 'Would you mind showing us the way out?'

Chapter Thirteen

Monday, April 17, 2017
Heathrow Airport, London

Dan Jackson walked back from the bar in the United executive lounge, carrying a whisky for himself and a white wine for his wife.

He passed the glass to her and sat down on the uncomfortable seat. 'You'd think United would be able to design a seat, wouldn't you? I'd much prefer to fly Virgin.'

His wife didn't look up from her magazine. 'We can't, not any more. It wouldn't look great if the newspapers found out.'

He took her free hand and leant over to kiss her on the side of the head. 'What would I do without you?'

'Probably a lot more, and with a younger model too.'

He took a sip of his whisky. Laphroaig. At least they had decent Scotch.

She put down her magazine on the table in front of her and turned to him. 'Are you sure you want to stand?' she asked out of the blue.

He put the Scotch down. 'Where's this coming from? You were the one who persuaded me I should.'

She shrugged her shoulders. 'Cold feet, maybe. Meeting that woman…'

'Mrs Sinclair?'

'Her.' She made a little moue with her mouth that he had always found adorable. 'Well, it made me realise we'd be giving up a lot. Our privacy, our freedom, the chance to be alone.'

He looked around the packed lounge, full of overweight executives trying to pile as much free food and drink into their mouths before take-off as they could. 'Air Force One would make up for it… nearly.'

He stared at the fingers intertwined in his. They had been married for 24 years now, after meeting at Yale. She was reading medicine and he finishing his MBA. It had been love at first sight for him, but not for her. As she always told him, he had the air of a street fighter about him in those days, and not a handsome street fighter. After much persuasion, she had eventually agreed to a date. He had taken her to the movies, *Scent of a Woman* with Al Pacino, trying to put his arm around her shoulders during the tango scene. She had slid out from under his flailing attempt at intimacy, saying, 'Not so fast, buster.' Even since, hearing tango music immediately made him want to take her in his arms.

'Don't joke. We have to be sure.'

He thought for a moment. This wasn't like her at all. She had been so keen, so determined he should stand. 'What's worrying you?'

She sipped her white wine. 'I wonder if it's worth it. We have so much already…'

'I think I want to stand. But only if you agree. We could do so much together, to make a difference. It was you who convinced me that we need to change America, return it to the ideas that made it great in the first place.' He took another sip of his Laphroaig. 'We've been training for this all our life, Catherine. It's our time.'

A minor singing star entered the lounge from one of the popularity contests, followed by her retinue of managers, hair stylists, personal assistants and assorted hangers-on. A photographer was constantly taking shots of her, the flash exploding in her face, highlighting her exquisite cheekbones.

'We'd have to put up with that for the rest of our lives.' She flicked her blonde hair back in the direction of the reporters.

'That's why we have to do this together. It's not my decision alone.'

'And the children, do they get a say? Shouldn't you ask them?'

Dan Jackson thought for a moment. She was making sure he understood it was not just him making a commitment to this. 'We'll ask them when we get home. They have to say yes too.'

He thought about his family. A grandfather he barely remembered, a father he had hardly seen. Family was so important to him, yet he knew nothing about his own. 'It's strange not knowing who I am or where I'm from. Not like you at all.'

She laughed. 'My family goes all the way back to the *Mayflower* and we have the ugly noses to show for it.'

He leant forward and kissed her forehead. 'I love your ugly nose.'

She smiled and let the smile drift away from her lips. 'You have to find out before you decide. I couldn't stand a mad troop of Birthers digging up anything sordid from your past.'

He kissed her again, this time on the lips. 'Don't worry, we'll find out soon. Now we just have to convince the kids.'

She looked at him mischievously. 'Oh, did I forget to tell you? I asked them already.'

'Really?'

'I had a chat with them. Tammy wants to turn the White House pink and Charles has decided he wants his own Secret Service man to play basketball with.'

He kissed his wife again. God, how he loved this woman.

Chapter Fourteen

Monday, April 17, 2017
Somewhere beneath the streets of London

'Sir, they are on the move again.'

He adjusted his position to look at the screen. CCTV had spotted them running down Fleet Street, towards the city.

'Get Blake and his men out of their holding positions and after them.'

'Yes, sir.' The operative spoke into his microphone.

'Bring other units in from the west.' He brought a map of London up on his screen. 'Take them along the Strand and the Embankment. We'll shepherd them to here.' He clicked to leave a marker on the map.

'Got it, sir.'

Ostransky smiled to himself. Keep them moving, keep them off guard, keep the pressure on. This time, shepherd them past the Royal Courts of Justice to Temple Underground. The irony was delicious. 'You'd better bring up the Underground CCTV, we don't want to lose them down there.'

'Yes, sir.'

He picked up his green tea and lifted the lid, placing it on the edge of the cup to prevent the leaves from entering his mouth. He would be able to make a positive report this evening to the Organisation; the Führer would be pleased. As head of operations, it was his job to ensure their plans went smoothly and this one was going exactly the way he wanted it.

Perhaps now he would finally receive the recognition that had been held from him. Perhaps he would be promoted to one of the twelve chairs around the world.

It was time; he had waited so long.

He took another sip of tea, feeling the grassy liquid slip down his throat. He had always wanted to live in Japan. There was something stark and minimalist about Japanese culture that appealed to him. Mishima was one of his heroes. Now he could follow in the man's footsteps. Only this time he would have power.

Real power.

Chapter Fifteen

Monday, April 17, 2017
St. Brides's Church, London

Jayne ran out of St. Bride's Church and along the narrow lane leading to Fleet Street. Alongside her, David limped along grimacing with every step.

At Fleet Street, she looked both ways down the street. Which way to go? Left or right? The sanctuary of St Paul's or the Courts of Justice? She remembered the conversation of their pursuers. They were searching the area around St Bride's Theatre. That was on the right, back towards the river. She turned to David. 'How's the ankle?'

He nodded his head. 'It's been better, but I'll survive.'

'This way.' She grabbed hold of his arm and hustled him to the left. Behind her, the sound of a police siren cut through the noise of the heavy traffic.

Were they after them again? How had they found them so quickly?

She looked over her shoulder. Nobody was chasing them.

Yet.

'Hurry, David, we have to keep moving.'

Two elderly women stopped and stared at them, stepping aside as Jayne and David ran past, shaking their heads.

Jayne ran on with David limping beside her, past the assorted banks, sandwich shops, Starbucks, pubs and wine bars, offices, dentists and pharmacies of this part of London. No more newspapers were based here, though, they had left for the delights of Wapping years ago.

David was still keeping up with her, despite panting heavily.

Behind them the sound of police sirens was getting louder. She knew they were after them now, but how?

At the corner of Fetter Lane, she stopped. Should they go right here, or carry on down Fleet Street?

'Where are we going?' David gasped.

Jayne thought for a moment. The truth was, she didn't know. Her whole world was Manchester and she didn't like London at all, finding it a cold place to live, inhabited by cold people.

She had lived in London once for three months when she was sixteen. A time of teenage rebellion against the harsh strictures of her mother. She still remembered the cold, lonely nights of that winter as she struggled to survive, eventually having no choice but to return home.

Her father was ecstatic at her return, her mother exultant at her embarrassment.

Not a happy time.

David noticed the confusion on her face. 'We could go to a flat the company keeps for guests in London. Senators and congressmen who want somewhere quiet to stay.'

'Sounds perfect, where is it?'

'Not far, near the American Embassy.'

The wail of the siren was right behind them now, changing pitch as it swerved between the oncoming traffic.

'Come on, we've got to keep moving.' As she grabbed David's arm, Jayne noticed a large green metal pole standing on a traffic island. She looked up. The camera mounted at the top panned down and pointed straight at her.

So that's how they were keeping track of them. They had access to the capital's CCTV. Who the hell were they dealing with? Who was after them?

She urged David to run faster. There was a squeal of tyres and brakes behind, followed by the blare of car horns.

They had to get away from the cameras. She started to remove her coat. 'Take off your jacket,' she shouted at David.

'What? It's Armani.'

'I don't care if it's the best from Burton's, take it off.'

Reluctantly, David removed his jacket, stuffing his passport and wallet into his trouser pockets. Jayne snatched it from him and threw it and her coat across a drunken tramp sleeping in a doorway.

'Down here. Now.' She grabbed his arm and ran through the narrow gate of a mock Tudor building into another alley. Behind her, Jayne could hear shouts and running feet.

'Quick, this way.' They hurried down the alley into an open courtyard dominated by a large round church. In the centre, a group of Chinese tourists were taking acres of photographs in front of the stone walls, ignoring the attempts of a tour leader with a red flag waving above his head to keep them under control.

'I recognise this. It's the church in the film...' David panted.

The Da Vinci Code, but no time to sightsee.' Jayne weaved through the chattering tourists, heading for another alley on the right-hand side of the courtyard.

'Why did we take off our coats?'

'The cameras. I'll explain later.'

She stopped, waiting for David. He was breathing heavily. 'My ankle...can't go much further.'

Jayne checked right and left. A Chinese tourist approached her with a camera. She waved him away. Now was not the time for a bloody selfie.

She glanced backwards over her shoulder. Nobody was following them, but she could still hear the sound of police sirens on Fleet Street.

Then there was a new sound, in front of her, but still far away, coming from the direction of Westminster.

'Keep moving.' She grabbed David's arm again and ran down Pump Court through a quadrangle surrounded by cramped offices. She knew this area well, having delivered sandwiches to the many barristers' chambers in these buildings. Fusty, ancient places, filled with the stench of old paper, old men and old money. The sandwiches she sold were as old as the buyers. A terrible job, but it had kept her alive during her exile away from her mother in London. The stale sandwiches left over at the end of the day were her one source of nourishment.

David limped after her, crossed the quadrangle and emerged into the bright sunlight of Middle Temple Lane, his elegant shoes dragging on the ground.

In front of them, a group of barristers were discussing a case, their white wigs reflecting the sun and their black gowns blowing in the breeze. The cobblestoned road sloped down towards the river, with more barristers and their besuited solicitors and clerks walking up towards them. No cars were allowed here. At least the fake police would be unable to drive after them.

'Can't go much further.' David put his hands on his knees, his breath coming in huge heaves. 'The ankle... hurts too much.'

'Not far to the Underground, come on.'

Jayne seized his arm and pulled him along with her. He almost tripped and fell, but she managed to keep him upright.

'Not far, keep going.'

They were halfway along the street when she looked back over her shoulder. A man had just come out of their alley and stopped on seeing the barristers. He brought his sleeve up to his mouth and began talking.

'Come on.'

David limped after her.

She looked over her shoulder again.

The man was walking after them, taking his time, not running. He looked like another solicitor making his way back to his chambers.

Then the clear sound of police sirens coming from both sides, the right and left, getting closer with every disorienting wail.

She glanced back again.

Three more men had joined their pursuer. This time, each was dressed in a dark suit and black tie. They spread out in a line across the street and advanced towards her and David, ignoring the billowing black clothes of the barristers.

'Hurry, David,' Jayne shouted, throwing his arm around her neck.

They ran under the arch of an ancient building dressed in white stone, and through a pair of open iron gates. In front of them lay a formal garden and beyond it the busy road of the Embankment, with the grey, silent Thames glistening in the distance.

David stopped moving, leaning into Jayne and readjusting his position. 'Can't... keep... going...' he gasped through gritted teeth.

'A hundred yards, that's all, David. Temple Station is down here.'

She hooked her left arm under his armpit and hurried him along the path through the garden.

People sitting on the benches at the side of the path ignored them, continuing to eat their sandwiches and chat, or simply enjoy the rare sun. One man even took the opportunity to look away, pretending they didn't exist, returning to peer into his *Daily Mail*.

Jayne looked over her shoulder again. The men were still striding relentlessly towards her, confident smiles etched on to their faces.

Why weren't they running? Why weren't they chasing after them?

Jayne realised instantly those men were the sheepdogs, herding their flock towards the area they wanted them to be.

She and David just happened to be the sheep.

A motorbike appeared on the right of the garden, revving its engine. Behind the handlebars sat the two riders who'd murdered Jack Wayne, their black helmets staring straight at her.

They weren't going to make it.

The sign for Temple station, with its red circle and blue bar shining out, was up ahead. Already, the cars were pulling to the left to make way for the police.

The sirens were screeching louder and louder, closer and closer. The motorbike was revving its engine, ready to let loose the cogs of war.

Behind her, Jayne could feel the steady march of the men herding her to the river.

The motorbike slipped its engine into gear. The sound changed from a throaty purr to a high-pitched snarl, grit erupting from behind the rear wheel.

The bike was racing towards them, the black visors of the riders reflecting light, revealing nothing about the men behind the glass.

The sirens were close now, deafening. A police car screeched off the Embankment and up on to the pavement, its tyres slewing wildly on the red grit.

The motorbike slammed into the side of the police car, throwing the rider over the top of the bonnet in a graceful somersault. The pillion passenger hit the blue glass of the flashing light on top, instantly smashing it.

The siren stopped.

People stood still for a moment, before finally rushing to the rider lying on the floor. Even the *Daily Mail* reader had looked up from his paper to find out what was going on.

Jayne grabbed David's arm. 'This way.'

She dragged David to the left, urging him to keep going. The men in suits had started to run after them now, finally breaking their formation.

David broke her grip on his arm, 'No, this way.' He limped through the stalled traffic across the road to the opposite side, opening the door of a black cab which had stopped for a moment.

'In here,' he shouted.

Jayne ran to join him, diving into the back of the cab.

'Where to?' the cabbie asked as another police car accelerated past them on the other side of the road, its siren blaring.

'The American Embassy in Grosvenor Square,' ordered David.

'You a yank?' asked the cabbie.

David nodded at the pair of eyes looking at him through the rearview mirror. A police car zoomed past them on the other side of the road, it's lights flashing and siren blaring.

'They don't half make a blooming racket, don't they. I bet it's louder where you live though, mate.'

'It sure is,' said David, 'but not as dangerous.'

Chapter Sixteen

Monday, April 17, 2017
Somewhere beneath the streets of London

'Blake is reporting that he has lost them, sir.'

Ostransky scratched his hand once more. The eczema was active today, its constant itch an irritation as he tried to concentrate. Once again she had managed to disappear. 'How?'

'An unavoidable accident. Two operatives are down.'

'More incompetence.'

The operator did not relay his comment to the men in the field.

'How did they get away?'

A quick conversation and the operator reported back to him. 'A black cab, sir. They didn't get the number.'

'Fools. And worse, incompetent fools.'

'Shall I convey the message, sir?'

He waited for a moment before answering. 'No. Tell them to stand down until further notice. Get on to the taxi companies, find out where they were taken. They may be stupid enough to go directly to the address, but with this woman, I doubt it.'

'Which identity should I use, sir?'

'I think Interpol for this inquiry. A detective from Holland inquiring into the drugs trade. Give them our contact number in the Met and warn him he may get a call. Make sure he's well briefed.'

'Yes, sir.'

'And get him to think of an excuse for today's actions. Something that would justify so much police activity.'

'A terrorist threat?'

'No. Something less memorable. Leave it up to him.'

'Yes, sir.'

They had lost them for now, but he was sure he could find them again. Blake was an incompetent fool. Time to terminate him. All he had to do was herd the two of them into the Underground. From there, Ostransky could have followed their every move on the CCTV without them knowing.

He scratched the reddening skin between his thumb and his index finger. The eczema was flaring badly today. Damn Blake and his incompetence.

Chapter Seventeen

Monday, April 17, 2017
Manchester Square, London

Jayne peered out of the curtains on to the empty street. The apartment was on the second floor of a building overlooking Manchester Square. It had amused her when David had told her the address. Wherever she went, Manchester was always involved somehow.

Perhaps there was more to David than met the eye. He had been the one to tell the cabbie to drop them half a mile from here even though it was painful for him to limp to the safe house. A clever move, hiding their final destination. Jayne should have thought of that, not him.

Their progress had been slow, Jayne constantly listening for the ominous whine of a police siren approaching in the distance.

It was the first time she had ever been afraid of that noise. In her previous life as a Manchester detective, she had loved the moment when, racing to a crime, they had switched on the siren. It had always given her a childish sense of power and control, the excitement of not knowing what they would find when they arrived.

But today had destroyed all that. Now the sound only produced one reaction in her. Fear.

She put her head round the curtains again. The street and the gardens beyond were empty. Only a solitary yellow light illuminated the scene.

'Are you sure this place is safe?' she asked, without taking her eyes off the square below.

David was resting on the couch, his sprained ankle raised on a cushion. 'Only I have the keys. Senators, congressmen and others have stayed here but they are unlikely to have told anybody.'

Jayne let the curtain fall back into place. She suddenly felt immensely tired, as if a huge weight had been placed on her shoulders, pressing her into the deep carpet.

The apartment was small but expensively furnished with all the blandness and lack of character of a modern hotel.

She slumped down into one of the armchairs. Her body felt like the bones had been removed and all that was left was the floating pain of sheer exhaustion.

'How's the ankle?' she asked.

'Painful.'

She dragged herself up from the comfort of the armchair and over to where David lay on the couch. She slowly removed his shoe and sock, watching him wince as she did so. 'Can you move your toes?'

His feet flexed upwards, the toes moving together. She placed her hands on his swollen ankle, gently pressing down with her fingertips. The skin was soft, almost feminine, not how she had imagined it at all. 'It doesn't seem to be broken, you probably stretched the tendons when you fell over.'

'It's painful, whatever it is.'

She pulled his trouser down to cover the ankle. 'I'll get some ice from the kitchen. Just rest it for now.'

She stood up and a twinge of pain shot through her back. *You're getting too old for this sort of stuff, Jayne*, she thought.

Inside the fridge were three bottles of champagne, and two each of a passable white and red. There was also a block of off-white cheese, a shrink pack of prosciutto and three packs of condoms.

Why would they keep condoms in the fridge? She was going to ask David but then she realised exactly what use the congressmen and senators must make of the apartment.

In one small freezer compartment she found a bag of ice, and in another, two Kit-Kats and a Hershey Bar. Just what she needed. Not the best chocolate but it would do.

She went back into the living room. David lay with his head back and eyes closed. She placed the ice pack on his ankle and instantly he shot up. 'What the —'

'Relax, the ice will help bring down the swelling.'

She snapped off one of the sticks of chocolate and offered it to him. He shook his head.

She bit into it. The sugar hit her immediately, giving her body a wonderful rush of energy.

Better.

'What are we going to do?' David stared at her, waiting for an answer.

Get control of yourself, Jayne. Get back to work. Think like a detective.

THINK.

She reached into her bag and took out the folder from their meeting, placing it on the coffee table. 'We need to go through today. Try to understand why your boss was murdered. Was he working on anything else?'

David shook his head. 'As far as I know, he wasn't.'

'He was going back to Washington this evening?'

'I booked the flight myself.'

'The motorcycle was waiting for us when we came out of the restaurant. Who knew we were meeting there?'

'Well, obviously myself, Mr Wayne and you, and Daniel Jackson. Nobody else.'

Jayne thought for a moment. 'The restaurant?'

'I booked it under a false name. Money talks, especially on a Monday.'

'Somebody must have known we were meeting there.' Her brain felt as woolly as a down fleece. She needed more chocolate and she needed it now.

'I don't think so,' he mumbled.

'Had you used it before for meetings?'

David nodded.

'They could have found out through the restaurant. Or they could have followed you both. Or one of the waiters may have told somebody. But something else is troubling me...'

Jayne thought back to the motorcyclist and his passenger, the dark, smoking barrel of the pistol, the metallic click of the hammer striking metal.

A shudder tsunamied down her spine. 'Who was the target? Was it all three of us or just Jack Wayne?'

David sat up straighter, adjusting the ice pack on his ankle.

A deep crease formed between Jayne's eyebrows. 'They didn't stop after they killed him, wanting us all dead. Which leads to my next question: why?'

'Look, the only thing I've been doing for the company is checking out Dan Jackson's family history. It's the most important project at the moment.'

Jayne sat back in her chair. 'Neither Jack Wayne nor yourself ever told me what your company does, David.'

The young man let out a long sigh. 'We're lobbyists. I know it's not the most popular profession at the moment but we do serve a purpose.'

'Which is?'

'To keep the concerns of our clients at the top of the political agenda of the Washington establishment.'

'And who are your clients on this case?'

He shrugged his shoulders. 'Above my pay grade, I'm afraid.'

'Let me remind you somebody tried to kill us today, so take a guess.'

'I don't know. It could be Dan Jackson...'

'Possible. But why go through your firm? He could have hired a genealogist like me himself. Who else?'

'His financial backers...'

'Financial backers?'

'Look, an election in the States costs a billion dollars. Somebody has to stump up the cash. That's what the meeting is about on Friday. Dan Jackson wants the support of a particular group of Bilderberg billionaires but he needs their money even more.'

'Bilderberg?'

'An annual meeting of some of the richest men on the planet. They discuss world events in secrecy. It's a private club for the rich and powerful, and their political friends. Occasionally, they will provide financial backing for their favoured candidates in an election.'

'And they look for a return on their investment?'

'Again, above my pay grade. But these are extremely rich businessmen. You do the math.'

Jayne opened the folder on the coffee table in front of her and stared at the picture of the young Boy Scout. 'Who else?'

'Who could be our clients? Anybody with an axe to grind against Dan Jackson.'

'Hold it. What do you mean? He's your client.'

'But we may also have a client who wants to work against him.'

'You'd take them on?'

'Of course, as long as they paid us.'

'And how would you feel about that?'

'Oh, I wouldn't know. It would be kept compartmentalised, and besides, it's —'

'Above your pay grade. I get the picture. Who else could have employed you?'

David took his time to think. 'One of the other political parties. Or somebody who wants to see how easy it is to find out any dirt.' David threw his hands up in the air. 'Look, I don't know who the hell it could be. It could be the CIA for all I know.'

Jayne realised she had pushed him too far. She softened her voice and changed tack. 'What about Jack Wayne? What was his plan?'

David sighed. 'Jack wasn't a great sharer, Mrs Sinclair, especially not with someone like me.'

'What do you mean?'

'Listen, let's lay our cards on the table. I'm only working for the firm because my dad got me the job. It's called connections. My dad and Jack's boss go way back. I'm just a glorified intern. Next year, I'm starting film school in New York. This is simply to tide me over till then.'

There was a silence between them.

'Thanks for the honesty, David,' Jayne finally said.

'If it's any consolation, I'm a better director than I am a lobbyist. Well, at least I think so, anyway.' He took the ice pack off and gingerly placed his leg on the ground, wincing slightly as it touched the floor. 'Shall I rustle us up some food? We usually keep some in the freezer in case a congressman or his "friend" get hungry.'

The empty wrapper of the chocolate bar lay open on the table; it was the only thing she had eaten all day. 'That would be great, David, thanks.'

'It'll have to be simple, I'm afraid. Hopalong Cassidy cooking.'

Jayne watched as he limped into the kitchen.

After a short while, he shouted, 'How does a steak sound?'

'Moo?' Jayne answered.

His head appeared around the kitchen door. 'And here was I thinking you had no sense of humour, Mrs Sinclair.'

Chapter Eighteen

Monday, April 17, 2017
Somewhere beneath the streets of London

Felix Ostransky took the key from around his neck and unlocked the door to a room on the lowest corridor of the basement. The door had no number and no name. The room it led to wasn't even included in the schematics of the building.

But it did exist. He visited it every evening at 8 p.m. precisely.

After closing the door behind him, he was confronted by two screens fixed in the centre of a solid wall.

He placed his right palm on one of the screens and stared directly into the other. A band of vibrant green light scanned both his hand and his face.

'Speak,' ordered the screen.

'Ostransky, Felix.'

'Voice recognised. Proceed.'

The wall on his left slid away to reveal a round conference room. There was no table, just a single chair on a raised plinth. On the walls, twelve flatscreen televisions leant slightly forward to face the black chair. They were arranged clock-like in a circle at head height. Beneath each of the screens was a single word: Britain, South Africa, Japan, America, Russia, Argentina, Australia, China, Brazil, Sweden, Egypt.

Ostransky hated the chair. He hated the impersonal nature of the screens. He hated being interrogated. He hated facing the single screen with nothing beneath it.

He strode over to the black chair and sat in it, adjusting his jacket so it didn't ride up as he spoke. It was important to look the part.

One by one the screens flashed on. But there were no faces; instead the logo of the snarling wolf appeared, each one a different colour. Only one man knew who the twelve heads of the movement were. Even to Ostransky, they were simply disembodied voices.

Finally, the screen at the twelve o'clock position was illuminated. An elderly man, grey hair neatly parted on the left and swept back off a high forehead, came into view. The eyes were blue, a piercing blue. Ostransky immediately felt uncomfortable, shifting nervously in his seat.

The man began to speak. A voice with a slight hint of a German accent. A commanding voice, one that knew it was going to be obeyed. 'America sends its apologies, it cannot be with us tonight. Ostransky, your update.'

Ostransky shifted in his seat once more. He must be confident, precise. A suggestion of weakness, the slightest hesitation, would be fatal. 'It is proceeding as planned, sir.' Enough, say no more. He must be seen to be in control.

The commanding voice again. 'The Jacksons are on their way back to America as we speak. The newspapers have been informed of the possibility of his candidature.'

'Ostransky.' A female voice came from the television with the word 'Argentina' beneath the screen. 'Are you sure everything is going to plan? Has the woman…?'

'Her name is Jayne Sinclair,' Ostransky filled in the pause.

'Yes, that woman. Has she found anything yet?'

Ostransky had to be careful here. Had Argentina heard a different story? 'Not that I am aware of, madam,' he answered confidently.

'Are you sure?'

'Argentina,' the leader interrupted, 'do you have differing information?'

'No, I—'

'Well, I think we should rely upon the answer of our Chief of Operations, don't you?'

A chorus of agreement issued from the speakers.

The leader continued. 'He understands the consequences of failure, don't you, Ostransky?'

The threat was there. When Ostransky was no longer of use to the Organisation, the end would be silent and lethal, a successor already in place as he drew his last breath.

He took a deep breath and answered. 'I do, Führer. But I would like to repeat my counsel from our previous meeting. The destruction of all documents and the termination of the individuals involved would be a much more effective solution to the problem.'

'But not a final solution, Ostransky. What about the documents we are unaware of? As Don Rumsfeld said, "There are known knowns. These are things we know that we know. There are known unknowns. That is to say, there are things that we know we don't know. But there are also unknown unknowns. There are things we don't know we don't know." It's the unknown that is important. The threat of discovery would always be there hanging over us. We must be certain that all possibilities have been covered before the meeting with the Bilderberg group on Friday. At the moment, our candidate needs their money and political connections. Without their backing, he will not succeed.'

'I understand, sir.'

'Execute the plan, Ostransky. Keep them moving and off balance. Find the unknowns.'

'Yes, sir.'

'Ladies and gentlemen, the day is nearly upon us. The day we have been waiting for since 1945. I am the fourth Führer of the Organisation, but I won't be the last. I am determined that during my leadership there will be no more skulking in basements. No more hiding behind television screens. No more concealment of our beliefs, policies and ideology. The course set by the first Führer must be followed through and completed. We now have the opportunity to create the Fourth Reich. A Reich which will bring pride back to the Aryan peoples all over the planet, raising them to their true status as the leaders of the world. We must not fail now.'

A chorus of approval came from the screens.

'We will succeed. We must succeed.'

The leader's screen went blank.

Ostransky stood up, his arm shooting straight out, as stiff as an airplane wing. '*Heil Führer.*'

A chorus of '*Heil Führer*' echoed around the room, before the logo vanished from each screen.

Now to get to work, thought Ostransky, *time to find the woman.*

Chapter Nineteen

Monday, April 17, 2017
Manchester Square, London

'You can cook.' Jayne placed her cutlery back on the plate and wiped her mouth with a napkin.

'Just a steak and salad. Nothing to boast about.'

'You'd be surprised how many men can't make a simple meal.'

'Like your husband?'

'Paul? He can't boil an egg without burning it.' A frown creased her forehead. 'You seem to know a lot about me, David.'

He laughed. 'I suppose I do. We performed background checks before we hired you. The recommendation of John Hughes clinched your appointment.'

'You will also know myself and my husband separated when he moved to Brussels.'

David looked down. 'It did come up in the research.' He reached for the wine and attempted to pour some more for her. She covered the top of her wine glass with her hand.

'But I know very little about you, other than you think you are a better film director than you are a lobbyist.'

'Not much to know really. I grow up in Connecticut. Dad taught at the University and Mom was a homemaker. Two elder sisters, both married with kids. A classic American suburban childhood, I guess; apple pie, TV, proms, band classes, baseball, high school, college.'

'Except?'

'Except?'

'In everybody's life there's always an except.'

He smiled. 'Except I was adopted by my father and mother when I was child and brought to America.'

'You've never met your birth mother since?' Jayne interrupted.

'No. I don't want to either. No point. My real parents were the ones in Connecticut, David and Sally Mercer.'

'No memories of your childhood before America?'

'Some.' He reached for the bottle again and tried to pour some wine for her.

Jayne shook her head. 'We should get back to work.'

While David cleared the table, she reached for the folder given to her by Jack Wayne, pulling out the copy of the naturalisation certificate of Dan Jackson's grandfather.

Beneath the elaborate border and those easily recognised block letters for the United States of America, a long description followed in a flowing typeface. The description was interrupted by the information typed in gaps that were left specifically for it:

Personal description of holder as of date of naturalisation. **Age: 36 years. Sex: male. Color: white. Complexion: light. Color of eyes: blue, Color of hair: blond. Height: 5 feet 8 inches.- Weight: 155 pounds. Visible distinctive marks: scars on right shoulder and left temple.**

Marital status: Single. Former nationality: British.

I certify that the description above is true and the photograph offered hereto is a likeness of me.

Jayne stared at the signature. It looked shaky and uneven, as if the grandfather were ill when he signed it. A badly taken photograph of a man wearing wire-framed spectacles was also signed beneath in the same spindly signature. The picture was ordinary – bland, even: the sort of man you wouldn't notice in a crowd.

The rest of the certificate gave all his American details:

State of New York
County of Albany

Be it known that at a hearing of the Superior Court of Albany County held pursuant to law at Albany Court, Eagle St on January 11, 1955 the court hearing found that Thomas Caldwell Jackson then residing at Bedford Road, Albany intends to reside permanently in the United States (when so required by the naturalisation laws of the United States) and has in all such respects complied with the applicable provisions of all such naturalisation laws and was entitled to be admitted to citizenship, thereupon ordered that such person be and was admitted as a citizen of the United States of America.

In testimony whereof this seal the court is hereby offered this eleventh day of January in the year of our Lord nineteen hundred and fifty-five and of our Independence the one hundred and seventy-ninth.

It was signed below by a judge and stamped with an official looking seal. It all looked authentic as far as she could see.

David limped over and sat down beside her. At least he was moving slightly more freely than before.

'What are you doing?' he asked, brushing his long black hair away from his forehead.

'Looking for clues to Dan Jackson's family history.'

'You're not going ahead with it, are you?' David threw his hands up. 'You still want to carry on with your research? Are you crazy?'

'Listen, David. This all started when Dan Jackson wanted to find out about his grandfather's past. It seems to me that if we carry on looking for the truth, we may also find out why Jack Wayne was murdered and why we were shot at.'

'But—'

'And anyway, I agreed to do a job. I'm not a quitter. We need to find out if the investigation is linked to Jack's death.'

David opened his mouth as if to speak, saw the determined look on Jayne's face and decided it would be better to keep quiet.

'Does that thing work?' She pointed to the laptop sitting on the desk in the corner.

'Of course, the senators need access to their files and emails.'

He went over and booted it up, quickly typing a password into the field. 'The password is "True Grit" in case you need to use it later.'

Jayne joined him at the desk. 'Was that Jack Wayne's idea?'

'Actually, it was mine – a joke. Jack didn't approve.'

She sat down and logged on to FreeBMD.com.

'What are you doing?'

'Checking your research. This site will give us the file number of his birth, if it exists.'

'It won't show the birth certificate?'

'No. But with the file number, we'll be able to apply for the birth certificate. Dan said his grandfather, Thomas Jackson, was born in Hereford around 1920.'

She typed the name and date into the field and pressed search. The result came back quickly: "Sorry, we found no matches."

She expanded the dates to cover 1914 to 1924. The same message was repeated.

'I told you we would find nothing.'

Jayne thought for a moment. 'Let's broaden the search.' She took out Hereford and left it blank. 'Now we're searching the whole of the UK. Jackson as a surname is a bit of a nightmare for genealogists. Far too common, but not as bad as Smith.'

Jayne pressed enter. A total of 4009 entries came back, all using the name Thomas Jackson.

'It's going to take years to go through all these one by one. We don't have the time.'

One last search. She logged on to findmypast.com and checked the 1939 Register.

'What's this website?' David asked.

'Just after the war began the British Government registered all citizens living in the United Kingdom, giving details of their professions, age, sex and date of birth. It's a wonderful resource for the period.' She typed in the name Jackson, adding a search string for Hereford.

Nothing.

Once again, she expanded the search and received over 3000 hits.

'It didn't help much, did it?'

She shook her head.

'You've reached the same point I did. I hit the wall when I tried to find out who he was and where he came from.'

She closed the laptop firmly. 'I need to think.'

She got up from the desk and walked over to the window, opening the curtain slightly to peer outside. The streets were still quiet, with just a pair of lovers walking hand in hand, staring into each other's eyes.

She turned back to David. 'Let's check the news. We need to find out what's happening in Jack's case – there's bound to be something. After that, I'll call a friend in the police. Somebody I trust. It's time we made a statement about today, but only to someone I know.'

She picked up the remote, switched on the TV, and searched the news channels.

Nothing on the 24-hour BBC channel, although apparently President Trump was reviewing designs for his wall. Sky News was equally blank. She found the local London channel.

Nothing.

A man had been shot dead in the centre of London and nobody was reporting it.

Jayne surfed across all the channels available.

Nothing.

Then she hit CNN. A handsome middle-aged man was sheltering his wife as they hustled out of La Guardia airport in New York through a mob of reporters.

'Mr Jackson, is it true you're going to stand as an independent in the 2020 election?'

'Mr Jackson, any comment please?'

'Mr Jackson, what are your next steps?'

There was a wobble to the feed, a blaze of flash-lights, and the long arm of a security guard covered the camera as a black Lincoln Town Car raced away from the kerb.

The image cut to an announcer standing in front of a brown townhouse, somewhere in Manhattan. 'CNN sources have informed us that Daniel Jackson, Chairman of internet security company Indios, is considering running as an independent in the 2020 presidential elections. Mr Jackson has built up his company from nothing over the last twenty years, and has been the angel investor in many of the most famous internet start-ups; Facebook, Uber and Google, to name a few. A spokesperson for Mr Jackson had no comment. We understand an announcement on the candidacy will be made next week.'

The camera cut back to a man wearing far too much tan make-up in a studio. 'In sports news, the LA Dodgers...'

Jayne switched it off. 'They've already begun speculating about the candidacy. I thought they were going to wait until I had finished my research on Friday?'

David sat up. 'They are trailing the news.'

'Trailing the news?'

'It's like throwing bait into a pond to lure fish to begin feeding. The fish, in this case, being the world's reporters.'

'It seems the clock has already started ticking without us knowing.'

'What are we going to do?'

'I think we have to find out who is behind all this. And the only way to do that is to do what Jack Wayne asked me to do.'

'Investigate Dan Jackson's background?'

'Exactly. But first I have to make a call to an old friend in Scotland Yard.'

And then it hit her. Her father. She had been on the phone to him when the motorcyclists had attacked.

'Make that two calls.'

Chapter Twenty

Monday, April 17, 2017
Manchester Square, London

London Jayne took the cordless phone into the bedroom and dialled her father. Once she told the police what she had seen, there would be no time to ring him.

The phone was answered quickly, as if he were sitting waiting for her to ring.

'Hello, who is it?'

'It's Jayne, Dad.'

'Thank goodness. We were talking and then all of a sudden we were cut off. What were the banging noises I heard?'

Jayne thought about telling her father exactly what had happened, but decided not to. It was too complicated to explain, and she didn't have an explanation.

If she told him everything he would worry about her and, knowing her dad, would insist on coming down to London to protect her as if she were still his five-year-old daughter.

'I'm sorry, Dad, I dropped my phone.' It was a bad lie and she knew it, but could think of nothing better. 'It smashed on the road.'

'I tried to ring you back, lass, but there was no answer.'

'I know, I'll have to buy a new phone.'

Her father's voice softened. 'When are you coming back, lass? You know me and Vera miss you.'

'I'll have to stay in London a couple more days. How is Vera?'

'She's fine, lass, sitting here with me now, having a cup of cocoa and a few biscuits.'

This was her father's habit. Since he had given up drinking beer at the ripe age of 65, the nightly cup of cocoa helped him sleep. 'Sounds like you're enjoying them.'

'Can't beat a baked biscuit.' There was a pause at the end of the phone. 'How's the case? Did the client brief you yet?'

'Okay. It's difficult. Not enough information.'

'Keep digging, you'll find it, lass. Always remember, the answer is out there somewhere, you just have to look in the right place.'

'I remember. Dig and you will discover.'

'That's it, lass. You were always my best pupil.'

'I'll tell you all about it when I see you. Got to go, Dad. Love you.'

'Love you too, lass. Look after yourself. Them people in London don't care for nobody. I can't abide the place myself. One time, I was...'

Jayne interrupted. 'Sorry, Dad, I've really got to go now.'

'Okay, see you soon.'

She hung up the phone quickly. She hated lying to her father, but it was for the best. He could do nothing to help and she didn't want to put him in any danger. She was in enough trouble as it was.

She looked into the living room. David was just sitting down on the couch and adjusting the ice pack on his ankle. Had he been listening to her call? She wasn't certain. But if his ankle hurt so badly, why had he moved?

She dismissed him from her mind. There were far more important things to do right now, like calling Harry.

She had met Detective Sergeant Harry Rimmer at the police college in Bramshill, on a course covering cyber crime. It was the latest police fad and, as one of the more computer-literate coppers in Manchester back then, she had inevitably been sent on it. They had hit it off immediately, sharing the same sense of humour and commitment to the job. It was obvious to Jayne that Harry had wanted to take the relationship further, but she was married to Paul at the time. For her, adultery didn't feel right. You were either loyal to someone or you weren't, there was nothing in between.

After the conference they still stayed in touch, helping each other with cases and fighting the rampant bureaucracy of the police with the best weapon they knew: humour.

'Hello.'

It was his voice, she recognised the cockney geezer vowels. 'Hi, Harry, it's Jayne,' she said tentatively.

'Jayne, great to hear from you, darlin'. It's been a long time. How's Paul?'

At the sound of her husband's name, Jayne winced. 'We've separated, he's living in Brussels now. But that's not why I'm calling...' she added quickly in case he got the wrong idea.

'Sorry to hear, Jayne.'

'Actually, I'm calling to check up on something.'

'How can I help?'

'I'm checking on an incident that happened earlier today in the city.'

'I'm on the job at the moment, let me get to the log page.' Jayne heard the rapid clicking of keys. 'What's the incident?'

'A shooting, around two p.m.'

There was a pause, followed by more clicking. 'Nothing on the log, Jayne. Are you sure?'

'Positive. On Dorset Rise.'

More clicking. 'Nothing here. We had one shooting yesterday but that was in Eltham. Some geezer topped himself with a shotgun. Not a pretty sight, apparently.'

'Are you sure? What about police called to an incident on Fleet Street around four thirty? Or a crash along the Embankment just after that time?'

Silence on the other end of the phone, followed by another fevered bout of clicking.

'Nothing. No incidents in the area at those times.'

'Are you certain?'

'Look, Jayne, I do know how to check a log, you know. I've even checked the Traffic log for any accidents in the area at the times you said.'

'And?'

'Nothing. Not a sausage. And a car crash on the Embankment would've been reported. I know my job.'

'Yeah, sure. Sorry.'

'Hang on...'

She heard the fevered clicking of a computer keyboard followed by a quiet chuckle. 'You were right, something's popped up on the screen just this minute.'

'What is it?'

'There was a film company shooting something or other in the area. Must have been one of those cops-and-robbers shows. You know, I've been watching one recently. *Line of Duty*. Biggest load of bollocks I've ever seen.'

Jayne interrupted him. 'A film company?'

'That's what it says here. And the times match what you thought you saw. They're all over the place these days, promoting London, they say. We had to close down Waterloo Bridge last week, all so some pint-sized star could walk over it pretending he'd single-handedly wiped out a terrorist mob. You wouldn't believe the chaos it caused.'

'Are you sure?'

'Am I sure the star was pint-sized? I met him, came up to my shoulders. Proper cocky geezer he was too.'

'No, I mean are you sure it was a film company?'

'Well, that's what it says here. And we've had no reports of shootings or gunfire anywhere. What with the state of alerts these days in London, we would have been all over it like a bad case of measles.'

Jayne knew what she had seen. And anyway, she still had Jack Wayne's blood on her clothes. He had been murdered. She had been shot at, whatever Harry said.

Her friend's voice changed in tone. 'Are you okay, Jayne? Do you want to meet up for a drink or something?'

That was the last thing on earth she wanted. 'Fine, Harry, fine. Thought I saw something this afternoon, in the City but I must have been mistaken. Like your log says, it was probably a film company. Anyway, thanks for your help and sorry for bothering you on the job.'

'Any time. If you need anything, you know where to find me.'

'Thanks for all your help. You've been a mate.' Jayne put down the phone quickly before Harry could ask any more questions. He was a smart copper and would quickly work out something wasn't right.

She walked back into the living room. David was still sitting in exactly the same position on the couch. 'The police know nothing about this afternoon. It's like it didn't happen.'

'How can somebody get shot on the street in the middle of London and the police know nothing?'

'I wish I knew, David. I wish I knew.'

Chapter Twenty-One

Sunday, October 4, 1936
East End, London

As Thomas looked around him, he could see most of the others sleeping on the bus, with one or two snoring loudly.

They had started off from Manchester with a few songs, and a crate of beer was handed around. Some of the men had been drinking before they got on the bus, and those were the first to fall asleep. The rest gradually followed, drifting off to the discordant lullaby and vibration of the engine.

Thomas Green and Johnnie Hawley sat at the front, just behind the driver. They were both wearing black uniforms. Johnnie's had the specially designed black shirt with its buttons on the side, modelled after the one worn by Sir Oswald himself. Thomas wore a plain black shirt Mutti had picked up at the market for 2/6.

It didn't matter, though – they were on their way to march through the East End, to show everyone the power of patriotism and the Will of the Nation.

As they neared London, the sky was beginning to show the first darts of dawn. The city was both bigger and dirtier than he had imagined, with lines of nondescript streets and dilapidated tenements. It reminded him of a less glamorous version of Hulme. It wasn't until they drove past Westminster Abbey, the Houses of Parliament and along the river that he could understand why this was called the mother of all cities.

The driver kept up a running commentary in his broad Birmingham accent. 'Here's the abbey, where the king was crowned in 1911, Lord bless him. And

103

here's where them there MPs sit. Waste of time, the lot of them, if you ask me. Big Ben is still on top over there, counting out the hours. They don't have much time left, do they?'

This elicited a big cheer from the back of the coach, though a few slept through it all. Johnnie would talk to them later about maintaining standards.

The driver dropped them off at the Tower of London. 'Now, this is where we meet at six p.m. this evening to go back to Manchester. Anybody not on the bus then will be left behind. Is that clear?'

There was mumbled agreement.

Harry bundled up the banner and clumsily threaded it through the door and off the coach. He could see the other BUF members assembling around them, a crowd of black shirts interspersed with the odd man in mufti.

They unfurled the banner and stood beneath it. The white letters, 'British Union of Fascists, Manchester Branch', stood out against the black background. At the top was the logo of the single lightning bolt, the flash in a circle, supposedly designed by Sir Oswald himself.

'There's not that many people; I was expecting more,' said Thomas, looking around at the assembling marchers.

Johnnie was quick to set him to rights. 'The Reds and the Jews are preventing people getting through to us. Don't worry, thousands of East Enders will join us when we start marching.'

He walked away to chat with one of the marshals, who was resplendent in a black shirt, black jodhpurs, knee-high boots polished to a silvery gleam and a BUF armband with the same lightning-bolt.

Thomas took it all in. The marchers were standing outside the old Royal Mint with the Tower of London behind them. There were banners from a few other cities: Birmingham, Exeter, Norwich, and even one from Liverpool, with a small crowd of Scousers making the high-pitched babble that groups of Scousers always do. Not that many marchers, though. Where were all the members?

Surrounding them was a phalanx of blue policemen, three deep, their pointed helmets topped with shiny silver buttons reflecting the sun of a late autumn day.

At the front of the column were six police horses and a marching band. Off to the left, Thomas could hear the muffled sounds of screaming and the crash of bottles being thrown, but he could see nothing, hidden as the Reds were behind the blue surge fence.

The band struck up a tune – a negro spiritual Thomas had only ever heard played in church.

Johnnie marched up to him. 'We're to assemble in the middle of the formation. Can you carry the Union Jack?'

'Me?'

'As the youngest, we thought it fitting. It's quite an honour, you know.'

Thomas picked up the flag and waved it in the air. As he did, a man dressed in black stepped out of the crowd and approached him, flanked by four burly guards and two photographers to capture his every action.

'Wave it high, son.' The voice was patrician and educated.

Thomas stuck an arm out horizontally from his body and brought his heels together as Johnnie had taught him to do. 'Mr Mosley, sir. It's a great honour...'

The fascist salute was returned by a slight wave of the arm. Sir Oswald Mosley continued walking past Thomas, inspecting his troops.

The march began to move forward, shuffling in one spot until enough ground had been made up at the front. Thomas lifted the Union Jack and waved it high. After twenty yards, they stopped.

'What is it? What's wrong?'

Johnnie peered over the top of the heads and waving flags. 'It's Cable Street up ahead. The Reds have blocked it with a tram. There's thousands of them.'

As they spoke, the mounted police horses galloped forward. Thomas could now see the crowds of people thronged around the stalled tram. The horses ploughed into them, officers' truncheons raised, striking down on unprotected heads, again and again.

The crowd thinned as people ran to escape the horses and the mahogany batons of their riders. Seconds later, it returned to reoccupy the space around the tram with even greater numbers. A white horse reared up on its hind hooves, throwing the blue-suited rider. Immediately, the policeman was surrounded by a mob of kicking and screaming demons. Three other policemen rushed forward, striking left and right, pulling their colleague from under the swinging feet and fists.

This human and horse dance flowed backwards and forwards for the next hour, neither side gaining or giving ground.

Thomas looked across at Johnnie, staring at the clashes further down the road. 'There seems to be a lot of them, and not so many of us.' He let the Union Jack drop to the ground, his arms tired from holding it up.

They waited in the same spot on the street in front of the Royal Mint for another hour. Up ahead, the noises were becoming louder. Again and again, the police charged into the crowd, only for it to vanish before them and reform in another place.

But still the way forward was blocked.

Then the order came to about face. Thomas raised the Union Jack high and saw it catch the wind, waving gently in the breeze.

They turned on their heels and began to march the other way, away from the East End.

A loud roar came from the assembled voices behind the tram.

Once more the police charged into the middle of the crowd, striking left and right, dragging men and women out by the collar and beating them as they lay on the ground, bodies curled up to protect themselves.

The band started up again, this time playing a marching song. The column moved off along the Embankment.

Thomas raised his flag even higher. Behind him he could hear shouts and screams, bottles being smashed, the high shrill of a woman being beaten, the blast of police whistles, the thud of batons on heads.

Johnnie rushed back. 'Mr Mosley has decided to march towards the City.'

'We're not going through the East End? I thought we wanted to show the Jews how powerful we were?'

Johnnie looked at him strangely. 'We don't question the leader, do we, Thomas? We are his to command, aren't we?'

'It's not that, it's just...' As Thomas spoke, the sound of fighting seemed to increase. Bricks and bottles began landing behind them, where they had been standing a minute ago.

Johnnie took his arm. 'We should get out of here. It's becoming too hot for my liking.' Thomas passed the flag to another man as Johnnie pulled him into a small street heading off to the right. It was strangely quiet, a restricted haven away from the batons of the police, the screams of the protestors and the drums of their band.

They both stopped for a moment. 'Shouldn't we go back?' said Thomas.

'Later, let it all quieten down first.'

A young woman walked past them, an expensive Leica camera slung around her neck.

'What are you doing?' Johnnie shouted across to her.

'What's it to you?'

He pointed to the black armband he wore with the word 'Steward' printed on it. 'You can't go down there.'

'Why not?'

She raised the camera to her face and clicked the shutter.

'The march, it's—' Thomas began speaking and then stopped as Johnnie grabbed the woman's arm.

'Let me go...!' She struggled to break free.

Johnnie held on tighter, pushing her back against the wall.

'I'm a photographer...' She fought to loosen his grip.

'You're a filthy Jew, that's what you are.' Johnnie punched her in the stomach and she collapsed on the floor. He pulled the camera from around her neck and examined it. 'Leica, excellent German workmanship. Too good for the likes of you.' He gave her another kick as she lay on the ground.

Thomas watched him, doing nothing to stop the assault. Johnnie kicked her again, stamping on her right leg.

Thomas felt the vein on his temple pulse and throb, his fists tightening and untightening.

Johnnie stepped back, still holding the camera and taking pictures of the woman as she lay on the floor.

For a second, she raised herself on to her elbow, blood streaming from her mouth. She struggled to say something through her broken lips and teeth, reaching up to take back the camera.

Thomas swung his boot as hard as he could, feeling the point of the toe connect and smash the bridge of her nose. He kicked again and again, stamping down on the inert body lying beneath him, crushing it into the pavement as one would crush a cockroach.

He stepped back, staring down at the small body, now curled into a foetal position, waiting for the next blow to land. Her shoe had come off, sitting upright on the pavement as if she had placed it there. He kicked her in the stomach once more, then stopped and looked at her. Her skirt had ridden up to reveal the sheer fabric of an expensive pair of stockings, the weave glistening in the light.

And then he was on the ground, a man on top of him raining down blows. Thomas covered his face and arms, but still the blows struck down.

Where was Johnnie? Why wasn't he helping?

Off to one side, the sound of a police whistle being blown. A gruff voice, the weight of the man lifted from his chest. A blue arm raising him to his feet and twisting his arm behind his back. A surge of pain though his shoulder and the whispered words in his ear: 'You're nicked.'

As Thomas was marched away, he glanced backwards over his shoulder. The woman lay unmoving against the wall, her leg twisted at a strange angle and a pool of blood forming under her head.

Chapter Twenty-Two

Tuesday, October 6, 1936
Magistrates Court, London

Thomas Green stared at the green-glazed walls of his cell. The place stank of a strange mixture of piss, shit, human sweat and fear. Lots of fear. Most of which came from him.

He didn't smoke, but he would love to have had a cigarette right now. Anything to break the monotony and torture of sitting here, waiting for them to come for him.

The only natural light came from a single pane of dimpled glass not more than six inches square, set high up where the wall met the ceiling. But the glass was so dirty hardly any light penetrated into the cell.

At night, they switched on the lamp above the door, but during the day, the cell was kept in a shadowy gloom. A place to suffer.

He sat on the edge of the concrete ledge, tugging his black shirt tighter around him. What would his mother think? What would she say? He imagined the hand-wringing and the whine in her voice, the German accent getting stronger as she became more emotional.

'Why did ju do it, Thomas? What haf I done to deserve a son like dis?'

Thomas tried to drive the image out of his mind. Had Johnnie done anything to get him out of here?

When he was being marched off by the copper, his arm twisted halfway up his back, he had seen Johnnie vanishing around a corner, running hell for leather. At least he got away.

He brushed his hair away from his eyes. The woman's face appeared in his mind. The look of fear in her eyes. The soft, forgiving thud as his boot smashed into the middle of her stomach. The blood, wet and dripping, from her mouth where the teeth had once been.

A shiver of pleasure ran down his spine. She had got what she deserved; no more, no less.

'Green, Thomas S.,' a sergeant shouted through the metal door.

'Yes,' answered Thomas, putting his hand up like an errant schoolboy.

'A visitor.'

A large key was inserted into the lock and the metal gears turned with a loud clunk.

Who was it? His mother? Or Johnnie?

Instead a small, fat man with four strands of hair combed over his bald pate stood in the doorway. 'Thomas Green?'

He put his hand up once more.

'I'm your brief. We haven't got much time, so listen carefully.'

He turned back to the sergeant. 'You can leave us now. Please turn on the light, I want to be able to see my client.'

'Yes, sir.'

Thomas turned his head away when the light was switched on, its brightness burning his eyes.

The barrister sat down on the concrete ledge next to him. 'When we get you in the dock, you are to answer exactly how I tell you, do you understand?'

'But I... who?' Thomas stammered.

'Come along, man. We haven't got all day. Do you understand?'

'Yes, whatever you say.'

The barrister stank of a heavy, sweet cologne. Not a bad smell, but when mixed with the putrid scents that sweated from the walls of the cell, it was a mix that was far too rich for Thomas's stomach. He gagged.

'If you're going to be sick, I'll leave now and you can enjoy your three-month stretch, do I make myself clear?'

Thomas nodded, covering his mouth with his hand and swallowing the vomit back down into his stomach.

'Here's what you are to say.'

Thomas listened attentively as the barrister outlined the strategy. 'Do you understand?' he asked a few minutes later.

Thomas nodded.

'And put this on before you are called.' The barrister passed a freshly laundered white shirt to him.

'What should I do with this?' He pulled off the bloodstained black shirt his mother had bought for him.

'Use it as a hankie for all I care. But get rid of it.'

And then he was off, leaving a peculiar aftersmell of cologne as the only indicator of his presence.

As Thomas was rehearsing his lines, the sergeant returned.

'You, Green. Out now. You're up before the beak. It's Mr Turner, a right bastard, and Charlie here tells me he's in a foul mood.'

Another policeman appeared by his side. 'His dog was run over this morning. He's not an 'appy camper, is our Mr Turner. Well, what are you waiting for? Stand up straight, lad, and follow me.'

They walked the length of a lime-hued tiled corridor. The government must have bought a job lot of these tiles, Thomas thought, eventually walking up some wooden stairs into an open court.

Facing Thomas was an old man dressed in a suit, feverishly scribbling something in a notepad.

A clerk stood up and said, 'Thomas Green, you are charged in this court with causing an affray on the morning of October fourth. How do you plead?'

Thomas remembered the words of his barrister. 'Not guilty, your worship,' he stammered.

'Speak up, man. You're in a court of law, not the whispering gallery of St Paul's,' the magistrate admonished from the bench.

'Not guilty,' repeated Thomas more loudly.

'Not another one; third this morning. Are you sure, man?'

Thomas looked at his barrister, who was standing on the right. The man nodded.

'Yes, sir. Not guilty, sir.'

'Is this another communist?'

The clerk checked his notes. 'No, sir, this man is a member of the BUF.'

'Sir Oswald's organisation?'

'That is correct, sir.'

The magistrate scrambled through the papers on his desk. 'I have a note from him somewhere… Ah, here it is.' He stared at Thomas. 'What did you say your name was?'

'Green, sir. Thomas Green.'

The magistrate cupped his ear. 'Speak up, man, I won't tell you again.'

'Thomas Green,' he shouted.

'There's no need to shout. You're in a court of law, not a fish market.' The magistrate scribbled furiously in his ledger. 'Well, get on with it,' he hissed at the clerk.

'The prosecution calls PC 769, Josiah Smith.'

The constable who had arrested Thomas climbed into the witness box.

Thomas felt a sympathetic twinge of pain shoot through his shoulder as the man appeared.

The prosecuting barrister stood up. Thomas noticed him for the first time. When he spoke, a long, lazy drawl came from his throat and his top lip didn't move beneath the caterpillar of his moustache. 'You are PC 769. You arrested this man' – he looked down to check his notes – 'Thomas Green, on the fourth of October?'

'I did, sir,' Josiah Smith answered in a fine Welsh baritone.

'Can you describe to us what happened?'

'I was assigned to the central area of the march. During the confrontation with the demonstrators, I was—'

'By demonstrators, you mean the communists who blocked the march of Sir Oswald's men?' the judge asked, peering over the top of his spectacles.

'Yes, sir. They were all over Cable Street and up as far as High Aldgate.'

'And was this a legally constituted march?'

'Oh, I wouldn't know, sir, I'm a constable. You'd have to ask the Commissioner.'

The prosecutor stood up and interrupted. 'The Commissioner was advising Mr Mosley and his marchers, sir.' He coughed. 'Due to the presence of so many rioters, they eventually turned away from the East End and marched along the Embankment rather than the original route.'

'Disgraceful.' The magistrate scribbled in his ledger.

The prosecutor continued. 'Tell me what you saw, Constable Smith.'

'Well, sir, like I said, I got separated from my colleagues, see, and I was trying to rejoin them when I saw a man dressed in black standing over a woman.'

'Which man in black?'

The constable pointed directly at Thomas. 'Him.'

His barrister stood up and straightened his wig. 'May I point out, your honour, that the man in the dock is not wearing black.'

'Quite correct, Mr Wright. Are you sure this *is* the man you saw, Constable?'

'Look, you, he was still standing there when I arrested him five seconds later, so it must have been him, see.'

Thomas's barrister was on his feet again. 'I'm sorry for the interruption, Your Honour, but I must point out once more, there were many men dressed in black on that particular day.'

'I'll ask you again, Constable Smith. Is this the man you saw?'

'It is, my lord... I think.'

'It is or isn't, man, stop wasting the court's time.'

'It is, Your Honour,' the constable said finally.

The prosecutor stood up again. 'Please continue to tell us what happened, Constable Smith.'

'Well, sir, the woman was bleeding from the mouth and the leg, sir, and she wasn't moving. The accused was standing over her in a threatening manner as if he were about to strike her. So I tackled him, see, to stop him hitting her again.'

'And then you arrested and charged him?'

'Well, I arrested him but the duty sergeant at Wood Street station actually charged him.'

'Yes, of course, Constable.' The prosecutor sat down.

Taking his time, Thomas's barrister adjusted his wig, hitched up his gown and gripped the lapel firmly with his right hand. 'Constable Smith, you had been fighting with the communist demonstrators, had you not?'

'Well, yes, sir. Proper barney it was, that's why I was separated from the other men, see.'

'And you saw the defendant standing over the victim.'

'That's correct, sir. Threatening her he was.'

Mr Wright turned to the court. 'Did you actually see the defendant strike the victim?'

'Well… not really, sir. But she was bleeding and he was standing over her, as if he was going to hit her.'

'Has the victim come forward to confirm she was struck by the defendant?'

'No, sir. I went back to find her later, but she was gone already.'

'And have you found the victim since?'

The policeman's head went down. 'No, sir, she's vanished.'

The barrister turned to the magistrate. 'Your Honour, this case has no merit at all. There is no victim. My client was not seen striking the non-existent victim. In fact, he will testify under oath he was trying to help her to her feet when he was tackled by Constable Smith. And finally, there is the possibility of an incorrect identification, as Constable Smith has stated clearly many men were dressed in black that day. Taking into consideration all these facts, Your Honour, I would respectfully suggest that my client has no case to answer.'

The magistrate looked at the clock. 12.20. His stomach rumbled. 'Thank you, Mr Wright. I would agree with you. The evidence is far too shaky to convict on such a heinous charge as affray.' He picked up the letter from his desk. 'Sir Oswald tells me the defendant has no previous convictions and seems to be an upstanding member of society, so we will dismiss this case.'

'But, sir, I saw him—'

'And a word for you, Constable Smith. Be more circumspect about whom you "tackle" in the future. The streets of London are not a field of rugby. Case dismissed.'

'I'm free to go?' said Thomas.

His barrister reached over and shook his hand. 'Free as a bird, Mr Green. But I would leave quickly before His Honour changes his mind or returns from his luncheon.'

Out of the corner of his eye, Thomas saw Johnnie waving.

He left the dock and immediately his friend was by his side. 'It's wonderful isn't it? Sir Oswald promised that Mr Wright would get you off, and he's been true to his word.'

'Sir Oswald paid for all of this?'

'He always looks after his people. Now we must celebrate your escape from the long arm of the law with some oysters and a bottle of champagne. I know just the place.'

'But how do I get home? And what about the job? I've been missing for two days. Mr Bronstein is bound to sack me.'

'Oh, don't worry. Father has cleared it all with old Bronstein. You're as free as a bird and you don't need to go back to work until next Monday. So how about some oysters and champagne? We could even try a black velvet.'

'I've never had oysters or champagne before. And I don't even know what a black velvet is.'

Johnnie's arm appeared on his shoulder. 'Well, then, you're in for a real treat, young Thomas. A treat well deserved after what you did to the Red tart. Come on.'

Chapter Twenty-Three

Monday, April 17, 2017
Manchester Square, London

Jayne took a deep breath. 'Our problems started when you briefed me to investigate Thomas Jackson. It strikes me that they are connected.'

'Connected?'

'Somebody is trying to stop Daniel Jackson's grandfather's background from being researched. And will go to extreme lengths, including murder, to make sure it isn't.'

David sat up on the couch. 'What are we going to do?'

'*I'm* going to carry on. The one way to find out who is behind all this is to discover what they want to hide. And that means looking into the secret past of Dan Jackson's family, finding out who this elusive grandfather was and why he wanted to hide his identity.'

He stared at her. 'I'm with you.'

'David, that isn't a good idea. This is going to be dangerous. Even worse, these people have the political connections, resources and power to cover up a murder in central London.'

'Who could do that?'

'I don't know, but I mean to find out.' She paused for a moment. 'On my own.'

Jayne watched as David's jaw clenched. Gone was the preppie New Englander and something stronger, more forthright emerged.

'I think you are forgetting, Mrs Sinclair, that it was my boss, Jack Wayne, who was murdered this afternoon.'

'I'm not forgetting at all, but—'

'And I am still your client. I am the one who briefed you about this job.'

'But David...'

He held his hands up and his tone softened. 'You're the professional and you are in charge, but as the client, I want to come along. Is that clear?'

'Despite your ankle?'

'This will be fine tomorrow. I'm a lot tougher than I look.'

Jayne thought for a moment. It would be useful to have somebody else to help. This case was bigger than one person and she could always lose him later if he started to get in the way.

She nodded.

'It's agreed.' He pushed himself up from the couch and limped across to the desk. 'I must ring the office. They've got to know what happened to Jack.'

Jayne put out her arm to stop him. 'I wouldn't do that, David.'

'Why not?'

'Somebody had to tell the killers about the meeting in the restaurant this afternoon. It wasn't me and it wasn't you. And if you booked it under an assumed name, it can't have been the owners of the restaurant. So who was it?'

'I don't know. Maybe Jack told somebody at the office.'

Jayne held her hands up. 'Perhaps he did. But until we find out more, I wouldn't tell anybody about anything we're doing. It's too dangerous.'

It was his turn to nod at her and sit back down on the couch.

She picked up the photocopy of the naturalisation certificate again. 'Where did you get this?'

'The US Customs and Immigration Service. Anybody can apply, you just pay sixty-five dollars for a search.'

'Has the visa information come through yet?'

'I'll check.' He tapped the keys on the laptop and a Gmail account popped up. He peered at a long column of emails before selecting one. 'It's here.'

'But how did you do that? It takes weeks for anybody to get information from them.'

'Having contacts high up at the Department of Homeland Security helps. Information any time, anywhere.'

He clicked the attachment and the pages of a document flashed on the screen. 'This seems to be a visa application to the embassy in London. The visa itself, a health certificate and a character reference are attached to the file.'

Jayne pulled up a chair and sat down beside him.

He separated all the documents, bringing them up side by side on the screen.

She checked the visa application. The man from the naturalisation certificate, albeit a younger version, stared out at her from a photograph. 'There's no birth certificate?'

'None was in the file. I guess he never gave one to the embassy.'

Jayne pointed to the birthplace that had been typed on to the application: Hereford. Beneath it was an address: 49, Fylde Road. 'Dan said he was born in this town around 1920 and this is where he was living in 1945.'

'He didn't move very far.'

'People didn't in those days. We should be able to find his family through the address.'

Jayne tilted the laptop towards her, opened a new tab and typed in findmypast.com. She went back to the 1939 records and entered the address. A message saying 'Sorry, we couldn't find any results' came up on the screen. She played with the fields for another five minutes, trying all possible combinations of name and address, getting the same response every time.

Finally, she brought up a modern Google map of Hereford and entered 49 Fylde Road.

'No record of any Fylde Road in Hereford.'

'Are you sure?'

She Googled the road's name and Hereford. 'It doesn't exist.'

'The road's name wasn't changed?'

Jayne shook her head. 'I can find no record of it ever existing in the town.'

She sat back in the chair as David checked for himself. Nothing.

'What's going on?' he asked.

She ran her fingers through her hair. It was greasy and thick with dried sweat. 'It seems Dan's grandfather may have lied to the embassy about his address in Britain.'

'Why?'

She shrugged her shoulders. 'Your guess is as good as mine.' She thought for a moment. 'Show me the other documents.'

'The health certificate and the character reference?'

Jayne nodded.

David clicked one of the documents and it filled the screen. The health certificate was in letter form with a doctor's name and address printed at the top:

I, Dr Stanley Conway, have examined Thomas Jackson on January 2, 1946 and found him healthy in both mind and body. He possesses two healed scars. One to the right temple and another to the left shoulder. Neither scar poses a danger to his health.

Signed, Stanley Conway.

'The letter is headed with an address in London,' Jayne said.

'He could have been living there after the war. Many people were displaced at that time.'

'Bring up the character reference.'

This time the heading on the letter was in an ecclesiastical script: St Columba's Roman Catholic Church, Ardwick Green, Manchester.

To whom it may concern,

I have had the pleasure of knowing Thomas Jackson since his birth in Ludlow, even baptising him in the rites of the Holy Church when he was six weeks old. He comes from a reputable and distinguished family, all of whom are devout Catholics, attending mass every Sunday.

I am happy to write this letter for this fine, outstanding young man.

Yours faithfully,

Antony O'Mahoney, Parish Priest

Jayne scratched her head. 'It doesn't make sense.'

'Why?'

'How could a parish priest in Manchester have baptised a young boy living over a hundred miles away.'

'Perhaps his family drove him there?'

'In 1920? Not many cars around then. And people didn't make such long trips simply to baptise a baby when a local church would have been much easier. The priest also wrote that the family attended church regularly, which was also impossible if they

122

lived over a hundred miles away. And even harder if the address didn't exist...'

Jayne leant back away from the computer. Her body ached and she was exhausted. She couldn't think straight enough to work all this out. But something was still nagging at her mind like a dentist with a drill. What was it?

And then it hit her. 'The birthplace.'

'I don't understand.'

'Open the visa application form again.'

David opened the folder and brought up the image.

She quickly scanned the visa before stabbing the screen with her finger. How could she have been so stupid? 'Look, in this visa form he states his birthplace was Hereford, but the priest says he was born in Ludlow. The two places are not far apart, both in the Midlands near the border with Wales, but they are very different towns.'

She quickly brought up the FreeBMD site and changed the place in the search field to Ludlow.

Within a second, one response popped up. She read it out loud. 'Thomas Jackson, born between March and June 1919. Mother's maiden name was Caldwell. This must be him.' She quickly found the naturalisation certificate 'See here,' she pointed to the affidavit given to the judge, 'the full name is given. He must have used his mother's surname, Caldwell, as his middle name.'

'So are we going to order the birth certificate?'

'No point, it would take at least a week to get here. There's only one thing we can do. Go to Ludlow itself and check the parish registers.'

'How do we know which church and which register?'

'We don't. But Ludlow isn't a big place. There will only be one or two churches at most. She quickly

Googled: 'How many churches in Ludlow?' The answer came back in 0.59 seconds.

'Well, apparently there are three. But I'll start with that one.' She pointed to St Laurence's. It's Church of England, the most likely.'

'When do we leave?'

'Tomorrow morning. I'm shattered and we need to give your ankle time to recover.' She stood up and stretched. 'I'm going to take a shower and then sleep. We'll make a start tomorrow morning. Are you sure the car is working?'

'It's always ready for the senators and congressmen.' David pulled a bunch of keys out of his pocket.

'We'll start early. Should take us about three hours to drive to Ludlow.'

'I'll sleep on the couch, you take the bed.'

'Very gallant, Mr Mercer.'

'We Americans do have our saving graces.'

'And for once, we both agree. I'll see you in the morning.'

'Good night, Mrs Sinclair.'

She turned to go into the bedroom and then stopped. 'One thing bothers me. If the grandfather was born in Ludlow, why did he say it was Hereford on the visa?'

David shrugged. 'Maybe it was a mistake, and he remembered it incorrectly.'

'Or maybe the grandfather lied?'

There was a moment of silence between them as the implications of her statement sank in.

'You'd better print out the documents.' She was about to go into the bedroom, but stopped and added, 'David, for a novice, you did well today. We'll be able to crack this, I know we will.'

He sat down at the computer. 'I hope so.' He checked his watch. 'We have just four days left before the meeting and the decision.'

'Won't they call it off if Jack Wayne has been killed?'

'Maybe, but I don't think so. It's too important to these people. You don't know them, Jayne, and neither do I really.' His voice tailed off.

Jayne tried to think, but tiredness was racing round her brain, clobbering every cell it met. 'See you in the morning.'

'Night, Jayne. Sleep tight.'

Chapter Twenty-Four

Monday, April 17, 2017
Somewhere beneath the streets of London

'We have contact, sir.' The operator looked up from his screen.

'Where?'

'Tracing the IP address. Mercer has logged on to his email account.'

'Stupid, very stupid.'

It always amazed him how the most intelligent people could do the most stupid acts. Logging on to your own account was like a schoolboy in a crowded assembly of 500 putting up his hand to say, 'It was me, sir. I did it. I wrote "The headmaster is an idiot" on the wall.'

He faced a choice. He could leave them where they were, just monitoring their activities. Or he could keep the pressure on. He remembered the Führer's instructions. There were only four days to the meeting.

'It's in Manchester Square, sir. I can't pinpoint the exact address as it's in a block of three apartments.'

He made a quick decision. 'No matter, we'll take out all three. Tell Blake to get his men there. No sirens this time, we don't want to wake up the rest of London.'

'Yes, sir. He's on his way.'

He relaxed back in the chair. Manchester Square wasn't far from where the taxi company had reported the cabbie had dropped them. He thought they may have been heading for the American Embassy, but apparently not. The woman was getting slack, making mistakes now – she must be tired.

He took another sip of tea.

'Blake reports the men are outside and ready to go on your orders, sir.'

'Has Mercer logged off yet?'

'Not yet, sir.'

Felix Ostransky stared at the computer in front of him. It had been so long since he had worked in the field. This time he should get closer to the action, see the location for himself.

'Tell them to wait. I will co-ordinate the mission personally.'

'But, sir, Blake's men are ready to go now.'

'Tell them to pull back and wait for me.'

If he wanted something doing well, it was better to do it himself. And besides, it was always better to rouse people in the hazy, middle-of-the-night time. They would be drunk from sleep and their reaction times so much slower.

He looked at his watch. 'I will be there in thirty minutes. Prepare to launch the mission on my arrival. Time to spook our mice once more.'

The operator spoke quietly into his microphone.

They would remember this moment in the years to come. The night when they had begun the long journey back to power. A power they had relinquished on that fateful day in late April 1945, when the first Führer had perished.

The Third Reich was dead. Long live the Fourth.

Chapter Twenty-Five

Tuesday, April 18, 2017
Manchester Square, London

Jayne lay in bed, desperately willing her eyes to close and discover the blessed relief of sleep. She glanced over at the bedside clock. 2.30 a.m.

She had taken her shower, letting the warm water wash away the sins of today. Looking at herself in the mirror afterwards, she saw a forty-year-old woman who looked younger than her years.

She kept herself fit with weekly visits to the gym and yoga, avoiding the dreaded computer spread from spending hours in front of her laptop. Her only indulgences were wine and chocolate. Even these she limited, allowing herself only the best chocolate and refusing to drink on at least three days each week.

Despite her aching body, sleep still would not come to her. What was it? What was annoying her?

She was tired, having nearly missed the obvious clue in the priest's letter. What else was she missing?

She thought back to everything she had seen that day. Was it something in the picture? Was it a document or a search she had missed? Was it something about David?

She jumped out of bed and wrenched open the door. David was sprawled out on the couch, a fawn blanket covering his body. The computer was still on, its screen showing the list of emails for a Gmail account.

Shit.

She ran over to him and shook his shoulder. 'Wake up, we've got to get out of here.'

The urgency in her voice communicated itself to him, despite his desperate tiredness.

'Wassup, what's happening?'

'Get dressed, we have to leave now.' She yanked the power cord from the computer and raced to the window, peering out through the side of the curtain.

Manchester Square seemed exactly how it had been two hours ago, only quieter, with no people to be seen.

Was she over-reacting? Was there nothing to worry about?

A figure dressed in black ran quickly across the street from right to left and vanished from sight.

They were here.

David pulled the blanket around himself and sat up. 'Whassup?'

'Get moving, David. Now.' She ran back to the bedroom, pulling on her clothes.

'Jayne, what's going on? I thought we were leaving in the morning.'

She quickly threw all the notes and photocopies into her bag. 'You logged on to your email account?'

'You asked me to.'

Jayne realised how stupid she had been.

'Slow down a minute, tell me what's going on,' he said.

She took a deep breath. Why didn't men just do as they were told? Why did she always have to explain everything? 'You downloaded the visa file from your Gmail account,' she enunciated slowly. 'They must have accessed your emails, putting a trace on the account to find the IP address of the computer which accessed it. With the IP address, they can find out where we are.'

David's face fell.

'Understand? They are outside now. We have to get out of here.'

David rushed to get dressed, grabbing his clothes and an old jacket from the wardrobe. 'Where do we go?' he asked as he was pulling the shirt over his body.

'I don't know. Anywhere but here.'

Outside they heard the faint crash of glass falling on to the ground, followed by silence.

They both stood still to listen for a second, before Jayne said, 'They're inside.'

David hopped around, pulling on his shoes.

'Is there another way out of here?'

'The back stairs. Out through the kitchen. Leads to a basement room, the servant quarters in the old days. Upstairs downstairs and all that.'

On the ground floor, a door was slammed open and they heard shouts.

'Is there an exit from the basement?'

David nodded. 'Into a rear courtyard, the old delivery area.'

Jayne grabbed the bag and shoved David into the kitchen. 'Show me.'

They ran out of the lounge through the kitchen to the back door. Just as he was about to open it, she grabbed his hand. 'Let me go first.'

'We'll have to go past the other apartment.'

She placed her index across her lips. Slowly she opened the door and listened. There was the sound of raised voices from the apartment below. A man shouting, a woman's muffled scream.

She stepped out on to the landing, being careful not to make a noise. The stairs led downwards in an internal staircase.

More noise from the apartment downstairs: a woman being slapped, the sound of a hand striking repeatedly across a face.

Jayne moved quickly down the stairs, turned right at the bottom and waited. A door with glass panels was on the left. Through the panels she could make out the shape of two burly figures.

Above, there was another crash as the door to their apartment slammed open.

Jayne grabbed David's arm and hurried past the door and down some more steps into a basement. Behind her she heard a muffled shout. 'Down here.'

Not a Russian voice this time, definitely American.

'Where's the exit?'

'Through here.'

They ran through the first room of the basement, light from the corridor throwing shadows into the dark room. David pulled open an internal door. 'This way...'

Then he stopped.

In front of him was a solid brick wall.

Chapter Twenty-Six

Tuesday, April 18, 2017
Manchester Square, London

'What's going on? There was a door here, I'm sure there was.'

The heavy stomp of footsteps coming down the stairs reverberated around the basement. Jayne's heart was beating so fast it was almost coming out of her chest.

She looked around. Obviously this had been a working kitchen in the past, where servants laboured to provide meals for the family upstairs in the days before the house was converted. Even the antique call bells still hung on a panel above the door.

And then, for a moment, she was suddenly back in the past. A heavily muscled woman was kneading bread on a marble table. A man in tails walking through the busy kitchen carrying a silver salver. A scullery maid struggling to put an immense cast-iron pot on the stove. The house was full of servants preparing for the evening meal. And at the centre of it all, a wizened butler was supervising the unloading of a cart in the street, sliding hessian sacks of vegetables down a delivery chute.

'Jayne... Jayne...!'

David's urgent shout forced her back into the present. It had happened to her before. It was like she was transported into the past for a few seconds, seeing the place as it was when it had been full of life and energy. She didn't know if it were imagined or real, only that it happened.

'Jayne...'

David's urgent shout galvanised her into action. She looked around the dark, dank, empty basement, so different from the one she had just imagined. But there was the opening, low down on the wall near the floor.

The footsteps were getting closer, coming down the steps to the basement.

'Quick, this way.'

She ran over to the iron cover and made to wrench it open.

It wouldn't move.

'Help me.'

David grabbed hold of the handle and pulled.

Still no movement.

A shout behind and slightly above them.

David put his foot on the wall and levered his whole body against the cast-iron door. A loud screech erupted from the tired hinges as they reluctantly opened.

'Inside, quick.'

Jayne pushed him inside and followed herself. A metal chute led up for eight feet to a wooden door at the top.

'Up there, quickly.'

David began to shimmy up the chute, using his hands and knees, pressing his back into the metal roof. Dirt, dust, cobwebs and God knew what else slid down the chute past Jayne.

More shouts behind them, in the basement now.

Suddenly there was a sharp squeak and a blaze of eyes like fireflies shining in the dark. Something jumped at Jayne's face, something warm and furry. She stifled a scream as it slammed off her neck and down between her legs, scurrying out through the open metal door.

Jayne could feel her heart beating like the rat-a-tat-tat of a drum against her ribs. Surely they must be able to hear her too?

Another shout behind them, followed by a pistol shot. She heard the same voice clearly again. An American accent, no longer Russian.

'No shooting. Why'd you shoot?'

Another voice, also American, shouting back, 'This place is full of rats. I hate rats, they scare the shit out of me.'

'Check the rest of the basement.'

'They're not here. Nobody would come here.'

'Search it. Start over there.' The last voice was authoritative and commanding. An order.

The footsteps walked away into another part of the basement.

Jayne crouched in the dirty metal tube, waiting to be discovered. Her breathing was heavy and her heart was fit to burst.

Suddenly, there was a draught of fresh air and a shaft of thin moonlight lit up the inside of the delivery chute. David scrambled out through the open top, turned and reached for Jayne's hand, pulling her up and out.

She was free.

A shout from above them. 'They're in the courtyard. Outside.'

Jayne and David ran for the door leading to the street.

Please let it be unlocked. Please!

A window opened behind them. A muffled, indistinct sound like the soft thud of a cosh on human flesh. A loud crack as the bullet struck the brickwork beside the door.

Jayne reached for the handle and it swung open.

They ran into the alleyway behind the house.

'This way. We keep the car over here.'

Thirty yards away, a Volvo C90 was parked in a small alcove. David fumbled for the keys.

Another shot hit the ground at Jayne's feet, ricocheting off the tarmac and lodging itself into the metal of the car.

David wrenched open the door and Jayne jumped in on the passenger side. His hand shook as he tried to insert the key into the lock.

Their rear windscreen shattered with a crash. A man was standing at the entrance to the courtyard, firing a gun at them.

The engine started and coughed. David stamped on the accelerator and the car surged away from the pavement.

The man was running after them, firing as he did.

Jayne looked back through the empty rear windscreen. The man was getting smaller by the second, eventually giving up the chase and standing in the middle of the road. A broad smile spread across his broader face.

A face she recognised immediately.

It was the same man who had masqueraded as a policeman when Jack Wayne was shot. A heavy, thickset man with a livid scar running down across the eye and cheek.

David accelerated around a corner. 'Where are we going?'

Jayne thought for a moment. They had to get out of London. She couldn't go back to Manchester, not yet anyway. They would be looking for her there. Where should they go?

'Jayne, where are we going?'

The only way to get rid of these men was to find out what they wanted, to discover the truth about Dan Jackson's grandfather.

'We need to go to Ludlow.'

'Now?'

'It's the only clue we have.'

Chapter Twenty-Seven

Tuesday, April 18, 2017
Manchester Square, London

'The woman has escaped.' Blake's voice was clear and calm in the headphones of the mobile command centre parked in front of Manchester Square. He had remained here when the men had entered the house. He wanted to be close to the action but not directly in the line of fire. That's what he paid people like Blake to do.

'Good. You made sure the threat was real?'

'I did. Encouraged them with a few shots.'

'Which direction did they run in? We'll pick them up on CCTV.'

'They didn't run.'

'But you said—'

'They had a car hidden in a rear alleyway, sir.'

The last 'sir' was insolent in its tone.

'Did you get the number?'

'Unfortunately not, sir.'

'Why not?' he shouted and immediately regretted such an outburst of emotion. He had to remain calm at all times. Blake was making too many mistakes. Time to remove him from the team.

'I'm sorry, sir, but it was too dark and the car was moving too fast.'

There it was again, the tone that said I don't really care what you think. 'Make of car?' His voice was back in control now. He would deal with Blake later.

'A Volvo C90.'

No 'sir' this time. 'Colour?'

'Black.'

He reached forward and typed in the universal code that controlled the traffic cameras in the area.

The bank of monitors in front of him slowly filled with the feed from the traffic cameras. They presented the orange-illuminated scene of a sleeping London. But still traffic jams clogged some of the busier streets.

People were coming home from clubs. Or work. Or visiting friends. Or just aimlessly driving around looking for other lost souls.

Most of the vehicles on the road were the ubiquitous black cabs. Their square compact shape, illuminated yellow lights and hunched drivers, the vampires of the London night, constantly on the lookout for their passenger prey.

But he could see no black Volvo.

Without the car's registration number, they would have to check each of the camera feeds visually. A job that could take hours. With the number, the job would have taken seconds.

Damn Blake and his incompetence.

He spoke to the operator back at HQ. 'Check each camera from the area around Manchester Square. We need to find them.'

'Yes, sir,' Whitaker's distant voice replied.

Where would Jayne Sinclair head next? She had proven a better, smarter opponent than he'd expected.

No matter. He was sure he could find her again. He could always find people.

He tried to put himself in her shoes. Where would she go next? Back to her home in Manchester? He didn't think so, but he needed to cover it, though, just in case. 'Make sure you check the cameras on the M6. She might be heading towards Manchester,' he said to the operator.

'Yes, sir.'

'Send me a copy of the computer files from the Manchester Square house.'

'I'll compile them for you now, sir.'

'Just the last week, I don't want to go back further.'

'Yes, sir.'

He rubbed a reddening patch of skin where his hairline met his forehead. Perhaps there would be a clue to their destination in the emails.

What would the woman do next?

Chapter Twenty-Eight

March 30, 1938
Manchester, England

After the court case, Thomas didn't spend as much time with the BUF as he had done before. But one fine Spring day in 1938, he was walking along Market Street when Johnnie came from nowhere and grabbed his arm.

'You haven't been to any meetings recently.'

Thomas tried to walk past him, but a hand went across his chest.

'Been too busy lately, too much to do.'

'So the party doesn't matter any more?'

He could see Bill and Harry standing behind Johnnie. He tried to laugh about it. 'It's not like that. I've a lot to do and now I've got a girlfriend, so not much time.'

Johnnie's finger poked him in the chest. 'The party and Mr Mosley stood by you when you were in trouble. Now it's your turn to repay the favour, got it?'

'Sure, I understand. I'll be there...'

Johnnie stroked the lapels of the suit Thomas was wearing. 'Nice, we are dressing above our station. Who you seeing, anyway?'

'It's Tilly, the girl in Accounts.'

'She giving you any?'

'I... I... I don't know what you mean.'

'You're a proper wide boy, you are! You played with her chassis yet?'

He tried to walk past but Johnnie stuck his arm out again. 'I was asking, because if you needed any help in that department, Bill and Harry would be only too happy to oblige, wouldn't you, lads?'

Bill and Harry said nothing.

'I... I...'

A long laugh from Johnnie. 'You should see your face. I was only joking.' A long arm snaked over Thomas' shoulders. 'Having a laugh with a friend, that's all.'

'I'm going to be late.'

'Meeting Tilly, are we? Mustn't be late for your bit of skirt, Thomas, couldn't be *en retard*, could we?'

Thomas manoeuvred himself out from under the arm and walked away.

As he turned the corner, a shout came from Johnnie. 'Don't forget the meeting on Friday.'

* * *

The day came and he thought about giving it a miss. Tilly wanted to go to the pictures, some Deanna Durbin movie or other.

But as he left the factory, Johnnie was waiting for him in the Alvis.

'I'll give you a lift, old sport, hop in.'

Thomas climbed into the car. The seats were slung close to the ground and he had to squeeze himself into the passenger seat. 'Nice motor.'

'Daddy bought it for me. A beauty, isn't she? Three and a half litres, coachwork by Cross and Ellis, and she goes like a bat out of hell.' The last words were shouted as he stomped on the accelerator and the car took off with a deep roar from the exhaust.

Thomas hung on to the door as Johnnie weaved in and out of the traffic, narrowly missing an old woman crossing a road.

'Shouldn't you slow down a bit?' Thomas shouted against the engine noise and the roar of the wind.

'What's the point, old boy? I like to see the look on people's faces as they realise this car is going to stop for nobody.'

'Watch out!'

Johnnie swerved the car round a small fat woman pushing an enormous perambulator across the road. Thomas looked over his shoulder. She was shaking her fist and shouting at the retreating car.

'Nearly got that one. Would have earned me ten points.'

Thomas gripped the door handle more tightly as, once again, the car surged forward on a stretch of open road.

They finally slowed to a stop outside the meeting hall. Johnnie switched off the engine and leapt out of the car. 'Come on, we're going to be late.'

Thomas shook his head. His ears were still ringing from the engine's noise and the rush of the wind across his face.

'The speaker's talking about the new Germany. He's actually been there. Afterwards, we can go down the pub. We need to talk, something exciting has come up.'

Thomas climbed out of the car and followed Johnnie into the hall.

The speaker was more interesting than most, at least he didn't rant and rave. Instead, he spoke force-fully of the changes in the new Germany, how the whole country was uniting behind Herr Hitler and his desire to bring order and stability back to society. New roads were being built, no unemployment, factories at full capacity, and even the trains ran on time.

Afterwards, Johnnie took him by the arm. 'Let's have that drink. My mouth's as dry as a fast bowler's jockstrap.'

'I have to get home, Mother's waiting.'

'A few drinks, won't be long.'

The arm went around his shoulder again and he was encouraged to go into the Rose and Crown, where Bill was already waiting for them.

As they sat down with their pints, Johnnie leant forward. 'How's it going with Tilly? You getting your leg over yet?'

Thomas blushed a bright red.

'He has, Bill. Thomas has popped his cherry, hasn't he?'

The ever-silent Bill remained quiet.

'Well done, old sport. You always remember your first, even if it's some spotty girl in Accounts. But anyway, we're not here to chat about your love life, adventurous though it no doubt is. No, instead, myself and Bill have a proposal for you.'

Thomas eyed him suspiciously. 'What's that?'

'Well, you speak German, don't you?'

'A little...'

'But your mum's German, isn't she?'

'She came here in 1919.'

'Still, she taught you German, didn't she?'

'As I said, a little.'

'Great, it's settled then.' Johnnie picked up his pint and took a large swallow.

'What? What's settled?'

He placed the glass back on the table. 'Mr Mosley is looking for volunteers to go to a summer camp in Baden Baden for two weeks. Think of it; two weeks of sun, sex and national socialism, all paid for by the party. You couldn't miss out, could you?'

'Why don't you go?'

'Oh, I am, Tommy boy. Myself and Bill are definitely going, but we have room for one other and you being a German speaker and all – well, it's only right you come too, isn't it, Bill?'

Bill simply lifted his pint to his face and buried his face in the warm brown suds.

'I don't know. How can I get time off work?'

'Oh, don't worry. I've spoken to Father and he's already agreed to give you two weeks off.'

Thomas thought for a moment. He'd always wanted to visit Germany. His mother had spoken so often about the cleanliness and the order of the place compared to scruffy old England. And the speaker had excited him about the changes in the country. Normally, he would never be able to afford it in a million years. But with the party paying, he could finally take the trip he had been dreaming about his whole life.

He would have to chat with Tilly, of course, but he was sure she wouldn't mind. He could bring her something nice back from Baden Baden, a bottle of perfume perhaps.

Johnnie clapped him on the back. 'What do you say, Tom? Are you in?'

Thomas picked up his pint, holding it in front of his mouth. 'When do we leave?'

Chapter Twenty-Nine

Tuesday, April 18, 2017
Somewhere beneath the streets of London

They had vanished from view.

His men had tracked them from Manchester Square to the M25, but then they had disappeared.

'They didn't use the M1 or M6, sir. I've checked all the cameras visually but I can find nothing. Two others double-checked the recordings. No black Volvo was on either motorway during the time specified.'

'They must have taken A-roads.'

'I agree, sir. Unfortunately, the traffic cameras on those roads are on different systems.'

'It doesn't matter. Get them.'

'But that means visually tracking the A-roads of four counties; Surrey, Berkshire, Buckinghamshire and Hertfordshire. It could take days.'

'Nonetheless, do it. We need to find them again.'

'But they could be anywhere, sir.'

'No, Whitaker, they couldn't. They are somewhere and it is your job to find them, do I make myself clear?'

'Yes, sir.'

'And send a team to Hereford. They may be checking up on Thomas Jackson there.'

The operator turned back to his console and began tapping at his keys once more.

Ostransky could feel the patch of eczema at his hairline spreading across his forehead, the itch increasing in intensity.

He picked up his green tea and drank to cover his annoyance and calm his mind. His people were becoming inefficient and ineffectual. They would have to be changed, upgraded as one would upgrade an application in a phone. Only the best were good enough. Only the best could carry on the traditions of the Organisation.

He stared at the bank of screens in front of him. The first rays of a dull dawn were beginning to join the neon lights illuminating the roads.

Where was she? It shouldn't be this difficult to find someone, not in this day and age. Normally, he would use their phone signal, tracking them wherever they went with ease. But she had already dumped the phones. Mrs Sinclair was proving to be a formidable opponent, but he would find her in the end. People were stupid or careless, and they always made mistakes.

'Have you finished compiling the computer files from Manchester Square?'

'Sending them to you now, sir.'

'Add the file on Thomas Jackson.'

'Yes, sir.'

'Any use of their credit cards?'

'Nothing. I've put a tap on them. We'll get a notification if the cards are used.'

He picked up his tea. The leaves floated in the bottom of the cup like seaweed. He needed a fresh pot.

They would have to use their credit cards soon to pay for fuel or food or simply to get more cash. When they did, he would know and they wouldn't escape again.

People were stupid, they always made mistakes. Not like machines. Machines only saw the world in 0s and 1s. No margin for error or mistake.

Mrs Sinclair would not disappear again.

Not again.

Chapter Thirty

Tuesday, April 18, 2017
Ludlow, Shropshire

Ludlow was already waking up when Jayne Sinclair and David Mercer pulled in to a car park off the main square. It was a busy market town with a centre showcasing the glories of Tudor and Georgian architecture, and a typically English olde-worlde atmosphere.

Jayne had been to the area many times with her husband, to eat and take in the sights of this paragon of English towns. She missed those days early in her marriage, when they had spent so much time together.

How had they drifted so far apart? She realised she was as much to blame as he was. Work, her breakdown, more work. She knew there was something about her personality that meant she threw herself into everything she did, leaving nothing behind. But when the thrill was gone, there was always the aching sense of loss. In her case, she fell out of love just as deeply as she fell in love. Unfortunately, Paul was the one to suffer.

In front of the car park, the market's stallholders were setting up their pitches, as they had done in exactly the same place every day for the last five hundred years. Off to the right, the ruins of Ludlow Castle dominated the town, the grey battlements hazy in the early morning sun. Opposite the castle, a café was opening its doors to welcome the first customers.

'A coffee?' It was David who spoke first. He must be one of those people who need the spark of caffeine to become vaguely human in the morning. Having travelled all night down quiet backroads to the town, Jayne could sympathise with the need for a kick of energy.

'We'll go to the church afterwards,' he encouraged her. 'I'm sure it won't be open to the public yet.'

They went into the café. Jayne ordered herself a macchiato and David went for a double shot latte. Both had blueberry muffins with their coffee, attacking them like a wolf ravages a sheep.

'Jayne, can I ask you something?'

'Go ahead.'

'How did you get into this line of work?'

'Being a genealogical investigator?'

David nodded.

She thought for a moment. Should she tell him the truth? She decided she would. After all they had been through together, she owed him that at least. And if he had done his research on her properly, he probably knew part of the story anyway. She took a deep breath.

'I was a detective inspector with the Manchester police. A good job, and I loved my work, maybe too much.' She took a sip of her coffee. 'One day, myself and another detective, Dave Gilmour, were on a routine check of some houses in Moss Side. I stopped to tie a shoelace while Dave knocked on the door. Next thing, there was a loud bang and he was on the floor clutching his chest and a shotgun was being pointed at me.'

'What happened?'

'I disarmed the shooter, but Dave died later that day in hospital, leaving a wife and two young kids.' She took another deep breath. 'So I'm afraid I had a breakdown. Spent days in bed; I couldn't leave the house. I was sent to a police psychiatrist and diagnosed with PTSD. Anyway, to cut a long story short, after six months off work, I went back into the office and realised I couldn't trust myself to do the job any more. I mean, what if the same thing happened again? How would I cope having the death of another copper on my hands?'

David was silent for a few seconds. His hand reached across the table and covered hers. 'It seems to me you've coped pretty well over the last day or so. At least we're still alive.'

She pulled her hand away and stood up. 'We're not out of the woods yet. Those men are still after us. It's time to get back to work.'

She walked over to pay at the till.

'But... but I've not finished my coffee.'

'Too late,' she said over her shoulder. 'We need to check the church.'

Chapter Thirty-One

Tuesday, April 18, 2017
Ludlow, Shropshire

'Come on, St Laurence's is this way.' Jayne strode down a narrow alley opening up at the bottom to a magnificent church, squashed between the buildings.

'Is this it? Not what I expected. Why have they hidden it away?' said David, looking up at the tall spire towering above him.

They had hurried through the narrow medieval lanes of the ancient town and found the church hidden behind a pub and a shop selling children's clothing.

From the outside the architecture was restrained, with large stained-glass windows set into a facade of honeyed stone.

Once inside, they were immediately surrounded by the peace, serenity and emptiness of an English church; solid wooden pews, an intricately carved rood screen behind an elegant pulpit, light streaming in through stained-glass windows and over it all a beautiful, elegant calm touching the heart and soul.

From somewhere, an organ began playing some Bach, the rich tones filling both the space and Jayne with a sense of joy. She could stay in such a place for hours, feeling the past in every carving, every mark on each pew, in every grain of wood.

But they had work to do.

A man dressed in a long black cassock bustled past, distributing hymn books for the morning service.

'Excuse me, are you the vicar?'

The man stopped and eyed Jayne. 'The deacon, actually.'

149

'I wonder if it's possible to look at the parish register.'

The man checked his watch. 'The service is going to start in half an hour…'

'We won't be long. I'm a genealogist and this man has flown all the way from the States to try to discover his long-lost ancestors.'

David waved. 'Howdy,' he said in an exaggerated Texan accent.

The deacon looked at them and then at his watch. 'I suppose it will be okay, but you'll have to be quick if you want to see it now. Or you could come back after the service?'

'We'll be quick, won't we, Mr Mercer?'

'We sure will.'

The deacon took one more look at his watch before sighing. 'Come this way.'

He led them to a room off one of the chapels, where he reached up and opened the doors of an immense oak cupboard. Jayne could see a row of parish registers, some dating back to the sixteenth century. How she would love to spend hours with these…

'What date and name are you looking for in this search?'

'Fairly modern, I'm afraid. A Thomas Jackson born in 1919. The mother's maiden name was Caldwell.'

'The name sounds familiar.'

'My ancestor came to America in 1946,' added David.

'That's good, the older registers are rather fragile, I'm afraid. I don't like handling those.' He ran his fingers over the books, finally choosing one of them and laying it on a table. 'Here's the register for 1917 to 1920.'

'Could I look at it?'

'I'm afraid not. We don't allow anybody to touch the registers except parish officials.' He opened the book and slowly turned the pages, finally getting to 1919. He ran his finger down the page. The writing was spidery with a heavy lean to the right. 'The vicar then didn't have the best handwriting, I'm afraid, but here it is. Thomas Caldwell Jackson.'

Jayne and David leaned in to see the entry.

Born 12 June, 1919 and baptised in this parish six weeks later, on the 28th July. Parents, Arthur Jackson and Maria Caldwell, witnessed by Roger Jackson and Alfred Caldwell.

'It looks like we've found your ancestor, Mr Mercer.'

Jayne smiled at him. The man did exist – they had found him.

'Could I take a quick note of the register?'

'Feel free, Mrs...?'

'Mrs Sinclair, Jayne Sinclair.'

'I'll leave you for a moment.'

The deacon stepped outside.

'He definitely exists. But why can't we find anything else about him?'

Jayne shrugged her shoulders. 'I don't know,' she said, carrying on writing the details down in her notebook. 'But now we've confirmed his name and date of birth, the rest should be easy.'

The deacon reappeared at the door. 'Mr Mercer, I thought you said your ancestor went to America in 1946?'

'That's right. He was my grandfather,' David lied with a straight face.

The deacon frowned. 'Could you come with me?'

They followed him as he crossed the chapel, bowed in front of the altar and walked over to the far wall. 'I knew I recognised the name. I pass this every day on my way to the sacristy.' He pointed to a brass plaque on the wall of the church with letters etched into the surface of the metal.

Thomas Caldwell Jackson
Born 12th June 1919. Died 3rd February 1922.
A child unto God.
From his grieving parents.

Chapter Thirty-Two

Tuesday, April 18, 2017
Ludlow, Shropshire

'Jayne, I don't understand. What did it mean?'

They were sitting in the same café as before, huddled over more cups of coffee. An air of gloom hung over them like a dark, depressing blanket. Jayne took another sip of her latte without answering him.

David persisted. 'How can a man who was born in 1919, and who supposedly went to America in 1946, have a plaque commemorating his death in 1922?' David shook his head. 'I don't get it.'

Jayne put down her cup and took a deep breath. 'Here's what I think happened. Now I have no proof, but what I think we have here is a clear case of identity theft.'

'Identity theft?'

'It's a common practice. When somebody wants to assume a new identity, what they do is go round graveyards looking for children who passed away at a young age. They then take the child's name and date of birth and apply for a passport using the child's identity but attaching their photograph.'

'There are no checks on this?'

'Not in the 1940s. Even today, it's still possible to do. You see there's no link between birth registration and death registration...'

'So as long as I know a name and a date of birth, I can apply for a passport, birth certificate and anything else I need for proof of identity.'

'Once you have one of those two documents, it's simplicity itself to get the others; a visa to America, for example.'

'So you think Dan Jackson's grandfather used this dead child's identity to get a new passport?'

'Probably, or somebody did it for him.'

'What do you mean?'

She took another sip of the coffee. It was cold now and almost tasteless. 'Well, it strikes me that ever since you briefed me to find out about his grandfather, we've been shot at, chased all over London, forced to climb out of a delivery chute, tracked by security cameras and witnessed at least one murder. What's even more worrying is the police are not even aware a crime has been committed.'

'But what you're saying is unthinkable. It means they can manipulate security, police and governments at the highest level.'

'You said "they", David.'

'Well, it has to be more than one person, doesn't it? We were attacked by at least four people at Manchester Square.'

'A conspiracy? But why? What do they want? And what do they have to gain from killing me and you? There has to be something you're not telling me.'

'Jayne, I swear on my mother's life, you know everything I know.'

She stared at him for a long time, before finally nodding.

'We're screwed, aren't we?'

She thought for a long time before answering. 'Back in 1946, somebody wanted to give Dan Jackson's grandfather a new identity in order for him to go to the United States,' she said slowly, thinking through the problem. 'Which means there was something wrong with his existing identity.'

'Something that would have prevented him from entering America?'

Jayne nodded again.

'But it all happened over seventy years ago. All we know now is our man died in 1922.'

'But we have more, David.'

'I don't understand.'

'We have this picture of his grandfather taken before the war and we have these.' She tapped the folder lying between them. 'A character reference and a health certificate written to help his visa application. And we know one more thing.'

'What's that?'

'We know that the priest and the doctor who signed these statements both lied.'

'But these people will be dead by now.'

'It's our only hope of finding the real man behind the fake identity.'

'So which way are we going? North to Manchester or back to London?'

'First we go back to civilisation, David. Otherwise known as Manchester.'

'There's just one thing. How much money do you have?'

She checked her purse. 'Five pounds, enough to pay the bill here.'

He opened his wallet. Inside Jayne could see one solitary ten-pound note sitting forlornly surrounded by plastic. 'I know you said don't use cards, but how are we going to get to Manchester. We need petrol.'

'How much do we have?'

'Enough for about thirty miles, not more.'

'That won't get us there.' She drank another sip of her cold coffee. It was terrible. 'Right, we're going to have to use a credit card, but let's cross over the border into Wales before we do. At least we can try to confuse them about our final destination.'

Chapter Thirty-Three

Tuesday, April 18, 2017
Somewhere beneath the streets of London

Ostransky had spent the last four hours reading the files copied from Manchester Square.

A happily married senator had stayed at the house last weekend, apparently on a fact-finding mission to the UK Parliament. From his emails, it soon became apparent that the real reason was to continue his affair with an English reporter.

He saved the relevant emails in a file for further use. One never knew when such information would be of use to the Organisation.

David Mercer's emails were of more immediate concern. He and Jayne Sinclair had managed to obtain copies of Thomas Jackson's original visa application to enter America in 1946, from a source in Homeland Security. Perhaps the Führer had been right after all. The woman was unearthing documents they didn't know existed.

He sipped his green tea, finding the grassy taste vaguely relaxing, like drinking a beautiful English lawn.

The American chapter of the Organisation had been terribly lax all these years. They had so much time to create a better backstory, supported by the correct documentation, but they had failed. No matter; he had already set the process in action. The visa documents for Dan Jackson's grandfather would mysteriously disappear from the American files.

An accident? A fire? A misfiling? He hadn't decided yet. Either way, the hastily assembled story that had allowed Thomas Jackson to enter the United States in 1946 would vanish in a puff of smoke.

Then the new story would be constructed. An Irish connection perhaps, to encourage the Mick vote? A long-lost cousin found in some cottage in Kerry. A story of losing the rest of the family in the bombing of London, the Blitz claiming yet another set of victims and all the family documents.

Americans loved their tragedies. Well, he would give them a soap opera to make their candidate seem like Jesus resurrected from the fires of the Blitz.

And the election itself? A foregone conclusion. Their algorithms and messaging were now so complex and fine-tuned that individual content could be formulated for every voter, delivered via their mobile phones, computers, televisions and radio – not forgetting the candidate himself, so telegenic he made Johnnie F. Kennedy look like Richard Nixon. It would be like a friend whispering in your ear, telling you exactly what you wanted to hear. He would be a candidate who would appeal to everyone.

He smiled to himself. A friend is the wrong word. More like Iago whispering poison in Othello's ear. Yes, that was exactly it: an online Iago.

'We've got a hit on the credit card, sir.' The operator interrupted his thoughts.

'Where?'

'A service station in a place called Welshpool.'

He brought up a map of the UK on his screen. Welshpool was in North Wales. Why had they gone there?

And then it hit him. He quickly scrolled back to the visa documents. What had the priest written? He'd baptised Thomas Green in Ludlow, not Hereford.

More mistakes.

He checked the map again. Welshpool was just 34 miles from Ludlow. Had she spotted the anomaly in the priest's letter too and gone to the town to invest-igate?

He should have worked it all out more quickly. He felt his fingernails bite into his palm. He didn't allow himself mistakes. In his line of work, mistakes were dangerous.

Mistakes were deadly.

'Move the team from Hereford to Ludlow imme-diately. Ask around the town to find out if anybody saw them. Plus check the Ludlow CCTV. I want to know where they went and what they found out. Despatch the helicopter and Blake to Welshpool.'

'Yes, sir.'

He could hear the operator speaking into his mi-crophone. The chopper was always kept fuelled and ready, but it would be at least half an hour before Blake could get anywhere near the town. Ostransky checked his watch; probably forty minutes.

With a fully fuelled car and money from an ATM, where would they go?

He checked the map again. Was she going to carry on north-west towards North Wales? Why would she go there? He traced his finger along the map to a large island off the coast. Were they going to Holyhead to take the ferry to Ireland? Or were they heading north, to the place she knew best. Man-chester?

He had to cover all eventualities.

'Send another team to Holyhead. Monitor all pas-sengers on ferries to Ireland.'

'Yes, sir.'

'Anything from the team in Manchester?'

'They're still outside her house, sir. Nothing so far.'

'Tell them to stay vigilant.'

'Yes, sir.'

For once, he felt uncomfortable and it was not a sensation he enjoyed. Information had always been his source of power. Knowing more than anybody else. His control of computers and their data had given him information, allowing him to always stay one step ahead of the competition. It was why he was made the Chief of Operations, reporting directly to the Führer.

But this time there were gaps in the information, like pieces missing from a jigsaw puzzle.

He didn't like this feeling.

And for a man who didn't have the capacity to feel anything, it was very disconcerting.

Chapter Thirty-Four

Tuesday, April 18, 2017
A train heading to Manchester

Jayne relaxed back in the seat on the train from Shrewsbury to Manchester. David sat opposite her, staring out of the window as the Shropshire countryside whistled by, occasionally glancing in her direction when he thought she wasn't looking.

She knew that as soon as they used the credit card, they would reveal their position to their pursuers. So she had driven the car to Welshpool, refuelled it, making sure they were seen, taken as much money as she could from her ATM, and then dumped the car in a Tesco car park where it should stay hidden for a while.

They had walked into the centre of town, taking a bus to Shrewsbury station. As they boarded the bus, they noticed a chopper flying low overhead as if scanning the ground. Jayne wondered if it was looking for them and decided it probably was.

In Shrewsbury, they had connected with a direct train to Manchester, which would arrive in two hours. As long as nobody was waiting for them in Piccadilly station, they should be able to go to ground in Manchester. At least there she would feel safe.

She defied anybody to find her in her home city, where she knew every nook and cranny. And where she had coppers she could trust to cover her back.

The only problem was arriving in Manchester. Had they worked out her plan? Would they be waiting for her?

She didn't know. So far, she had done the best she could, somehow managing to keep them both safe from whoever was chasing them.

She wished she knew who they were. Who could have the power to tap into the nation's CCTV networks? They were run by many different organisations: police, local councils, traffic enforcement, private companies. And yet their pursuers had managed to use all of them.

These bastards could also monitor her bank account and David's email. How had they managed to hack into her account? Only GCHQ, the government eavesdropping department, had the power and it needed a warrant to do it, signed by a judge and authorised by the Home Secretary. Was the British government chasing them?

But why?

She was investigating the background of a potential American presidential candidate. Surely, it could have nothing to do with the British government, could it?

'What's the plan, Jayne?' David asked.

Always it was up to her. Why didn't he have a plan? She almost snapped at him, but stopped herself. Getting angry would not achieve anything.

'First, we're going to see an old friend of mine. With a bit of luck, he'll be able to tell us about this.' She pointed to the picture of Dan's grandfather in his Boy Scout uniform, which lay on the table between them.

'An old friend?'

'An old acquaintance. I nicked him for receiving stolen goods back when I was a copper. He's a fence, or at least he was then.'

'Sorry, could you speak English?'

She smiled and remembered the saying about America and England. Two countries separated by a common language. 'I nicked him when I was a copper. He was a receiver of stolen goods at the time.'

David smiled. 'So you think he'll know what this picture is?'

'With a bit of luck. He deals in militaria now. Went straight after his last stretch.'

'So he's a legitimate businessman now. Am I understanding you correctly?'

'Well done, we'll have you speaking English in no time. And he's supposed to be "legitimate".' She formed quote marks with her fingers in the air.

'And after that?'

Jayne sighed. She had a difficult call to make to her ex-husband. How was she going to explain to him that she needed somewhere to stay, that her own home was far too dangerous?

'We'll find somewhere to stay.'

'A hotel?'

'Too conspicuous. They need ID plus a credit card to cover the charges. We could stay in a flophouse, but that would be more dangerous than a hotel.'

'Flop-house?'

'A place for winos, drunks, street sleepers, or anybody looking for a bed to sleep in for the night who doesn't care too much about the condition.'

'I'm not sure I like that idea.'

Jayne had forgotten how WASP-like David was. His genteel manners were almost a return to a bygone age. 'Don't worry, we'll find a place to stay.'

'And tomorrow?'

'We find out about the priest on the letter by visiting the church he ran during the 1940s.'

'What about after that?'

Jayne threw her hands up in the air. 'I don't bloody know, David. You may or may not have noticed but I'm winging this, working out what we do as we find out more information. It's not a "Plan A followed by Plan B" sort of job.

'Sorry, Jayne, I...'

She immediately felt guilty, doing exactly what she had told herself not to do when the conversation began. Worse still, people in the compartment were looking at her, trying to work out why she had raised her voice to the man sitting opposite. Exactly what she didn't want.

She leant forward. 'I'm sorry, but this is tough, I —'

He put his hand over hers. 'It's alright, Jayne, I won't ask any more questions.'

Chapter Thirty-Five

Tuesday, April 18, 2017
Manchester

Jayne stepped down from the train at Piccadilly Station in Manchester, scanning the platform in both directions.

Passengers flowed past, desperate to find a connection to a tram, hurrying for a bus or simply looking for a toilet.

Nobody seemed to be coming for her or David. She grabbed his arm. 'We need to get out of here, quickly.'

He limped after her, the ankle still giving him some pain.

They found a black cab waiting at the rank, the driver reading the *Sun*.

'Cheetham Hill,' said Jayne, opening the door.

The driver put down the paper and waited for them to enter before accelerating away from the kerb, simultaneously turning on his meter.

'Who are we going to see?' asked David.

'A man called Herbert Levy. It's not far, as long as we don't hit traffic.'

The cab accelerated through the so-called Northern Quarter. A marketing ploy by property developers to make some poky, 'bijou' apartments in one of Manchester's oldest districts seem hip and happening.

They had succeeded in attracting a swathe of young and single hipsters, as well as a full English of trendy cafes, all with the same distressed furniture bought in a job lot from Oxfam. Most of the places had last seen a cleaner when the Manchester militia were charging the poor at the Peterloo Massacre.

In the doorways of these new cafes, the homeless lay wasted on spice or cider, killing the hours and themselves. The nouveau riche and the nouveau poor living side by side. One revelling in the atmosphere of decadence, the other just decaying.

They turned up Cheetham Hill Road, passing the brick towers of Strangeways Prison. Jayne had spent some time interviewing prisoners there. The smell remained with her to this day – a combination of sweaty socks, sperm, tired men and cabbage. It made her gag every time she went in there. It was one place she never wanted to see the inside of again, in this life or the next.

After five minutes dodging the red lights, Jayne leant forward and told the taxi driver to pull up in front of a Thai massage parlour.

David stared at the shop. 'Is this where he is? A massage parlour?'

She paid the taxi driver and took David by the arm, leading him to the door of the shop. As they entered, a bell rang above their heads. Two tired wo-men, both wearing mini-skirts that revealed the bot-tom of their buttocks, adjusted their low-cut tops and sat forward in their armchairs.

Jayne checked the taxi driver was pulling away from the kerb. 'Sorry, ladies, wrong address.' She closed the door quickly. 'It's not far from here. But if anybody asks him,' she pointed to the departing taxi, 'he's going to report that we went in here.'

She hurried him around the corner, down a deserted alley strewn with rubbish and out on to a small street lined with a terrace of shops.

In the middle, sandwiched between the kosher butcher on one side and an Oxfam reject shop on the other, she found what she was looking for.

Herbert Levy's shop door was painted a shade of bright green that had obviously once been used as camouflage paint. Around the outside, on the walls, more of the paint had been daubed on to create an effect like an army tent. In the middle of the jungle this would have been perfect camouflage, but in the middle of Cheetham Hill it was less than successful. The shop stood out like a high-vis vest at an undertakers' conference.

'Herbert Levy and Son', the sign above the green door proudly proclaimed. Beneath the name, the words 'Dealer in Militaria, Objets d'Art and Bric-a-Brac' were written in a cursive, almost illegible gold script.

'As you can see, Herbert likes to cover all his bases.'

She pressed the button for the bell at the side of the door and peered through the steel mesh guarding the glass. The window was so dirty it was like looking through the bottom of a bucket of mud.

'Come on, Herbert, I know you're in there,' Jayne shouted through the letterbox.

The door opened immediately.

'How'd you know I was here?'

The speaker was an aged man who smelt vaguely of cats. He hadn't shaved for at least two weeks and his face was as creased as an old pair of trousers. Above the sharp blue eyes, two white, hairy caterpillar eyebrows moved independently, neither co-ordinating with the rest of the facial muscles.

Jayne pushed past him into the shop. 'I didn't, Herbert, but when was the last time you went out?'

Herbert took this as a serious question. He stared up at the ceiling and considered his answer. 'Two weeks ago last Fursday. Had an arms and militaria conference. Did a lot of deals there, a lot of deals. But everyfing's done on the internet these days. No need to leave the shop any more.' The voice still retained the Cockney accent of his youth despite having lived in Manchester for the last fifty years.

'What do you do for food? No, don't answer. Let me introduce you to my associate, David Mercer.'

Herbert looked him up and down. 'They hiring a better class of copper these days?' He reached out and felt the lapel of David's jacket. 'A wee bit conservative for my taste but still, nice schmutter. Could do with a bit of clean, though. You a Yank?'

'How did you know...?'

'Got the eye, haven't I? Always have had. My dad, he—'

'When you two have finished with your mutual appreciation society, we'll get on with business.'

'I ain't done nuffin' wrong. On my son's life, I ain't.'

'You haven't got a son, Herbert. Nor a wife. Nor any living relatives as far as I remember.'

'You got a memory like a bear trap, Mrs Sinclair. Do you never forget nuffin'?'

'But the sign, it says "Herbert Levy and Sons",' said David.

'Ah, the punters love that. It suggests longevity and trustworthiness. A business handed down from father to son.'

'The only thing you ever handed down was some used underwear, Herbert.'

'That;s not a nice thing to say to a respectable businessman, Inspector Sinclair.'

'Now, I told you, I'm not a copper any more.'

'So it means I don't have to answer any of your questions?'

'That's true. But for old time's sake, I'm sure you will.'

'I ain't a sentimental man. All that nostalgia bollocks means nuffin' to me.'

Jayne was about to point out that the man ran a store specialising in 'nostalgia bollocks' but decided not to. A more straightforward approach would be best with Herbert.

'The old times' sake was when I nicked you back in the day for receiving. We left a lot of the charges off the sheet; a favour, I seem to remember. A quick phone call to Barry Knowles at Cheetham Hill nick might help. It's towards the end of the month, they're always looking for a few easy collars to make the crime statistics look better.'

Herbert rubbed his hands. 'Don't be like that to a friend, Mrs Sinclair. How can I help you?'

Jayne produced the picture of Dan Jackson's grandfather. 'What can you tell me about this?'

Herbert looked at the photo of the young man and shook his head. 'I don't have nuffin' to do with stuff like this.'

Chapter Thirty-Six

September 12, 1938
Baden Baden, Germany

He hitched up his brown leather woggle, making sure it was centred in the middle of the tan collars of his shirt. He checked the ends of his black neckerchief. They must be exactly the same length as each other, stretching to cover the cross strap of his leather belt. Hans Diderich had warned him that Baldur von Schirach was a stickler for the protocols of the uniform. He checked his shoes; a quick wipe on the back of the socks to make them shine even more. Finally, he fastened the belt around his black shorts. A new pair, bought just for this meeting.

Today was the big day and he was ready to meet the leader and editor of the movement's paper.

He had been in Germany for nearly six months now. Originally, Johnnie and the branch had only sponsored him for a two-week visit to the camp. But he had loved it and when the time came for him to return to England, he could find no reason to go back.

He would miss his mother and his sister, of course, but what did they matter in the greater scheme of life? He was here, at the centre of the greatest revolution mankind had ever seen. A revolution where the purity of the race mattered above all else. And, at its heart, the leader – the man who had changed everything.

Der Führer.

The camp had been specially created for Germans living abroad, the *Volksdeutsche*. The mix of people from America, England, Sweden, the Sudetenland, Danzig and other countries had opened his eyes to the world. One thing united them all; a love for Germany and the Führer.

At first, he had found living in tents and the relentless commitment to physical exercise exhausting, but after a few days he had come to love the morning runs, the mass gymnastics and the emphasis on health and vitality. He loved the newfound strength he found in his shoulders and his legs.

The instructors were superb with him, patiently explaining the theory and practice of National Socialism. For him, it wasn't just a few marches or picking fights with the Jews in the East End any more, but a way of government and a way of life, putting the state first and the individual second.

For the first time in his life he felt part of something bigger than himself. A mass of people committed to one goal: the rise and salvation of the German people.

And then there was Ilse. Meeting her was the final attraction, ensuring he never went back to the grey skies of Manchester. The camp had been showing Leni Riefenstahl's film of the Olympics, and he was seated in the third row from the front along with Otto from Danzig, Franc from Alsace and Swedish Sven.

He had noticed this girl sitting in front of him, her long blonde hair intricately braided and hanging down to the small of her back. She looked back at him once or twice before the film started, apparently checking who else was in the hall, but he knew she was really looking at him.

During the interval, she had stood up and dropped her kerchief on the floor.

He went to pick it up, bending down as she went to reach for it. Their hands had touched and he looked into her blue eyes and he was lost for a second, mumbling 'sorry' in English.

'You're the English boy, right?' she had said in a strong Pfalz accent.

'Yes,' he'd replied, not wanting to look at her face but instead staring at his polished shoes.

'Can we practise English together? I do want to learn, but at my school, the teacher has resigned and nobody's teaching it any more.'

'A Jew?'

'Half-Jewish. A Mischling. He had to go eventually.'

The music for the film began again. They had both sat down, but not before she had glanced behind her and smiled.

Later that evening, after the film had finished, they spent the time until lights out talking together about the future. She told him all about herself. How she had been selected for the Lebensborn programme because of her Aryan features and purity. 'My family couldn't have afforded the school otherwise,' she explained. 'But we are Echt Deutsch and so it's only right I get to go.'

She had a few complaints too. The Bund Deutsche Madel took up so much of her time; attending meetings on Wednesday and Saturday, community work in the evenings, classes on the duties of women in National Socialism, classes on physical fitness, outings and camps, but she supposed she had to give something back to the Fatherland that had given her so much.

They had kissed later in the evening too. Just a short kiss, but it sent a shiver through his body that went looking for a spine, and didn't find one.

They had been a couple ever since, seeing each other once a week on marches or when the Hitler Jugend and the Bund Deutsche Madel united for meetings, or to go around the town painting the Star of David on Jewish shops.

171

He was amazed these people still remained in business, hanging on to their threadbare existence when all Germans boycotted their stores. They wouldn't last long, though, he would see to that.

He was brought back down to earth by a shout from the Stammführer. The head of the Hitler Jugend, Baldur von Schirach entered wearing full uniform and supported by a phalanx of assistants, photographers, aides and the heads of division.

Thomas and the others stood to attention, shoulders back, chest out, eyes focused on an imaginary spot two feet in front of them.

Baldur von Schirach passed along the line, stopping in front of Thomas. 'You are from England, yes?' he said in clear, fluent English. 'I am extremely pleased with the latest edition of the magazine, *Wille und Macht*. It was your idea to do an English special?'

Thomas looked down at his feet and nodded.

A hand reached out and raised his chin. 'Do not be modest. The Führer is delighted, especially with the letter from Chamberlain. How did you get it?'

'I wrote to him and he replied.'

'Very resourceful. I can't imagine the Führer writing a long letter to an English newspaper.'

Von Schirach took one step back and held out his hand. An aide passed him a letter written on notepaper from 10 Downing Street. 'Listen, everyone. I have in my hand a piece of paper from Chamberlain, the English prime minister. The Führer is pleased, let me read it to you.'

He searched for a section in the typed letter. 'Here it is.'

He coughed twice and began reading the letter out loud. '"I welcome the attention of the German Youth Movement to devote a special issue of their magazine to the subject of England, and I gladly accept the invitation to contribute to a project which I regard as evidence of a growing desire for mutual understanding between our two countries.'"

Here he looked up directly at Thomas. 'Congratulations to this young man for extending the invitation.'

Thomas blushed a bright red, feeling the heat extend up his face to the roots of his blond hair.

Von Schirach coughed again and continued. '"In writing to you, the young manhood and young womanhood of Germany."' He looked up again and a smile spread across his face. 'The elderly fool was actually writing to a member of his own country. What a shame.'

The rest of the members of the unit laughed dutifully.

The head of Hitler Jugend looked for his place and then continued. 'The fool then quotes Shakespeare as if there were no other English writer we would know.'

Again, more laughter.

Von Schirach held up one elegantly gloved finger. The laughter ceased. 'But now, he comes to an important part. "All the hopes of Germany are set upon you; to your care is committed your national heritage and traditions, your national honour and your national prosperity. All this is committed to you for your safekeeping, and I am confident you will prove worthy of the trust."' Here, von Schirach looked at them each in turn. 'The old fool puts it well. You are the Guardians of the Reich. You are the future of the Reich. Your purity, honesty and strength will rebuild a German nation that was once on its knees. Do not take the responsibility lightly, nor show an ounce of compassion to the enemies of the Reich. Smash them as you would a cockroach.'

Throughout this speech, von Schirach's face became more and more contorted, the veins on his temple standing out in stark relief beneath his cap. Thomas thought he was going to burst a blood vessel.

Then, as quickly as he had become agitated, a bemused smile returned to the leader's lips.

'But this is not why the Führer is so pleased.' He returned to the letter, looking for his place once more, before reading aloud once again.

'"But your responsibility does not end there. You have a future for the responsibility of your country: but you have also, in common with the youth of other nations, a joint responsibility for the future of the world." And here the English becomes convoluted, almost as if it were written by a German...'

The unit laughed again but were stopped once more by an upraised finger.

'"It is already and in the future will be still more the happy fortune of youth now flourishing in many lands to foster - by means of mutual exchange of visits and otherwise - that understanding between nations that is so essential to the settling of differences and the appeasement of the world."' Von Schirach panted like a dog running out of breath. 'He goes on for a few more sentences and then signs the letter, Neville Chamberlain. Now, can any of you tell me why the Führer was so pleased with this letter?'

Suddenly, it was as if the sun had illuminated the darkest corners of Thomas's mind. He understood completely what he had to do with his life. He put up his hand.

Von Schirach nodded. 'Let the English boy answer.'

'The Führer is pleased because the letter shows the man's weakness. He understands the need to protect national honour and national culture, but then wants nations to get along and appease each other.' Thomas searched for the German words to express his thoughts. 'But there is no appeasement, only the ability of one people, one race, to dominate another. Germany doesn't want to "get along" with other nations, it wants to rule over them.'

Von Schirach clapped his hands. 'The Englishman understands it better than anyone. The German people must be free from the restraints imposed on them by Western liberalism and Jewish ideology. We have not been put upon this earth to appease, but to rule and conquer lesser nations, creating Lebensraum for all the German people. The Führer has made this clear in *Mein Kampf.*'

He stopped speaking and smiled again. 'Let me let you into a secret. Soon, this idiot will have "discussions" with the Führer regarding the intolerable position of the German people in the Sudetenland. He will appease and seek to understand; the Führer will dominate.'

He reached out his hand and the assistant gave him a badge, which he pinned on Thomas's chest.

'This is from the High Command. It was created specially on the orders of the Führer. You are an honoured young man. Heil Hitler.'

Von Schirach gave a salute and left the hall followed by his staff.

Thomas snapped to attention, returning the salute precisely; arm held out at forty-five degrees, palm down and fingers stiff and pointed forward.

He finally understood. England was ancient and weak and tired. Now was the time of Germany, a time to create a new Reich, and he was going to be part of the work, whatever it took.

As the others gathered round him, admiring the badge with its swastika and Union Jack displayed together, he saw Ilse staring at him. There was a fierce passion in her ice-blue eyes and he knew that evening he would have her.

Chapter Thirty-Seven

November 9, 1938
Baden Baden, Germany

They all jumped on the lorry together, the Hitler Jugend and the Bund Deutsche Madel. He could feel Ilse's body pressing against his. Up front, the flag of his unit – a black swastika against red and white horizontal stripes – flew proudly from the cab.

They were off to teach the Jews a lesson. Yesterday, Ernst vom Rath had finally died in Paris from the gunshot wounds he had received from the Jew, Gryndzpan. They had been warned to be prepared for action and this morning the call had come.

The lorry drove down Sophienstrasse and then along Lichtentaler Strasse.

People were beginning to gather in the streets. Everywhere, he could feel an electric tension in the air, like walking beneath the wires of a sub-station. You couldn't see the power but you knew it was there.

The weather was cold, but not too cold. None of them was wearing a coat, though. For some reason, they didn't need them.

The lorry was stopped by an SS man dressed in full military uniform. He pointed to a shop on the corner with a neatly painted glass window. 'Steiner Butchers. Specialists in kosher meat and sausages. The Jew who owns it has been arrested. You know what to do.'

The family of the Jew were huddled outside the door: a woman with a shawl over her head and two young children hanging off her coat. She sat on a battered suitcase not looking at anything in particular, staring into mid-air.

They clambered down off the lorry and Thomas was given a pot of yellow paint and a brush. He ran over to the wall behind the woman and began painting the words '*Juda Verrecke*' on the walls at the side of the shop. It was a slogan they had been taught in the youth camps. A slogan from history: *Deutschland erwache. Juda verrecke.* He had trouble understanding this in English, but to all his German friends it made perfect sense. He finally translated it as 'Germany awake. Jews croak.' He knew something was lost in the translation. But he painted it anyway. The local people would understand what it meant.

A crowd had begun to gather now to see what was going on. The Jewish woman jumped up and sheltered her children, moving them away from the shop and into the road.

Ilse and two other girls from the BDM had been given large hammers. As Thomas finished his sign, she raised the biggest hammer above her head and brought it down on the plate glass of the window. The window shook but didn't smash. The crowd groaned.

Her friend, Sylvie, took her hammer and threw it at the window. It immediately smashed into large shards of glass on the pavement. The letters, painted on the glass, jumbled together to form a giant, transparent jigsaw puzzle.

The crowd began clapping and cheering. Another hammer was thrown, smashing more of the window. Ilse stepped forward, reaching through where the plate glass had once stood, and took the meat lying on the marble slab. She handed it to a young girl standing with her father. 'Sorry, it's kosher, but it's meat.'

The young girl took it, saying thank you. The crowd surged forward past the Jewish woman and her children to reach in and grab what was left for themselves.

Up and down the long street, other shops were being given exactly the same treatment: a hardware store owned by a Loewenstein, a furniture store with the name of Bloch and Sons written above the door, and a jewellery shop proudly proclaiming it had the best watches from Switzerland.

Inside the jeweller's a uniformed SS man was desperately kicking an ancient cast-iron safe. He bent down and turned the handle but it still wouldn't open. Taking out his pistol, he fired two shots at the metal front. For a moment, the crowd stopped what they were doing and listened.

There was silence.

The SS man appeared at the door and shouted, 'You can't even get money from a Jewish safe.'

The crowd cheered and carried on looting the shops.

Thomas looked down the street. People were coming out of the stores carrying buckets and mops, chairs, mirrors, and spades. Two aged women were even carrying a wardrobe between them, struggling under the weight but reluctant to let go of their prize.

There was no anarchy, though. No fights or disagreements. The looting was orderly and disciplined; two policemen looking on made sure of that.

The Stammführer of his unit called him forward. 'Get on the lorry. We need to go back into town.'

Thomas grabbed hold of Ilse and pushed her up on to the flatbed. To him, she never seemed more beautiful than at that moment. Her hair, normally tied in a tightly woven plait, had come loose and flowed around her face. The top buttons of her blouse had come undone, revealing the top of her breasts, where a few drops of sweat glistened on the small blonde hairs that lined her body. She was breathing heavily; he didn't know if it was exertion or excitement and he didn't care. But what attracted him most was the energy in her eyes. A passion, a fire he had never seen before.

They stood on the top of the lorry and were driven back the way they had come. The crowds were thicker now, lining the streets. Some mothers were holding their children above their heads so they could see what was happening. Others were holding their hands, making sure they stayed close beside them.

Up ahead, near Leopoldsplatz, the road became totally blocked. They were ordered to dismount. As they did so, they heard cries from the crowd.

'The Jews are marching. The Jews are marching.'

The crowd surged forward. Thomas grabbed Ilse's hand and elbowed their way through. People moved out of the way when they saw his uniform. They reached the edge of the street just as the head of the column of Jews was turning into Sophien-strasse.

There were about a hundred of them formed into three columns, marching down the centre of the street, flanked on either side by burly SS guards. The Jews were all men, some young, some old, some middle-aged. All wore long coats to keep out the cold.

As they passed the Head of the Police standing by the side of the road, a loud order came to remove their hats. At first, a few hesitated. The order was repeated and all hats were taken off as they passed the man whose responsibility it was to maintain law and order in the town.

The crowd were mostly quiet at this point. A few students, whom Thomas recognised, were gathered around one of the teachers. They were shouting loudly, *Juda verrecke,*' again and again, encouraged by the watchful eye of their teacher.

The rest of the people were mostly silent, watching from the side of the road.

One man asked Thomas, 'Where are they going?', pointing to the marching lines of Jewish men.

Thomas shrugged his shoulders.

An SS Untersturmführer heard the question. 'They're going to the synagogue on Stephanienstrasse. Time to hear their lesson.'

Thomas grabbed Ilse's hand once more and ran alongside the march, dodging through the crowds lining the street. As they got closer to the synagogue, the crowd was denser, noisier, much more aggressive.

The building was large and imposing, with two square towers in each corner and beautifully intricate stained-glass windows, the colours shining brightly in the November sun. It looked more like a medieval church than anything else, a testament to the wealth of the Jewish population in the town.

He elbowed his way to the front, pulling Ilse behind him. There were people shouting at the Jews now, hurling abuse into their faces.

'Dirty Jew.'

'Get out of my town.'

'Bloodsucker.'

'Devil.'

One man even stepped forward to throw a punch at an eminent lawyer, shouting, 'Here's for what you did to me.' He missed first time, but his wife came forward then and she didn't miss. The lawyer fell to the ground, where he was helped up and quickly rushed away from the mob into the temple.

Thomas noticed the SS had spread three of the blue and white prayer shawls on the floor at the entrance. He had seen one before, hanging in the office of Mr Bronstein, where it waited for him until he went to his prayers.

The Jews of Baden Baden tried to avoid stepping on the beautifully fringed shawls as they entered the interior of the synagogue, but the SS forced them to tread their dirty shoes into the silk.

Soon, the bleached whiteness was covered in the dirt of the streets.

With Ilse in tow, he pushed past a black-shirted SS and into the synagogue. A row of fine wooden pews faced an intricately carved arch supported by two marble pillars. Beneath the arch, in front of a door, stood an elaborate lectern, behind which was an SS Officer carrying a large swagger stick.

'Let's watch from up here.' Ilse grabbed his hand and they ran up the stairs to a gallery overlooking the main hall of the synagogue. The Jews beneath were still filing in and sitting on the pews. Thomas leant over and looked down at the assembled men beneath him. Some had fine heads of black hair, others were bald. One had a large bald spot surround by tufts of hair like a monk's tonsure. He pointed this out to Ilse and they both giggled. The man looked up at them. Or rather the man looked through them as if they weren't there.

The SS officer tapped the lectern with his stick. 'Thank you for coming,' he said to the seated congregation in front of him. 'We will now begin this service with a song. You all know the words to the Horst Wessel song, don't you? Well, it's time to sing.'

He tapped the lectern once more and began to lead the song, conducting the choir like a Capelmeister, his stick a long baton.

'Die Fahne hoch! Die Reihen fest geschlossen!

SA marschiert mit ruhig festem Schritt.'

At first, the Jews looked at each other, not knowing what to do. The SS officer tapped his lectern as he sang and another ran around waving his arms upwards, encouraging the congregation to sing the Horst Wessel song.

Gradually, the men in the front row joined in, followed by the rest of the congregation:

'Kam'raden, die Rotfront und Reaktion erschossen,

Marschier'n im Geist in unser'n Reihen mit.

Kam'raden, die Rotfront und Reaktion erschossen,

Marschier'n im Geist in unser'n Reihen mit.'

Outside, the mob began to laugh as the singing became louder and the congregation joined in. One SS man at the side struck an elderly man who wasn't singing across the head. The rest took the hint and began to sing with more passion.

Thomas heard the words soar up from the people beneath him and echo off the curved roof. He pulled Ilse closer to him. The words filled him with joy. At last, this was a time to avenge all the petty insults he had received. At last, here was a people who understood the world. At last, here was a nation standing up for itself.

The SS officer at the front waved his arms to stop the congregation from singing. 'Enough, enough already. We can't have our national song desecrated in such a manner.'

The mob outside the door, looking in, laughed.

'Instead, we should have a reading from the Holy Book. You, you can be the reader.' He pointed at an elderly man sitting in the front row.

Thomas recognised him as a former teacher at the Gymnasium. A fine man, he had helped Thomas in his first days in Germany but had then vanished from the school.

The man stood up and walked to the lectern.

'But the book you will be giving a reading from is this.' The SS officer held up a copy of *Mein Kampf*, the Führer's face prominent on the cover.

'But I... it's not...'

The officer brought his stick up slowly. The man looked at it and blanched.

'I've marked the passages. It should be educational for your people.'

A buzz went round the mob at the back of the synagogue, who were gathered around the entrance.

The former teacher opened *Mein Kampf* at the marked page. In a whisper he said, 'I have received an order to read the following.' He began to read from the book in a voice so low and hushed it could barely be heard. Thomas had to lean forward to try to catch the words.

The SS officer brought his stick down on the back of the man's neck. 'Start again and read louder.'

Without looking up, the man began reading. '"How close they see approaching victory can be seen by the hideous aspect which their relations with the members of other peoples takes on".'

The stick crashed down on the lectern. 'Louder, louder. They can't hear you at the back.'

The old teacher coughed and carried on reading much louder now, almost defiant.

'"With satanic joy in his face, the black-haired Jewish youth lurks in wait for the unsuspecting girl whom he defiles with his blood, thus stealing her from her people. With every means he tries to destroy the racial foundations of the people he has set out to subjugate. Just as he himself systematically ruins women and girls, he does not shrink back from pulling down the blood barriers for others, even on a large scale. It was and it is Jews who bring the Negroes into the Rhineland, always with the same secret thought and clear aim of ruining the hated white race by the necessarily resulting bastardization, throwing it down from its cultural and political height, and himself rising to be its master."'

This reading continued for the next hour. When the SS officer became bored with one reader, he rapped the man on the back of the head and ordered another to take his place.

Ilse yawned as beneath her another man took his place at the lectern. She turned to Thomas. 'I'm starving, let's eat.'

'A few more minutes. Let's see what happens.'

She went quiet and leant into him, pressing her breasts against his chest. 'Are you sure you want to stay here longer?'

He was about to give in to her when the SS man rapped the lectern and shouted, 'Take them out, I've had enough.'

As the Jews filed out into the courtyard, a few asked if they could go to the toilet. The officer laughed. 'Of course you can, why are you asking me?' He pointed to the wall of the synagogue. 'Piss there.'

Two of the men could no longer control their bladders. They rushed to the wall and stood in front of it, a wet stain darkening the painted surface.

'See,' the officer shouted, 'these old men always piss on their own patch. It's in their nature.'

The other Jews filed outside, not looking at the wall or the two men standing beside it.

When they had finished, the elderly men buttoned themselves up and said a few words of prayer, before filing out of the door to join the others standing outside.

Thomas and Ilse climbed down the stairs, following them into the courtyard.

'I'm starving, let's eat,' she repeated.

'You're always hungry.'

She looked at him. 'And not just for food, Thomas, remember that.' She kissed him full on the lips in front of the doorway to the synagogue.

'When you two have finished, I have a job for you.' It was their Stammführer. 'Come this way.'

Outside, the crowd was watching the Jews being herded into the centre of the courtyard. Two buses pulled up on the road and a doctor stepped down. The Jews were hustled on board, with the doctor rejecting the sick, aged or infirm. Or at least, he pretended to examine them, but it was a cursory glance rather than anything else.

'Where are they going?' Thomas asked.

'I don't know, Dachau probably. The best place for them,' answered their supervisor.

The older Jewish men who were being released quickly melted through the crowd back to their homes. The younger ones sat on the bus, not looking out of the windows but staring straight ahead.

'Here,' the supervisor took a tarpaulin off a pile of wood and three cans of paraffin, 'you're to burn it.'

'Burn what?'

'That.' He pointed to the synagogue. 'It's time we showed them who's boss.'

Ilse and Thomas were joined by four of the other Hitler Youth. They picked up the wood and paraffin cans, carrying them into the synagogue. Thomas piled the wood beneath the central lectern and doused it with paraffin. The others ran around with the cans, spreading the liquid across the wooden pews and floor. Finally, the whole place stank of the sharp stench of petrol.

They gathered near the entrance and Thomas took a box of matches from his pocket.

'What are you doing?'

A worn-out elderly man seized his hand, trying to wrench the box from his grip. They struggled for a few seconds, fighting over the matches, before one of the other boys came to his senses and hit the old man across the back of the head with a stave of wood.

Instantly, Thomas felt the man's grip release. The old Jew sank to his feet and, as he did so, his soft pepper-and-salt beard brushed against Thomas's arm.

'Please...don't.'

A wave of revulsion flowed over Thomas. He gritted his teeth and smashed his fist into the man's face. The old Jew collapsed on the floor, curling up into a ball as the others stepped forward and kicked him again and again.

Ilse touched Thomas's hand. 'Can I?'

She took the box from his grip, opened it and took out a match. As the others kicked the elderly man, she held the match over the striking strip.

Thomas saw the small blue end of phosphorus move down and across, suddenly flaring into a bright orange and red flame. For a second, Ilse held it in her hand before launching it into a pool of paraffin on the floor.

The match died as it landed in the liquid, before there was a quiet whoosh and a thin blue wave of flame spread across the floor to the lectern beneath the arch. In front of their eyes, the flames licked the sumptuous fabrics. Soon they were ablaze and more flames engulfed the lectern, sending out tendrils of orange and red to seize the arch and the pews. A thick black smoke began to fill the chamber.

Ilse stood still, transfixed, as more flames began to taste the walls, bubbling the paint as they passed over it. The smell was intoxicating; wood and petrol and cotton and paint, all mixed together in one holy mass.

The heat flowed in waves from the burning walls and pews, getting fiercer with every second.

Thomas grabbed Ilse's arm. 'We should leave now.'

The others were already at the door, shouting at them to go.

Ilse stood there, staring.

He pulled her away and tripped over the prostrate figure of the elderly man. Ilse kicked him once more as she ran past.

The man didn't move, nor did he utter a moan of pain.

As he pushed Ilse out of the door, Thomas took one last look at the interior of the synagogue burning warmly in the Autumn stillness.

The body of the old man was still lying on the floor, flames licking his flesh.

Chapter Thirty-Eight

'It's the principle of the thing, Mrs Sinclair. My old dad would turn over in his grave if he saw me dealing in stuff like that.'

'What's the problem, Mr Levy?' asked David.

'What's the problem? It's German, ain't it? Nazi stuff. I has nuffin' to do with Nazi stuff. Big market for it too, I'll tell you. Easy to shift and nobody asks no questions.'

'Slow down. What the hell are you talking about?' Jayne held up the picture. 'What's wrong with this?'

'It's a picture of a member of the Hitler Youth, that is.' He put an eyeglass to his eye and brought the picture up close to his face. 'Probably 1938 or 1939 from the uniform.'

'How can you be so sure?' asked David.

'I might not deal in it, but I have to know all about it. And I'm sure Mrs Sinclair has told you I'm one of the best in the business. I knows my stuff, I does. See the badge with the black border? It's a Hitler Youth High Command decoration awarded to distinguished foreigners. He seems about eighteen or nineteen to me, so was probably called up in September. A lot of the Hitler Youth went into the SS, you know. He looks like butter wouldn't melt in his gob, but you never know what he got up to during the war, do you?'

'Thanks for the info. Anything else you can see?'

Again, Herbert held the picture close to his face, peering at it through the lens of his glass. 'That's strange... Never seen it before.'

'What's strange?'

'He's got a British flag on his shirt. The Union Jack. And it's crossed with a swastika. Maybe he could speak English or something. I could check up on it for you, if you want. I know somebody who deals in this stuff... and don't you worry, DI Sinclair, he's as straight as a badger. Pretty straight, anyway. Well, he hasn't been caught yet, if you knows what I mean.'

'He hasn't got a record.'

'No EP, no LP, not even a compact disc.' Herbert laughed and looked at David for support.

'Leave me to tell the jokes, Herbert,' said Jayne.

'Yes, Mrs Sinclair. Leave me your number and I'll call you if he knows anything. Mind if I take a picture and zap it over to him?' He pulled a dirty mobile from his pocket.

'You never cease to amaze me, Mr Tech-Savvy himself.'

'Got to move with the times. Anyway, it's free, innit? I likes machines, Mrs Sinclair, even got a microwave somewhere.'

'What's it for, darning socks?' asked Jayne.

'Nah, it's for some of the stuff I sell. Rub it with lemon juice, stick it in the microwave and five minutes later it comes out looking forty years older...' Herbert suddenly stopped speaking, looking furtively around him. 'You didn't hear that, did you, Mrs Sinclair?'

'Hear what, Herbert? Me, I'm as deaf as a donkey these days. So, what's your number?'

'I thought you always had my number.' Herbert laughed again, a peculiar croak like a strangled chicken laying an egg.

'No jokes, please.'

'It's here on my card.' He passed her a small camouflage-patterned card.

Jayne took a quick glance at it. 'Fine, you have a phone, I need to use it. Through here, is it?'

Herbert rushed forward to stop her but she had already pulled back a curtain guarding the entrance to a back room. Inside, she was confronted by stacked boxes marked with the brand name 'Samsung'.

'Like watching television, do we?'

Herbert stopped laughing. 'I'm looking after them for a friend.'

'Get rid of them.'

'Yes, DI Sinclair.'

'Where's the phone?' Jayne had a difficult call to make to her ex-husband and here was better than in some phone booth in the middle of nowhere, if she could find one that worked.

'Over there, near the televis—' Herbert cut his sentence short, pointing instead.

Jayne pulled the curtain closed behind her.

Time to call Paul.

Chapter Thirty-Nine

Tuesday, April 18, 2017
Manchester

The phone rang for an interminably long time. Jayne was about to hang up when Paul's voice came on the line.

'Hello.' The tone was abrupt and curt.

'Hi, Paul, it's Jayne.'

'What can I do for you?' There was no change in the tone or softening of the voice. They had only been separated officially for three months but they had been drifting apart for years. The end came when Paul insisted she move with him to Brussels. She didn't want to leave her work and why should she? She was an excellent researcher and it provided a comfortable living. Plus, her father was getting on and in the early stages of dementia; she couldn't leave him alone.

But she knew these were the rational reasons, the things we use to shore up our emotional decisions. When it came down to it, the truth was that she just didn't love Paul enough any more to make the sort of sacrifices he was asking. He, of course, in his own peculiarly male, self-centred way, didn't see them as sacrifices but as duties a wife owes to her husband.

That had been the final straw.

'Hello? Jayne... hello? I'm at the assembly plant now, it's quite noisy. What do you want?'

She took a deep breath. 'Paul, I have a favour to ask...'

The background noise in the phone suddenly vanished. He must have found somewhere quieter to talk. 'Ask away,' he said.

'Could I use your sister's house for a few days?'

'Why? What's wrong with our house?'

The house was still jointly owned. It was another point of contention between them. 'Nothing. There's nothing wrong with the house. I just want to stay somewhere else for a few days.'

Silence from the other end of the phone.

'You're going to have to trust me on this one, Paul.'

'Trust you? Why should I do that?' His voice had taken on the little-boy-lost tone which so annoyed her. The voice of a child who was used to getting his own way and had suddenly been denied.

'Because I need your help right now.'

Again, silence. 'What's going on? Are you in trouble? Do you want me to fly back?'

She smiled. That was the real Paul — the man who, in the days after the death of Dave Gilmour, had been her rock, her buttress against depression and sorrow and guilt. 'I'm fine.' She thought desperately about something to tell him that would help appease his fears. 'It's just a job where it would be best if I didn't stay at home for a few days.' She realised she didn't sound particularly convincing.

There was a long sigh on the end of the phone. 'You and the bloody genealogy work. It's a waste of your time, Jayne, hanging around with wasters researching their bloody family trees.'

'Paul, are you going to help me or not?'

Another long sigh. 'The key is under the plant pot at the back door.'

'Thank you.'

'But, Jayne, take care of the place. My sister wouldn't like it if you messed with her stuff.'

'She passed away eight months ago, Paul. Have you done nothing to the house?'

'I couldn't face it.'

'Do you want me to help you sort out her effects when I've finished this case?' Instantly, she regretted making the offer.

The whine in the voice became even stronger. 'If you could, Jayne, that would be wonderful.'

She paused for a moment, trying to think of what to say next. 'Anyway, thanks once again for the key.'

'Are you sure you don't want me to fly back? I could be in Manchester tomorrow.'

'Certain, Paul. I'll be fine. It's only for a few days.' She tried to make her voice artificially perky. 'I'll put the key back under the plant pot when I leave, don't worry.'

She put the phone back on the hook and kept her hand hovering over it. Should she call him back and tell him the truth?

There was a time when they had no secrets between them, everything was discussed, everything agreed. But that time was long gone. She decided not to call him back. Enough was enough.

She drew the curtain back. Both Herbert and David were standing there, trying to pretend they hadn't heard every word.

Herbert spoke first, revealing he had indeed heard. 'Mrs Sinclair, for a policewoman you have a very lax sense of security. Take it from an expert: under a plant pot is the first place a thief looks.'

'Thank you, Herbert, for your professional advice.'

'Happy to help. My mate has already come back on your photograph.'

'He's quick.'

'I only work with the best.'

'Thank you for your diligence.'

'Diligence is my middle name. Herbert Diligence Levy. Has a certain ring to it, don't you think?'

'A certain confidence and permanence,' answered Jayne. 'Even better than Herbert Levy and non-existent Son. It sounds almost professional.'

'I am a professional.'

'A professional tea leaf?'

'Mrs Sinclair. That's libel, that is, of my good name.'

'A couple of things, Herbert. It's slander when it's spoken, libel when it's written. And you haven't got a good name, so what's the problem?'

'The problem is your picture, Mrs Sinclair. My friend tells me it is a Hitler Jugend uniform, as I thought. But he thinks it might be a bit later than 1938, probably 1939 or 1940. It's the badges apparently. He's never seen a badge with a British flag before. He was keen to purchase it if you're interested.'

'I don't have it, but thank your friend for his help.'

'That's not all. He noticed something in the corner of the picture. A sign.'

'A sign of what?'

'A sign for Lichtefelde Training Camp near Berlin.'

'Our man was in training?'

'He was, or about to go into training. The problem is that camp was reserved for the Waffen SS.'

Chapter Forty

August 19, 1941
Lichtefelde Training Camp, Berlin, Germany

Thomas Green adjusted the strap on his backpack and picked up his rifle. The Rottenführer was in position with his bloody whistle, always with his bloody whistle.

A loud shrill noise and the man in front of him took off. He marched forward and stopped at the line. The Rottenführer was staring at him. The bastard dwarf had been a POW during the First World War. He had even picked up a smattering of English from some girls in Skegness. But despite that, he always tried to make life difficult.

'The Little Englander is late again.' Or, 'The Englander has not been listening in the Weltanschaulicher Unterricht. He needs to understand his National Socialism much better if he is to remain a member of the Waffen SS.' Or the worst: 'No leave for the Little Englander this weekend. He will instead be working with me on his march; it still lacks discipline.'

Thomas watched as the Rottenführer raised the whistle to his lips.

Wait for it. Wait for it.

Then he blew and Thomas, like the good soldier he was, ran as fast as he could to the first obstacle. His body, his mind, no longer his own but owned by the Rottenführer with the whistle.

Up and over. Easy.

The backpack was banging into his back with every step. He would have to adjust the straps later. Up ahead, a long stream of soldiers, each ten seconds apart, were attacking the obstacles. The man in front of him was already slowing down, Thomas was closer to him already.

He thought back to the day he had left Baden Baden. Ilse, in her white dress with the tiny blue cornflowers on it, standing at the station to see him off.

The night before, she had given him a new Leica II camera with its built-in rangefinder so he could take pictures of his comrades and his training and send them back to her.

He had been rejected by the Wehrmacht because 'he wasn't a true German', but the Waffen SS accepted him with open arms once he produced his *Volksdeutsche* certificate. He was a member of the German Race and he had papers to prove it. The training was at Berlin-Lichtefelde Barracks and he was to join the Leibstandarte Adolf Hitler, the Führer's own regiment. Ilse had been so proud of him when he received the letter, she had taken him into her parents' bedroom and they'd made love on the floor, beneath the portrait of her father.

He would always remember lying in her arms in the afternoon, the late summer sun shining through the window, highlighting the fine blonde hairs covering her body. And her smell; a perfume of summer meadow with a hint of something darker and more earthy, like grass after a shower. He would always remember that smell.

She told him she was pregnant after they made love. But he was not to worry because she was Lebensborn and so everything would be taken care of by the nation.

He didn't worry. Her pregnancy had nothing to do with him. Not now. He had more important work to do.

He arrived at the barracks on a summer's day in 1940. The German army had crushed France and

Britain, the Dutch and Belgians had surrendered. Norway was in their hands and Italy had come into the war on their side. From the Baltic down to the Mediterranean, the Aryan race ruled supreme and he was one of its members.

A *Volksdeutsche*.

The processing at the barracks was quick and efficient. His field-grey SS uniform and equipment were issued to him and he was tattooed under his left arm with his blood group: Type O.

He heard the Rottenführer's high-pitched whistle as he passed the Schutze in front of him. The sound was followed by a bellow. 'You've been beaten by the Englander, you should be ashamed!'

He saw the Schutze's eyes, they were red-rimmed and suffering. No fight left in them. He would quietly be packed off to some other battalion to become a policeman or a company clerk.

Thomas threw himself on the ground, his rifle cradled in his arms like a baby. Using his feet and knees, he wriggled under the wire. Above his head, he could hear the sounds of rounds from a Maschinenpistole 38 thudding into the soft sand banks on the right. The Unterscharführer said he used live rounds but Thomas didn't believe him. He kept his head down anyway, no point in taking any chances.

And then he was out from under the wire and running again. A long run to the rope swing, now across a balance beam.

He checked his breathing. Fine.

The pack was still hammering into his back like a demented woodpecker.

His legs and body were fine. The months spent on physical training in the Hitler Jugend had paid off. He wasn't an ill-bred product of the Manchester slums any more, but a fit, active, determined young man.

'Put your heart into it. Faster. Faster,' shouted the Rottenführer.

Thomas picked up speed, leaping up the nine-foot-high wall. His hand was grabbed by the man on top and he was hauled up to sit astride the top.

His *kamerad* jumped down and carried on running. Thomas waited for the next man, to help him over the wall.

From his position, he could see the obstacle course stretched out in front of him. Men were running and jumping, holding their rifles across their chests. Others who had already finished were encouraging their comrades. The Rottenführer was strutting around the centre of the course, barking commands.

Thomas knew he belonged here, with these people and with this nation. He would give up his life for it if necessary. He would fight and kill and maim and strangle to be here.

Nothing was going to stop him.

He had found his home. He had found his people. He had found his purpose in life.

Chapter Forty-One

Tuesday, April 18, 2017
Somewhere beneath the streets of London

It was going to be a difficult conversation.

'Get out, all of you.'

The operators began to get up and leave their seats in front of their consoles. Still the screens flickered on.

They had lost them. The genealogist and David Mercer had disappeared.

The teams at Holyhead and in North Wales had reported no sightings. Luckily, the car had been found by chance when it was reported to the police by a Tesco security guard for having a broken rear window. A patrol car had been asked to check it out and they had intercepted the message.

The helicopter had burnt gallons of fuel hovering around the area with only one result; a sighting by a member of the public of a flying saucer over Welshpool. They had released a report stating it was an atmospheric weather balloon.

Nobody believed it.

Finally, they had not been seen at the house in Didsbury, no more use of credit cards and no use of a mobile phone. Nobody had logged on to David Mercer or Jayne Sinclair's bank or email accounts.

Ostransky was stumped. How could they vanish off the face of the earth?

But he already knew the answer. By not taking part in any of the conveniences of modern life - computers, credit cards, mobile phones and social media.

Without these tools that proved their existence, a person was invisible. With them, they were as easy to

199

see as if a spotlight had been shone down on them from God.

In this case, he was God.

He picked up the phone and pressed 4 on speed dial. The call was answered immediately.

'I hope you're going to tell me our problem has been solved.'

'I'm afraid the targets have gone to earth. We can't find them at the moment.' He was conscious of how incredibly weak his voice sounded.

'That is not what I wanted to hear, Mr Ostransky. You were appointed to this position because you promised us efficiency and order. Your mission was to follow the woman wherever she went, destroying any evidence she might uncover. You were provided with ample resources for performing the task and yet you have failed. The selection of our candidate is only three days away. Your job was to ensure there would be no obstacles to the selection. You're telling me you don't know where the target is?'

'I know the area of the target, but I can't pinpoint their exact location at this moment.'

'So this is an example of indeterminate incompetence?'

Felix Ostransky winced at the savage sarcasm. 'I believe the statement is unfair. I am confident we will be able to pinpoint the target soon.'

'I'm glad you are confident, Mr Ostransky. You have exactly twenty-four more hours to find this woman and discover what she has found out, do I make myself clear? After that, I will make alternative arrangements.'

'I understand precisely, Führer. I have never let you or the Organisation down. I will not start now.'

'I am glad to hear it, Mr Ostransky. Find her, and find her quickly.'

The phone went dead. He put it back on the receiver and gestured for the operatives to return. How was he going to find her?

And then it came to him in a moment of utmost clarity. There was an extremely simple way to solve this problem.

Chapter Forty-Two

Tuesday, April 18, 2017
Heaton Moor, Manchester

The key was under the plant pot beside the rear door, as Paul had told them. Inside, the house was cold and unloved, with a blanket of damp permeating everything.

Jayne looked for a switch for the central heating. She had only visited the house twice in the thirteen years she had been married to Paul. Both times his sister had become 'tired and emotional', berating the men in her life, or the absence of men in her life.

Jayne had a low tolerance for women like her but, because of Paul, she sat listening to the whining and moaning and criticism of everything and anything but herself.

Paul, on the other hand, lapped it up. As if it returned him to a time when they had stood together against the neuroticism of their mother.

Families: why beat them when you have to join them?

It amused Jayne that she looked into the history of families even though she didn't know much about her own.

Her father had absconded when she was two, leaving behind nothing but his name attached to a young toddler. Her mother had coped as best she could until she met the man Jayne now called her father, Robert. The man she loved more than anybody else even though they had no blood relationship. For her, he was always her dad; her biological father was merely a donor of sperm.

She eventually found the central heating switch, and the boiler kicked in with a start of electricity. For the first time in two days, she finally felt safe. David sat in the chair and relaxed.

'You look whacked.'

'Whacked and hungry.'

'How's the ankle?'

'Better. Still sore but better.'

'Let me take a look at it.'

He took off his right shoe and sock, raising the leg on to the couch.

'It looks less swollen than before. I'll put a bandage on it to give some support. You can rest it tonight.'

She went into the kitchen and found a first-aid box in the larder. At least Paul's sister had been fairly organised.

She knelt down, using a damp cloth to wash David's foot and ankle.

'I feel like a client in a spa. Can you give me a massage too?'

'That is definitely *not* part of the service.'

She took out a large roll of white bandage and gently began to wrap it around the sole of his foot and his ankle. He only winced once.

'You look like you've done this before.'

'St John's Ambulance first-aid course. A lot of coppers take it.'

She finished by tying the two ends of the bandage in a neat bow. 'Better?'

'Nearly as good as new. You never cease to amaze me, Mrs Sinclair.'

'I thought you were calling me Jayne.'

He was silent for a moment, just looking at her with those large, soft eyes. She hadn't noticed how long his lashes were until now. Almost feminine in the way they curved away from the eye.

He smiled at her and was about to say something, but she spoke first. 'I'll order a pizza and take a shower while we're waiting for it. I need to wash two days of fear and loathing off my skin.'

She stretched and rotated her head, trying to ease the tension from her muscles.

'I know the feeling. Turn around,' he ordered.

She turned away from him. Strong fingers gripped the base of her neck and massaged their way across her shoulders.

Instantly she felt the hairs on the back of her neck rise in pleasure and her head tilted backwards. The fingers unravelled and smoothed her knotted muscles as they dug into her skin.

Despite herself, she felt her body relaxing. It had been a long couple of days, fraught with anxiety. Beneath his fingers, all the stress seemed to ooze from her body.

'Where did you learn how to do this?'

'Swim training. After every session the coach used to relax our muscles with a five-minute massage.'

The fingers dug deeper into her muscles. She arched her back in pleasure, lost in the moment. Then the clock on the mantelpiece sounded the hour loudly, one bell after another.

She pulled away from his hands. 'I'd better order the food.'

'Don't you want me to continue?'

'Maybe later, but...' She left the sentence unfinished.

She stood up and walked over to the phone. Was it too risky to order food at a time like this?

Whoever was chasing them had their tentacles everywhere. Were they monitoring phone calls using voice recognition? Perhaps they had already worked out that she would return to her home town, the place where she felt most secure.

But she needed food and there was none in the house. She had to make the call.

She picked up the phone and dialled Dominos, being careful to give a false name. Mrs Pocahontas had a nice ring to it. It was a risk, but the chances they could monitor all calls were slim.

She climbed the stairs to the bathroom, throwing off her clothes and letting the hot, steamy water run down her body. The massage had been wonderful, feeling the strife and stress flow from her body beneath David's strong fingers. He was an attractive man. Shame she hadn't met him in a different time and place.

She shook her head. *Can't think like that, Jayne. Not now. Concentrate on work. Men can wait, the work can't.*

She finished drying herself and searched her sister-in-law's wardrobe, finding a vintage sweatshirt and a pair of jeans only an inch or so too big.

When she went downstairs, David was asleep in the chair, his mouth open to reveal those perfect American teeth. Were people like him born with them? The top of his shirt had fallen open to reveal the curve of his muscular chest. She spent a few moments looking at him. In sleep, there was a softness, a gentleness to his body which she liked. At any other time…

The doorbell rang and she stood still.

Who was it?

Had they already found her?

Or was it the pizza she had ordered?

Quietly, she crept to the window and checked through the curtain. A large man was standing at the door. She looked down towards the road. No delivery bike parked in the driveway.

The bell buzzed again. She ran to the back of the house. If they were going to come in, there was the weak point. Whilst the suspect is occupied at the front, enter through the rear.

She looked out of the window.

Nothing.

The bell buzzed again.

Gingerly, she walked to the front room. The man was still there.

Get a grip, Jayne. If it were their pursuers, she would be dead by now, surrounded by armed men gloating over her body.

She opened the front door a crack, peering out around the corner.

A fat, spotty young man was standing there holding two large boxes.

'Pizza,' he said brightly.

She opened the door fully, checking the road on either side of him. 'Where's your bike?'

'Down the road, just made a delivery at number twenty-three. Pizza's hot tonight.'

'I thought it was always hot?'

He laughed. 'I meant popular as in like a hot chick.'

What was going on today? Was there something in the water? A full moon?

Whatever.

She paid the testosterone-fuelled delivery boy in cash. Two minutes later she was sitting at the table, the proud possessor of two Margaritas with extra cheese. After hunting around the kitchen, she found a bottle of red left over from Paul's sister's wake.

A Chilean Merlot. She wouldn't be seen dead drinking this as a rule, but beggars couldn't be choosers. She poured herself a large glass and went back into the front room.

David was still asleep, mouth still open, snoring gently. She was tempted to wake him, but she decided not to.

For the first time in two days, she was alone and had time to think. She took a bite of pizza and realised how hungry she was. It was the first food she'd had since the muffin that morning. She sipped the wine, enjoying the wonderful warmth that even bad red wine gave to a tired body.

What was she going to do? It seemed Dan Jackson's grandfather was in the Hitler Youth. But how could that be, wasn't he English? Dan Jackson was sure. No accent. No foreign twang at all.

So who was he? Obviously not Thomas Jackson. He had died in 1922. The grandfather must have illegally acquired a new identity in order to enter the States. Was it because of the war? Did something happen during the war that meant he had to escape from England?

Perhaps they would find the answers when they visited the church tomorrow. After that, there was only one other line of enquiry open to them – to return to London and find the family of the doctor who had signed the health certificate. Why had he lied about Thomas Jackson?

The warmth, the wine and the food made Jayne feel extremely drowsy. Before she dropped off to sleep in the chair, a thought popped into her head.

What would happen if she couldn't find out who he was before Friday?

She was asleep before an answer came to her.

Chapter Forty-Three

'Have you heard anything from England?'

'Nothing so far.'

Catherine Jackson picked up a forkful of quinoa salad, and looked at it a moment before popping it into her mouth and chewing. Her husband was sitting opposite her with a glass of Cabernet in his hand.

'You should have heard something by now.'

He did a quick impression of Groucho Marx, complete with imaginary cigar. 'Listen, doll, no noos is good noos.'

Despite herself she laughed and then continued. 'We're just a couple of days away from the biggest meeting of our lives and you're making jokes.'

His hand reached out to hers but she pulled it back before he could touch it.

'Listen, Catherine, if we get the ok on Friday, I'll run. But if we don't, then there's still the business, there's still the kids and there's still us...'

'You don't get it, do you? For the first time, we have a chance to make a real change in this country. A change my father worked for his whole life. And you don't care...'

The hand reached out again. This time, she didn't pull back. 'I do care, honey. More than you could ever know. I was raised to believe in the American Way. But it's been destroyed by a vast army of bureaucrats, politicians, and bloodsuckers who think the world owes them a living. We are going to change this country. Make a brave new America, a rugged country where people look to themselves, not to the government, to solve their problems. A return to the principles of the founding fathers. That's my dream.'

She looked him in the eyes. 'That's *our* dream. It's what we've worked for all our lives. If we don't seize the chance now, it might never come again.'

'We just need to wait. We can't lose patience and go running round like a bunch of headless chickens or the Marx Brothers in *Duck Soup*.' He did another impression of Groucho Marx. 'Remember, you're fighting for this woman's honour, which is probably more than she ever did.'

She laughed and then looked down to play with her food.

He stopped being Groucho for a second. 'I'll call them tomorrow morning and find out what's going on.'

'Find out what the woman, whatever her name is...'

'Jayne Sinclair.'

'That's it. Find out what she's been up to and what she's discovered so far.'

'She may have discovered nothing.'

'If she hasn't, that's great. And find out where she is. You're paying for this, you should be kept up-to-date.'

'I'll ask tomorrow. Now, have you finished with the salad?'

She pushed the bowl away from her. 'Yes, I've had enough of dieting. Such a bore.'

'Excellent, because there's some Rum and Raisin Haagen-Dazs in the fridge and a chocolate brownie calling your name.' He cupped his hand over his ear. 'Can you hear it? Catherine, Catherine...'

She turned her head to listen better. 'You're right. I can hear it screaming, "Make it two brownies and more Rum and Raisin ice cream." We can watch Hannity on Fox News while we eat.'

He saluted her. 'Orders received and understood, ma'am.'

'Thank you, Mr President.'

Chapter Forty-Four

Wednesday, April 19, 2017
Buxton, near Manchester

The men hurried into the reception area of the Buxton Nursing Home. There were two of them, both burly and well-muscled, with short, buzz-cut hair.

They showed their Metropolitan Police identity cards to the receptionist.

The taller of the two was obviously the leader. 'We'd like to speak with a Robert Cartwright.'

The receptionist glanced through the glass safety door separating the lobby from the residents' area. 'I can't see him at the moment. He's probably with Vera. What is it about?'

'I'm afraid the matter is confidential. We can only tell him.'

A stern-looking woman wearing a dark blue uniform appeared from an office behind the reception desk. 'How can I help you?' she said in a strong Glaswegian accent.

'These policemen are from London, Matron. They want to speak to Robert,' the receptionist explained.

'What does this concern?'

'As I explained to your receptionist, I am not at liberty to say. It is police business.'

The Matron folded her arms across her chest. 'And I am not at liberty to allow you to disturb the people in my care, unless I know why they are being interrogated.'

The tall policeman sighed. 'We are not here to arrest anybody. We just want to chat to Mr Cartwright.'

'And I will tell you again: these are fragile people, many of them suffering from dementia or premature senility. Robert has early-stages Alzheimer's. I do not want him disturbed in any way.'

The tall one began speaking again before he was pushed aside by the shorter colleague. 'Mrs…?'

'Miss Colquhoun. Matron.'

He leant forward and lowered his voice. The Matron found herself leaning towards him too. 'Miss Colquhoun, it's rather a delicate matter. His daughter, Jayne Sinclair, has been badly injured in a car crash. We are here to take Mr Cartwright to see her.'

'Why didn't you say earlier, man? All this silly hush-hush secrecy.' She turned to the receptionist. 'Go and find Robert. He will be out in the garden doing the crossword with Vera. Ask Jenny to pack an overnight case. I presume he will be in London for more than one evening?'

The short policeman nodded.

'Well, hurry along there, woman, we haven't got all day.'

The receptionist jumped up and pushed open the safety door.

'You can use my office to tell him. It'll be quieter there.'

She showed them into a room off the reception area. A plastic aspidistra sat in the corner, placed between two Swedish chairs and a Formica coffee table. 'Please sit down. Robert will be along shortly.'

In less than a minute, an aged man appeared at the doorway accompanied by a slightly younger and well-coiffured woman.

'What's wrong? What's happened to Jayne?'

'Sit down, Robert. These two policemen are here to help you.' The Matron pulled out a chair for him and gently pressed on his shoulders, forcing him to sit.

'What's happened? Ellen said she'd had an accident.'

Vera placed her hand on his shoulder and squeezed.

The shorter policeman dropped his voice a register. 'I'm sorry to have to tell you, Mr Cartwright, that your daughter, Jayne, has been in a car accident in London. She's undergone surgery and is in a stable condition in hospital. We have been sent to Buxton to take you to see her in London.'

Robert's face went bright red. 'Is she hurt? Is she okay?'

'All we know is she sustained head injuries, but is now in a stable condition.'

Robert tried to get up. 'I must go to her, Vera. She can't be alone now.'

The Matron held his arm. 'Calm yourself, Robert. Jenny is packing an overnight bag for you. You can leave when it's ready.'

'Can Vera come too? I don't know if I could manage on my own.'

'I'm afraid there's only room in the car for one person, Mr Cartwright.'

Vera took his hand. 'You'll be okay, love. You have to go and see Jayne.'

Robert suddenly looked confused. 'What about the wedding? What about us?'

'Don't you worry, dear. We can get married later. The most important thing now is for you to go and look after Jayne.'

Jenny appeared at the doorway, carrying a coat and a small blue bag.

'You're right, lass.' Robert stood up and a new strength seemed to suffuse his body. 'Let's go now. Can't waste any more time.'

The two policemen stood with him. 'The car's outside. We'll make a start.'

'Which hospital is Jayne in?' the Matron asked.

The smaller policeman looked confused for a moment before the tall one answered. 'Royal Holloway on the Edgware Road. We'd better hurry, Mr Cartwright, if we are to get there this evening.'

Robert kissed Vera on the cheek. 'I'll call you when I get to London, lass, let you know how Jayne is.'

'Take care, Robert.'

The tall policeman picked up the overnight bag, whilst the other took Robert's arm to hurry him out of the nursing home.

Vera ran to the door as Robert was being helped into the back of the Mercedes. 'Look after yourself, love,' she shouted.

But the car was already moving down the drive. In the rear, Robert stared ahead, his face and jaw as rigid as Derbyshire stone.

Chapter Forty-Five

Jayne and David knocked on the door of the vicarage.

They had spent the night sleeping in their chairs even though more comfortable beds were waiting upstairs. Jayne had found some clean clothes for David in a cupboard. Not the most modern designs, though – a beige jumper and a pair of trousers with flared bottoms, paired with a blue jacket with the largest lapels she had ever seen this side of the circus.

For herself she found a black jacket to go over the sweatshirt. At least she was warm now and the clothes were fresh.

Later, they might take a chance and buy some new clothes from Debenhams or Selfridges. One of the larger department stores where they could blend in with the crowd.

She knocked on the door again. Within seconds, it was answered by a wrinkled woman wearing a brown apron. 'Father Jeremy is expecting you.'

They were shown into a large, untidy room with an immense oak table at the centre. On the wall, yellowing photographs of bald-headed priests stared back at them, the names written beneath the pictures in a flowing copperplate script.

There were no comfortable chairs, just twelve wooden school seats arrayed around the table.

Jayne sat down in one of them while David wandered around looking at the photographs. He stopped beneath a particularly imposing image of a priest with bushy eyebrows and a fierce, determined stare. 'This is the priest who signed the certificate of character.'

'He was one of our lot. Fascinating man, if a tiny bit eccentric.' The elderly priest had come in silently and now stood before the open door. He was a small man with two white tufts of cotton-wool hair lying like powdered snow over his ears. He was dressed in a long black cassock with dark grey socks and black plastic sandals.

He glided over the floor and sat opposite Jayne, adjusting his position on the hard seat until he found a spot that was vaguely comfortable.

'You said on the telephone you wanted to talk to me. How can I help you?' The voice was a rich Irish burr.

'Thank you for seeing us at such short notice, Father.'

'I'm glad to see my parishioners. It's a small parish, quiet, don't you know. But I haven't seen either of you at Mass recently.'

David moved round the table and sat close to Jayne.

'That's because we're not parishioners, I'm afraid.'

'Oh, well, it's not surprising. Not many people are any more. Sure, there's churches closing all over the place and others being turned into luxury apartments. I mean, who would want to live in a church? Cold, draughty places at the best of times.'

'Actually, Father, we came to see you about that priest.' David pointed to the photograph on the wall.

'Father O'Mahoney? And what would you be wanting with him? The man's been dead for fifty years or more.'

'Do you know anything about him?' Jayne asked.

'Ah, well, quite a lot. He was a bit of a character, you see. And people remember characters. It's the rest of us they forget.'

216

The door crashed open and a woman stood behind a trolley laden with cups, a teapot, a sugar bowl and milk jug.

'You're going to have to learn to open the door a wee bit more quietly, Mrs Hobart.'

'I don't know my own strength sometimes, Father. It must be all the spinach I'm after eating.'

The priest turned back to Jayne and David as Mrs Hobart bustled in. 'I took the trouble of ordering some tea, I hope you'll join me.'

'That would be lovely. Milk, no sugar,' said Jayne.

'No milk, no sugar for me, Father,' added David.

'Have you no Hob Nobs, Mrs Hobart?'

'You finished the packet last night, Father. All of them, gone. I thought a mouse had got them when I came down this morning.'

'No, it was me, right enough. A mouse with a dog collar. I do like a Hob Nob.'

As the tea was being served, Jayne and David stayed silent, waiting for Mrs Hobart to leave. Father Jeremy stared into the depths of his brown tea as if waiting to discover something buried in it.

It was Jayne who restarted the conversation. 'As we were saying, Father, we've come to see you regarding Father O'Mahoney.'

The priest's eyes drifted up and to the right as if he were remembering a time long forgotten. A small smile crossed the thin lips. 'And before I tell you about him, do you mind telling me what is your interest in a priest who has already gone to his maker?'

Jayne looked at David before answering. 'I'm a genealogist investigating a man who went to America in 1946. A Thomas Jackson...'

'I thought I heard an American accent from your man here. Is he your relative?'

David smiled. 'Not really, I'm acting for his grandson.'

217

'We get a lot of people in here wanting to look at the parish registers even though we're not a particularly ancient church. People these days seem to spend an awful long time searching for answers in the past.' He stopped for a moment, pausing to sip his tea, then talking as if to himself, without looking at them. 'I suppose it's a reaction to this modern world of ours. Looking for something to hold on to when everything else seems so fragile and temporary.'

'I think it's more, Father. It's a desire to discover one's own place in the world. A result of all that has gone before. Family has become less important in the last fifty years, but family history has become more important. It's not a coincidence.'

'I'm sure it's not.' The priest took another sip of his tea.

'Anyway,' interrupted David, 'what about Father O'Mahoney?'

Again the smile appeared on the priest's face. 'Ah, Americans, such an impatient race, forever running around trying to change the world and solve its problems.'

'It's what we do, Father.'

'I wonder, wouldn't it be better if you stopped for a while, smelt the flowers, saw the presence of God everywhere, in everything? Wouldn't that be a better thing to do?'

'I'm sure it would' – Jayne leant forward – 'but you were telling us about Father O'Mahoney.'

'I was, wasn't I? I didn't know him, of course, all before my time, but the character of the man shines through in his writings and his sermons. And then, of course, he was detained by the British for two years.'

'Detained?' asked Jayne.

'On the Isle of Man. You don't know?'

Jayne and David shook their heads.

'Well, let me tell you about him.' The priest sat forward. 'But I'll first pour myself a drop more tea. The old throat gets dry with the talking these days. You should see me after Mass on a Sunday.' He poured the thick brown tea into his cup, adding three sugars from the bowl. 'Now, where was I? Father O'Mahoney, that was it. Well, you see, you have to understand the atmosphere of the time to understand him. He was an arch conservative, even by the standards of a church in Ireland, which was not known for its liberalism. In those days, if you were clever and poor, there was only one option available to you. The Church. He went to Maynooth, as we all did, and there fell under the influence of a Canon Simpson. Now, the Canon was famous for being to the right of Genghis Khan: Women are child bearers. The rich shall inherit the earth. Sex outside of marriage was a sin. Sex inside of marriage was a duty. Priests were to be obeyed in all ways. The Church was to be dominant in all phases of Irish life... I could go on, but I can see I'm boring you.'

'No, you're not, it's fascinating.'

'Mrs Sinclair, you were brought up a Catholic?'

'I was, Father.'

'I can see it in you. The natural obedience never vanishes. What was it the Jesuits said? "Give me a boy till he's seven and I'll give you the man." I always thought it was more like "...and I'll give you a Catholic for life". Shocking hypocrites anyway, those Jesuits.'

'You were telling us about Father O'Mahoney,' Jayne reminded him.

'I was, wasn't I? Anyway, the respectable Father ended up joining the Blue Shirts.'

'Blue Shirts?'

'The Irish version of Mussolini's Blackshirts and Hitler's thugs. Much more Irish, though. They prayed before they kicked people's teeth in. Anyway, when De Valera dealt with the Blue Shirts in 1934, Father O'Mahoney had to get out of Dodge fast, as I believe they say in your neck of the woods, Mr Mercer.'

David smiled.

'He was sent to this parish,' he looked upwards and spread his arms wide, 'to St Columba's. The church has an awful habit of moving its problem priests around, as we all know. Here, I'm afraid his conservatism developed into something more devout. He fell in love with the teachings of Hitler and Mussolini, while the events in Spain only encouraged him in his beliefs.'

'He became a fascist.'

'A card-carrying member of the British Union of Fascists.'

'How does a priest reconcile those beliefs with the idea of charity and forgiveness?' asked Jayne, a frown creasing her forehead.

'They can't, of course. But Father O'Mahoney did... somehow. He was deeply involved in Mosley's crew here in Manchester. So deeply involved that, like many others, he was interned on the Isle of Man in 1940.'

'What's that?' asked David.

Jayne explained. 'When war began, the BUF were seen as potential threats as supporters of Hitler. Many of the supporters were detained in internment camps on the Isle of Man. With true British irony, they were placed next to another camp full of German Jews who had managed to escape from Hitler.'

The men both stared at Jayne.

'A client's Jewish father ended up there. I found the details of his imprisonment for him.'

'You are correct, Mrs Sinclair. He was finally released and came back here in 1942, staying on as parish priest until his activities finally caused the Church to bundle him into a job where he didn't have contact with people. He became an archivist in the diocese, I believe, until he died in 1968.'

'Do you think he carried on his activities after the war?'

'As a fascist?'

Jayne nodded.

'I've read some of his writings from the period. His views didn't change. In many ways, they became more extreme, talking about the failure of the Germans to achieve the final solution.'

'Which was?'

'The slaughter of the Jews, Mrs Sinclair. For him, they were the murderers of Christ. He thought the Germans hadn't gone far enough to punish them for their sins.'

Chapter Forty-Six

28 October, 1942
Near Krakow, Poland

Thomas let the yellow ribbon slip through his fingers and fall to the wooden floor. He ran his hands through his greasy hair. They stank of cordite and were pitted with flecks of black gunpowder.

He was tired, so tired.

Around him, the rest of his unit were sprawled out on the floor of the village hall. Not so many as when they had started out at the height of summer. Some had been injured in the attacks, others had cried off sick, too tired or too confused to continue. The rest had stuck at the job.

They had been joined in the work by groups of Poles and Ukrainians who did most of the killing now, his unit just providing a guard for them. But today, the Poles had been sent elsewhere so his men had to do the work.

They were in a small village, miles off the beaten path, which his unit had just liberated from its inhabitants. Their bodies lay sprawled outside on a concrete path.

Not many this time, just sixteen. Anyone who could run had already fled into the forest before they arrived. Only the sick, old or infirm remained. They had shot them anyway.

He took another swig of brackish water from his canteen. Within seconds he was thirsty again. It was a thirst that couldn't be satiated.

He picked up the yellow ribbon. Despite the numbers of people he had shot in the last months – he had lost count at two hundred – this girl had stayed in his mind.

He didn't regret killing her, it was what he was ordered to do. It was just that there were so many of them. How could he and the few men in his unit keep on killing?

Two men had already refused orders from Leutnant Gerber this morning. They were sick of the death and the futility of it all. Was there no end to it?

He remembered how he had felt when he passed out on parade as a Schutze: Pride. Heroism. Honour. Unity.

He was going to help save the nation from the horror of subjugation by a foreign culture. He was going to protect the Fatherland from all those who would destroy it. He was going to be a hero of National Socialism.

And look at him now.

A wreck of a man.

He often thought of his mother and sister living in Manchester. Had they survived the bombing? In the *Völkischer Beobachter* he had read that Manchester had been obliterated by the devastation inflicted by the Luftwaffe during Christmas 1940, but he was sure that wasn't true. Cities survived. People survived.

He pushed the yellow ribbon back into the top pocket of his jacket. The badge given to him by Baldur von Schirach was still there after all these years.

All these years? It sounded like it was such a long time ago. But it was less than four years. An age and half a life away.

Leutnant Gerber stood in front of him, blocking the light from the window. 'Unterscharführer, get your men ready. We move to the next village immediately.'

Wearily, he rose to his feet, pulled down his uniform and set his cap on his head. He checked the safety catch on his pistol and slipped it into its oiled holster.

The men were sprawled around the room in groups of two or three, not speaking, just lying on the wooden floor.

'You heard the officer, time to get going. On your feet.'

Time to kill.

Chapter Forty-Seven

Wednesday, April 19, 2017
Ardwick Green, Manchester

'What was all that about, Jayne?'

They were standing outside the vicarage. The meeting hadn't lasted much longer. Mrs Hobart had come and reminded Father Jeremy he was due to do his rounds at the hospital at 12.30.

The priest had said something strange as they parted. 'You mustn't judge us, Mrs Sinclair. We priests are as normal and fallible as other men.'

'I don't judge you, Father. I'll leave that to God.'

'It's wonderful to see you still believe in God. Me, I'm not so sure myself.'

And then he was gone, out of the door as silently as he had arrived.

Mrs Hobart had shown them out. 'You mustn't mind the Father, he's a decent soul. Does far too much thinking, if you ask me. Thinking is bad for you, my old mum used to say. And she was right.'

Now they stood on the street. Jayne's mind was racing. What should they do next? The answer was obvious to her.

Then David repeated his question. 'What was all that about?'

'It seems our Father O'Mahoney was one of the leading lights in the British Union of Fascists. They were run by a man called Sir Oswald Mosley and, in the 1930s, they tried to bring Fascism to Britain. Didn't have much success, though. I don't think they managed to even get one MP elected.'

'First, Dan Jackson's grandfather is dressed as a member of the Hitler Youth although he's not a German. And now we find out the priest who signed

225

his character reference was a leading member of the British Union of Fascists. Was he involved with them? And how deeply?'

'We don't know, David, but we have to find out.'

'How?'

'You're not going to like this, but we have only one lead left. The doctor in London.'

'But he must be dead by now, it's over seventy years ago.'

'I checked with Yellow Pages this morning. There's a person with the same surname still practising medicine at the same address. I think it must be a relative.'

David ran his hand through his hair. 'But London, it means...'

'Going back to the area where we were attacked. I know it's worrying, but it's the only thing we can do. There are no more roads left open to us.' She paused for a moment before saying, 'You don't have to come...'

'No,' he said quickly. 'I want to. I can't let you face those thugs alone. When do we leave?'

'Soon, I've booked us on the train out of Manchester Piccadilly tomorrow at one p.m.'

'But it means we'll spend another night here. We're losing time, Jayne.'

'Can't be helped. Here is safe, plus we need some new clothes, unless you want to remain looking like a refugee from the 1970s.'

He pulled his flares out to cover his shoes. 'I feel like a sailor from some ghost ship.'

'And I need to go to Boots. Time to be a brunette for a change. Anything to confuse our watchers.' She pointed to a CCTV camera covering the road junction in front of them.

Instinctively, David ducked down.

'Too late. If they'd seen us, we'd already be hearing the sirens by now. But let's keep moving. A moving target is always more difficult to spot.'

'One more thing. How could you be so certain I would come with you?'

'I wasn't. But I knew we had to go.'

Chapter Forty-Eight

Wednesday, April 19, 2017
M6 Motorway, southbound to London

It was as they passed Birmingham on the M6 that Robert realised something was wrong. The tall one was driving. He hadn't said a word since they had left the residential home in Buxton. The shorter one was sitting by his side on the rear seat, looking constantly at his mobile phone.

Robert had tried to talk with them, to find out more about Jayne's condition and the accident, but he had received blunt replies.

'How did the accident happen?'

'We don't know,' said the shorter policeman beside him.

Silence.

'How badly injured is she? You can tell me now.'

'We don't know, mate.'

'But she is injured, right?'

'Head injuries was what we were told. That's all we know.'

'But she's going to be alright, isn't she?'

Finally, the shorter one looked up from his phone. 'Listen, mate. We were simply told your daughter was in an accident. Our job is to take you to London, that's all we know.'

'Right, sorry. I know you're just doing your job, but I'm worried about my daughter. She means more than life itself, does Jayne.'

Silence. The shorter one didn't even look up from his phone this time.

Robert decided to keep his mouth shut. Perhaps this was the way London coppers operated. He remembered Jayne's colleagues on the force. They wouldn't have been like this. And Jayne would have known what to do too.

The silence continued as the car rolled on down the M6. Robert looked out of the window. The English countryside flashed by, interrupted by blue motorway signs and the occasional advertising hoarding.

Robert looked back inside the car. The shorter one was still staring at his phone. Every five minutes or so, it beeped and the man pressed a key. In front of him, the tall policeman's head stared straight ahead, concentrating on the road as he sped in the outside lane. The car's engine was smooth and silent; Robert could only admire the quality of the engineering and the comfort of the interior leather seats.

He tried once again to make conversation. 'Fancy car this, for the police. In Jayne's day, they had nothing like this. The closest they ever got was a Vauxhall Vectra.'

'It's a hire car.' The tall man in the front spoke for the first time.

'A hire car? Must cost a pretty penny, to drive all the way up to Buxton and back down again, just for me.'

'It's what we were told to do, mate.'

'Told to do? I thought it would have been easier to call me, or get the local coppers to arrange everything.'

'That's not what happened.' The tall one's answer was surly and abrupt.

A frown appeared between Robert's eyes. 'Which station did you say you were from, anyway?'

'We didn't, mate,' the short one answered.

This was getting too much. 'Well, which station is it?'

'Listen, mate, if we told you, you wouldn't know, so what's the point?'

The car began to slow down as they travelled through the wasteland of brick and concrete and steel otherwise known as the City of Birmingham. The dark, forbidding, man-made towers stretched out as far as the eye could see on either side of the motorway.

Robert thought these were the rudest coppers he had ever met. He'd have to complain about them to their superior officer when they arrived in London. They shouldn't treat people like this, especially not those whose daughter was lying in hospital.

He'd had enough from these two. 'What did you say your names were?'

'We didn't,' the tall one said.

So bloody rude. 'I want to see your badges now. I've never been so badly treated in all my life. I've known coppers ever since Jayne worked in the force and I can tell you that you shower of shit are the rudest, most inconsiderate people. You should be ashamed to be police.'

Robert's face became redder as the anger took hold and his body shook. How dare they treat him like this?

'I think it's time, mate,' said the driver.

'What? What did you say?' Robert shouted at him.

He didn't see the short one sitting beside him pull out a small hypodermic from his pocket, unsheathe the needle and plunge it into the wrinkled skin below his ear.

Robert's hand immediately came up to protect his face from another blow that he felt sure was coming. 'What? What's going…?'

But the neurotoxin was already beginning to take effect. His tongue felt swollen and woolly in his mouth. His head seemed to wobble on the end of his neck and there was a strange ringing in his ears.

His body felt like it wasn't part of him at all, but some separate entity he had never met before.

And then the world went black.

'We should have done it earlier,' the tall driver said, 'I can't stand it when they get all chatty.'

'Yeah,' was the only answer from the short man in the back.

Chapter Forty-Nine

March 14, 1943
Krakow, Poland

The evacuation of the ghetto had started yester-day, and for the last 24 hours his men had not slept.

The orders from Untersturmführer Goth were simple. All those who could walk or work were to be gathered in Zgody Square for transportation to Plaszów Camp. The rest were to be eliminated.

His squad had marched across the stone bridge over the Vistula at noon, through the wall with its arched supports and into Podgórze, the district of the ghetto.

The Trawniki men, mainly Ukrainians from Galicia and its surrounding regions, had been at work since the morning.

Bundles of clothes lay discarded in the streets, like flotsam washed upon a concrete shore. Tell-tale plumes of black smoke betrayed the route of the Ukrainians through the area.

A line of ragged and starved men lined up, wait-ing for the truck to take them to the camp. A few carried their possessions, one even holding a large double bass, without its case, to his chest, defying anybody to take it off him.

But most stared into the air, looking through and past the soldiers as if not acknowledging their pres-ence or even their existence.

Their task was to sweep through the streets after the Trawnikis, picking up or executing the stragglers.

It was his decision on which were to live and which were to die. That day, most were to die. It was easier than marching them back under guard to Zgody Square. His men preferred it, and he didn't care. At least a bullet to the back of the head was a quick death.

Their progress through the ghetto had been slow at first. He had taken pictures of some of the scenes he had witnessed using the camera Ilse had given him.

He often thought about her. One day he would go back to Baden Baden to see her again. The baby would be one year old by now. Was it a girl or a boy?

She had sent him letters, which followed him to Poland months later. In them, she chatted about her life working in a factory making uniforms, but she never mentioned the child. Instead, she was worried that food was becoming harder to find and rationing was stricter but she was sure the Führer would lead them to victory in the end.

He stumbled over a body lying in the street. A young woman, no more than twenty, with wavy blonde hair. She didn't look Jewish at all. She was wearing nothing but a torn off-white slip and one stocking on her left foot. Thomas couldn't see her face. The Trawnikis had smashed it in with one of the pick-axe handles they carried.

He stepped over her and carried on walking down the street. He was hungry; soon it would be time to stop and eat.

One of his men suddenly raised his arm. Instantly, Thomas and the rest of the squad dropped down on their haunches, checking the towering tenements on either side of the street.

He waited for the bomb to be thrown or the machine gun to open fire, but nothing came. He could hear the raucous sounds of shouting and laughter up ahead.

He stood up and walked to the Schutze who was on point at the front of the column.

'Why did you stop?'

'The sounds, sir. I thought it might have been the resistance.'

'They are not going to be laughing and shouting, are they?'

The man looked down at his dusty boots.

The shouting stopped for a second. A long scream pierced the air, changing pitch. It came from the back.

'We should check it out.'

He signalled to the other men to stay where they were and entered a door on the right with the Schutze.

The place stank of piss and people. Clothes, buckets, paper, books and what remained of a piano were strewn in a pile at the foot of the stairs.

Up above, the shouts became louder and more raucous. Thomas stepped over the rubbish and mounted the stairs. The tenement was six stories tall. It was not until he reached the top that he found the source of the noise.

A group of six Trawnikis, with pistols drawn, had herded twenty women and children into a single room. There were no men.

One of the Trawnikis was manhandling a woman to an open window. As soon as he saw Thomas, he stopped what he was doing, letting the woman drop to the floor where she crawled back to the safety of the others.

A howl of despair came from the group. All began talking, shouting and crying at once. One woman, older than the rest, inched forward and touched Thomas's arm.

'We have done nothing wrong. It's all a mistake.' She spoke perfect German. 'Please understand. We want to work, we have done nothing wrong.'

The Trawniki took off his hat.

'What's going on here?' asked Thomas.

The Trawniki – a Ukrainian, of course – tried to explain using faltering German. 'We found new way.'

'A new way?'

'New way of killing Jews.'

One of his men joined him and they mimed grabbing an arm and a leg, rocking the invisible body between them and throwing it through the open window.

Thomas pointed at the children cowering behind the skirts of their mothers. 'And them?'

The Trawniki shrugged his shoulders. 'One day they will be big Jews.'

The woman touched his arm again, kneeling down in front of him. 'Please, we have done nothing wrong, done nothing wrong.'

A young girl wearing a bright red coat ran out from the group and down the stairs, the sound of her shoes receding the further down she went.

Thomas was so tired.

He looked at the woman still repeating her words over and over again. Slowly, he lifted his gaze to the Trawniki, standing in front of the open window, cap in his hand, a gap-toothed smile creasing his face.

Then he turned to go.

The squeals and shouts and moans of the women and children followed him down the stairs, punctuated by the deeper grunts of the Trawnikis.

As he reached the bottom of the stairs and came out into the street, another piercing scream came from the top floor. This time it was followed by a soft thud in the courtyard at the back of the building.

He assembled his men and they continued their trawl for male stragglers.

He found the red coat later than evening. The young girl's body was wearing it.

235

Chapter Fifty

April 17, 1943
Near Krakow, Poland

One moment Thomas was on his feet, ordering a Schutze to monitor the left flank, and the next he was lying on the ground staring up at white clouds scudding across the blue Polish sky.

The attack had come out of nowhere. The pop of a mortar from far in the distance and then an explosion on his right, fragments of shell whistling past his face.

A sharp pain in his shoulder and then nothing.

He woke up to watch the clouds. For a long time, he wondered why they were moving so quickly across the sky. Then he realised they were moving extremely slowly. Just that each time he closed his eyes, another five minutes passed before he opened them again.

A Schutze blocked out the light. 'A medic is coming, Unterscharführer.'

'What happened?'

'Partisans. All dead now. Leutnant Gerber too.'

Nobody would miss him, least of all Thomas.

He touched his right temple. A wet, sticky liquid covered his hair, soaking his ear. He brought his wet hand up in front of his eyes. His fingers were red with blood.

His blood.

He didn't want to die here. Not alone, not out here in a country he hated. *Help me*, he screamed at the Schutze, but no sound came from his lips.

His body started to tremble, a cold shiver starting in his legs and rippling up his body into his mouth. His heart was beating faster.

He felt the blood trickle from his temple over his ear.

His blood.

His teeth started to chatter. *Stop it. Make them stop. Where was the medic?*

As if hearing his call, a man leant over him, cutting away the left sleeve of his uniform.

What are you doing? My head, it's my head. Say something to me. Tell me what's going on?

I don't want to die here.

Not here.

He felt a sharp pain in his shoulder as the medic's fingers probed the wound.

It's my head, you fool, can't you see the blood?

Finally, the medic spoke to him. 'The shrapnel seems to have gone through the shoulder, exiting the other side.'

But what about my head?

'And don't worry about your head. It's just a superficial wound. You will have a scar, but nothing more.'

He felt something sharp dig into his left arm.

'I'm giving you something for the…'

He didn't hear the rest of the sentence.

Chapter Fifty-One

On the way back to Paul's sister's house, they stopped off to buy some new clothes and pick up an untraceable pre-paid mobile.

Whilst David was taking a shower, Jayne took the opportunity to call her father. It had been so long since they had talked and she had to make sure he was okay.

No answer.

She tried again.

Still no answer.

Strange. Her father always answered his phone, keeping it hung in a bag around his neck so he would never forget where it was.

She checked she was calling the correct number.

It was right. She rang again.

Still no answer.

The next time, she rang Vera's phone. It was answered in two rings. 'Robert, Robert, is that you?' Her voice was excited, breathless.

'Vera, it's me, Jayne.'

'Are you okay, Jayne?'

'I'm fine.'

'Which hospital are you in?'

Hospital? What was Vera on about? 'I don't understand.'

'We were told you'd had an accident, a car accident. You were in hospital. But we rang the Royal Holloway and you weren't there. Robert has gone to see you.'

'Hold on, say that again. Dad's gone where?'

'To meet you. Two policemen came for him. But we checked the hospital and you weren't there.' A note of suspicion entered Vera's voice. 'Where is Robert? Have you seen him yet?'

A shiver of fear ran down Jayne's back. They had taken her father. Why?

Vera's voice interrupted her thoughts. 'Jayne? Jayne, have you seen Robert? He is okay, isn't he?'

'Dad's fine, Vera.' She hoped her future step-mother would forgive this white lie, but Vera was too far away to offer any help. It was all up to Jayne now.

'Why doesn't he answer his phone? Can you put him on?'

'You know what he's like. Dropped it, didn't he?'

'Well, put him on then, I'd like to speak to him.'

'He's in the bathroom now. I'll get him to call you tomorrow.'

'He does spend a long time in there. As long as he's okay. He is okay, isn't he, Jayne?'

Jayne crossed her fingers, hoping Vera wouldn't spot the lie. 'He's fine.'

'And you're fine?'

'I'm good.'

'Then why did those policemen say you had been in a car crash?'

Lies, they always catch up with you. It was the same in police interviews. Catch the suspect in a lie, and invariably they start to make mistakes, compounding one lie with another until their statement made no sense. 'It was all a mistake.'

'They seemed very sure...'

'I have to go now, Vera. See you soon. We'll be back tomorrow. Bye.'

She switched off the phone, hoping Vera wouldn't call back.

What was she going to do now? They had her dad, the one man she cared more about than anybody else in the world.

Had they killed him already?

No, there would be no point. He was a bargaining chip against her. These people weren't thugs, they acted for a reason. But what the hell did they want?

She started pacing up and down the small living room, the anger building inside her. How dare they? Her father was off-limits. He had never done anything to hurt anybody.

Jayne punched the wall in frustration. What the hell was she going to do?

For the first time in a long time, she felt lost.

And then the mobile phone buzzed.

Chapter Fifty-Two

Wednesday, April 19, 2017
Somewhere beneath the streets of London

Ostransky looked at the screen of the old man's phone. He felt sure the number being displayed belonged to the genealogist. Her father only had sixteen contacts on his phone and this wasn't one of them. She was probably using a pre-paid SIM card.

Time to flush her out.

He typed:

Mrs Sinclair, we have your father

and pressed send.

The answer came back almost immediately.

Who are you? What do you want?

Before he could reply, another message appeared.

If you harm him in any way, I will kill you. Understand?

Incomprehension followed by anger, the classic response. Acquiescence would come soon, it only had to be encouraged.

He typed in:

We have no intention of harming him as long as you do as you are told.

Once again he pressed send and waited.

The answer took a little longer this time.

What do you want me to do?

Good. She understood her position exactly. He typed:

Discover all you can about Dan Jackson's family and make your report on Friday. After you do, your father will be released…unharmed.

The threat was there, out in the open.
The answer came back.

I don't understand, you want me to make my report?

He decided to keep the pressure on.

That is correct. Report all your findings on Friday. Failing to research or not making a report will lead to the termination of your father.

Ostransky congratulated himself on his stroke of genius. She would now understand and she would have no choice but to obey.

A pity none of them would leave the meeting on Friday alive. He quite liked the old man and had a sneaking admiration for Mrs Sinclair. But alas, in this mission, only the fittest would survive.

The phone buzzed with a two word message:

I understand.

Ostransky smiled. For the first time in a few days he felt no need to scratch the patch of eczema between his fingers.

Chapter Fifty-Three

Wednesday, April 19, 2017
Heaton Moor, Manchester

'What's wrong?'

Jayne looked up to see David framed in the doorway, his hair still wet from the shower. For the first time in a long while she felt alone and tired and full of fear.

'My father, they've taken him…'

David rushed across the living room and sat down beside her. 'I'm sorry, I don't understand.'

'They've kidnapped him. Threatening to kill him.' Jayne held up the phone with its messages.

David took it from her and read them quickly. He put his arm round her shoulders and pulled her closer to him. She could feel his hand stroking the back of her head.

'What are we going to do?' she asked.

He pulled her tighter to him. 'There's only one thing to do. We must go to London, continue the investigation, find out the truth.'

She pulled away from him. 'But that puts you in danger too. These men, they've threatened to kill my father. But you're not involved, you shouldn't risk your own life.'

He held her shoulders. 'Jayne, we're in this together. I'm coming to London with you, whatever happens.'

She nodded.

David read through the messages one more time. 'There's something I don't understand, though. Why do they want us to continue the research? Surely, they've been trying to stop us for the last three days? For God's sake, they shot Jack.'

'I don't understand either. But it's very clear. Continue the research and make the report on Friday.'

'No indication who sent this text?'

Jayne shook her head. 'It's from my dad's mobile, though. Whoever has that also has my father.'

David stared at the phone for a long time, then he made a decision. 'I'll book tickets on the first train to London tomorrow. The sooner we get started, the better. I'll also ring Dr Conway and arrange to meet her just as soon as we can.'

'What do you want me to do?'

'Nothing at the moment, let me handle it. The best thing you can do is find out more about Thomas Jackson. We know so little at the moment.'

'And if we can't find anything?'

'That's what we say in our report.'

'It's not enough, they will kill my father.'

'That's why you need to concentrate, Jayne. Use all your skills to find out the truth.'

Jayne nodded. In a softer voice she asked, 'After we have reported our findings to Dan Jackson, will they still release my father?'

David thought for a long time. 'I don't know, Jayne, I really don't know.'

For the first time since the death of Dave Gilmour, Jayne felt weak, vulnerable and uncertain. It was not a feeling she enjoyed at all.

Chapter Fifty-Four

July 12, 1943
Berlin, Germany

'You can stand easy, Unterscharführer.'

Thomas Green put his hands behind his back and relaxed his stance.

'You may as well sit down while you're here. You'll find us more informal than you are used to in your regiment.'

Thomas found a hard-backed chair positioned against a wall and brought it forward to Dr Hesse's desk. After being discharged from the hospital, and having two weeks' rest in the Schwarzwald, he had been ordered to attend this man's office on Von Der Heydt Strasse at 9.30 precisely.

'I see you have noticed my title. An honorary one, I'm afraid. I'm not a medical doctor. How are your wounds?'

'The shoulder still gives me pain, but the head has healed well.' He pulled his blond hair aside to let Dr Hesse see the scar.

'Excellent. A little wound for the nation. Something you should be proud of.' The doctor glanced at the folder on his desk. 'Unterscharführer Green, you are English, are you not?'

'I'm *Volksdeutsche*, Herr Doctor.'

The fat, balding man behind the desk waved his tiny hands. 'Yes, yes, I'm sure you are – but born in England, yes?'

'In a small village called Manchester.'

The doctor looked surprised. 'Village? I thought Manchester was a large city.' And then it dawned on him. 'Ah, this is English humour, yes? See, you are

English.' He laughed and his shoulders shook in unison.

'What can I do for you, Herr Doctor?'

'To business, you English say, don't you? So, let's get down to it. The Führer has made a decision based on my advice. We are going to create a British Free Corps from the POWs currently in camps in Germany.'

'A British Free Corps?'

'Part of the Waffen SS, which will be recruited to fight for Germany in the struggle against international Bolshevism.'

'Like the Norwegians, Dutch, Belgians and French in the Waffen SS now?'

'Exactly.'

Thomas sucked in his breath through his teeth. 'I don't think it will work.'

'Why? 50,000 Dutch have joined, along with 40,000 Belgians, 20,000 French and even 6,000 Norwegians.'

'But the British are different.'

'Do they not fear the Bolsheviks and the Jews?'

'Of course, but—'

'But the Führer has decided the British must play their part in the fight against communism. We have already started to look for former members of the BUF and dissidents in the ranks of the POWs. Some of them have been sent to a camp at Genshagen to soften them up a little with a more relaxed regime before we ask them to join.'

'What has all this to do with me?'

'We want you to write some pamphlets stating why you joined the Waffen SS. These will be distributed in POW camps. In addition, you will be stationed in Genshagen, helping to persuade men to join the British Free Corps.'

'I won't have to rejoin my unit?'

'Not unless you want to.' Doctor Hesse paused for a moment. 'I believe they are being sent to Russia next week.'

'All you want me to do is write some pamphlets…'

'And help to persuade the POWs to join the Corps. The Führer has decreed that when enough men have enlisted, a separate unit of the Waffen SS will be formed for the British in the Westland Division. So, we have a deal, yes?'

The man finally stood up with his hand out. Thomas took it and the man sat down again.

He adjusted his spectacles, pushing them back on to the bridge of his nose, and opened a ledger in front of him. 'You will begin your work now, Unterscharführer.'

'But my kit—'

'Has already been delivered to Genshagen.'

Chapter Fifty-Five

September 12, 1943
Genshagen, Germany

'Hello, I'm here tonight to talk to you about the British Free Corps.'

There was a groan from the men assembled in front of him.

'It's supposed to be a bloody film, not a bleedin' lecture,' one of them shouted in a Cockney voice.

'It is, but before we start I'd like to say a few words.'

Thomas had become slightly better at public speaking but it still didn't come easily to him. The words seemed to fall out of his mouth rather than trip off his tongue. He tried to remember the eloquence and gestures of the BUF speakers he had seen before the war. The repeated phrases, the pumping fist, the emotional call to action – but they all felt so unnatural to him.

The camp at Genshagen, south-west of Berlin, had formerly been a holiday resort catering for the workers and families of the state railway. Dr Hesse had commandeered it and, with a few minor alterations, it had become Special Detachment 517, reserved as a holiday resort for deserving British soldiers who had spent the longest time incarcerated. A place where these POWs could enjoy greater freedom and better food, away from the boredom, overcrowding and bleakness of the Stalags. At least, that's what they were told. In truth, the camp served as a recruitment station for the British Free Corps. While ordinary POWs had the chance to relax, prisoners with fascist views could be cajoled, intimidated or bribed into joining the new force. Unfortunately, not many had succumbed to the temptation.

He waved the leaflet he had written with McArdle's help and began reading from it.

'We of the British Free Corps are fighting for you! We are fighting with the best of Europe's youth to preserve European civilisation against the menace of Jewish communism.'

'Boring!' a voice shouted from the audience.

Thomas carried on anyway. 'Make no mistake about it, Europe includes England.'

'No it doesn't,' the same voice shouted again. The audience laughed.

Thomas ploughed on. 'Should Soviet Russia ever overcome Germany and the European countries fighting with her, nothing on earth could save the continent from Communism.'

'Germany saves... but Dixie Dean scores on the rebound.' The same voice again. Thomas was trying to work out where it was coming from when the camp commandant, Sonderführer Oskar Lange, entered the hall and strolled down to the front row.

Thomas finished reading the pamphlet, ending with a call for them to join the British Free Corps.

There was silence from the men. Eventually, a few began to clap, led by Courlander, Cooper, Brown and Maton, Britten and Chapple. All ex-BUF men who had already committed to joining the new unit. The other two hundred or so POWs were not so eager.

'Can the bloody film start now?'

'About bleedin' time too.'

The Sonderführer turned back and stared at the audience. The men who had been shouting immediately went quiet.

Just as the lights dimmed, the drone of aircraft engines was heard overhead and the air-raid sirens screamed the need to find shelter immediately.

The men began to run out to the hastily dug shelters.

'I was lookin' forward to Mae West tonight.'

'In your dreams, mate.'

'You should've sent a note to Churchill; don't bomb Berlin tonight, Mae West is comin' up to see us.'

Thomas and the men who had already signed up to the British Free Corps trooped out with them.

For the first time, he wasn't so certain about this war. Where was the Luftwaffe? If the British could bomb Berlin so easily, what else could they do? Invade Europe?

Whatever happened, he would survive. He always survived.

Chapter Fifty-Six

April 20, 1944
Hildesheim, near Hanover, Germany

'All present and correct, sir.' Thomas saluted his commanding officer, Hauptsturmführer Hans Roepke.

'I'll inspect the parade now, Oberscharführer.'

Thomas saluted back as smartly as he could. He had been teaching the other men to do it for the last two weeks. Some had got it straight away, others had been less willing to make the effort.

'I feel like a fuckin' puppet.' This had come from Freeman, one of the more senior men.

'It's easy. Heels come together, the arm shoots straight out at a forty-five-degree angle, palm down, chest out, back straight, head tilted slightly upwards.'

'It's not British,' said Bennett in his Birmingham whine. 'I thought we were supposed to be in the British Free Corps, not the German Army.'

'We are a separate unit attached to the Waffen SS,' explained Thomas. 'Like the French or the Dutch or the Swedes.'

'What about the Turnips?' joked Leister.

Thomas had ignored him. He had been promoted to Oberscharführer, the equivalent of a Staff Sergeant – he didn't have to deal with this crap.

'And where's the rest?'

'The rest of what?'

'The rest of the unit,' said Bennett. 'I was told at Stalag 1Va there were going to be thousands of Brits joining to fight the Russians.' He'd looked down the line of men assembled on the parade ground. 'There's only twenty-seven of us. Where's the rest?'

'They are being recruited.'

'And what about officers? I thought we were supposed to have British officers.'

'They are being trained separately,' Thomas had lied.

'So when are we going to see them?' asked Bennett.

Thomas strode towards him, confident he could take the stupid bastard if it came to a fight. 'Enough questions, you're members of the British Free Corps now.'

'It don't look like it...' Bennett had said, again looking up and down the line.

Most of the men had been dressed in the ill-fitting field-grey uniforms of the SS, but none of them, other than Thomas, had any unit insignia or patches. Some, like Bennett, wore no uniform at all, having recently arrived and preferring clothes constructed out of cast-off material by one of the POW camp tailors.

'For once, that's a great point. Tomorrow is the twentieth of April, the Führer's birthday. Today, we will be issuing the uniforms for the first company of the British Free Corps. March this way.'

Thomas had goose-stepped across the parade ground, the others ambling after him in a peculiarly British fashion.

In the store, Britten, the man assigned to be the tailor, had been waiting. In his hands he held a black lozenge-shaped patch for the right collar, showing three lions *passant gardant*, similar to those seen on the Royal Standard.

For the left sleeve, he had a Union Jack patch shaped like a shield, as well as a thin black armband to be worn above the left cuff, with the words 'British Free Corps' in English embroidered in a flowing Gothic script.

'Right then, give your uniforms to Britten, who will sew the badges on for you tonight, ready for the parade on the Führer's birthday tomorrow.'

Tomorrow had now arrived. Thomas had assembled the men on the parade ground, adjusted their uniforms so they looked vaguely martial, and ordered them to stand at ease until he returned.

Hauptsturmführer Roepke walked up and down the short line, adjusting a cap here or a collar there, before standing in front of the men with Thomas at his side.

'I have waited for this day for too long.' He spoke English with a slight Scots twang, having spent two years living in Glasgow. 'It fills my heart with gladness to see such a fine body of fighting men – English fighting men – standing before me. We have one mission, soldiers: to take the fight to the Bolsheviks, eliminating the evil of communism from the earth. From today, the British Free Corps will join the Waffen SS to achieve that mission. The training will be long, it will be hard, but we will achieve our goal. Britain and Germany fighting as one against the common enemy.'

Bennett put his hand up.

Hauptsturmführer Roepke's eyebrows raised almost to the peak of his cap at the interruption on parade.

'I just wanted to ask. We won't have to fight the British Army, will we? I mean, my brother's in the army and I wouldn't like to fight him.'

'Let me make it clear. The British Free Corps will only ever be used on the Eastern Front, never against the British Army. When Britain sees sense, as I'm sure she eventually will, the country will join us and together we will smash the communist hordes once and for all.'

He smashed his leather-clad fist into the palm of his hand. The slap echoed around the parade ground.

As if embarrassed by his vehemence, the words that followed were softly spoken, almost whispered. 'Carry on, Oberscharführer.'

With a quick salute, he marched straight back to his office.

Thomas stepped forward. 'We're going to spend the rest of today learning German drills.'

There was an audible groan from the men in front of him.

Thomas carried on anyway, showing them exactly the same manoeuvres he had been taught at Lichtefelde.

The day did not go well.

Chapter Fifty-Seven

Wednesday, April 19, 2017
Manhattan, New York

'Did you talk to the genealogist woman?' his wife called from her dressing room.

They were getting ready to go to a fundraising dinner for the homeless of New York. Dan Jackson always found it strange that people would raise money for the homeless by eating the best food the world had to offer, drinking expensive wines rather than Thunderbird, and wearing enough jewellery and furs to keep an army of homeless people fed and sheltered for tens of years.

But his wife had said it was important for his standing in the town to attend these sorts of events. He would even have to bid later for some atrocious piece of 'art', which would go into a store room as far away as possible from himself.

'Sorry, dear, what was that?'

She appeared at the door, dressed in a long Gucci gown of glistening emerald green constructed from a fabric that clung to her body, accentuating and flowing round her curves.

'You look stunning.'

'Thank you. I asked if you had spoken to the genealogist woman.'

She vanished back into her dressing room again.

'Not yet. I rang the number she gave me. No answer.'

Catherine reappeared at the door, holding two pieces of jewellery that sparkled in the light. 'Did you call David Mercer? He's with her, isn't he?'

She held up two drop earrings to her ear lobes. 'The diamonds or the citrine?'

'You know if I had my way, neither. We would do exactly as Hitler did in 1933; round up the beggars and the homeless, take them off the streets and into protective custody in internment camps. They would soon get the message.'

She placed a finger across his lips. 'Save your ideas for the campaign, dear. When you are President, you can do what you want to implement them.' A small smile crossed her lips, 'The wonderful thing is, anything and everything can be justified as a campaign promise.'

She checked herself in the mirror. 'The citrine, I think.' She vanished again, talking from inside the dressing room. 'I've told you so many times, dear, you're going to have to attend far more of these dinners once you decide to run. It's not the money raised, it's the presence. To be seen with people who matter, people who support you.'

She reappeared once again at the door. 'How do I look?'

He walked over and held her by the waist. 'As perfectly delicious as ever.'

He bent down to kiss her, but she ducked her head out of the way, wagging her finger in his face. 'You're not spoiling the make-up I've spent hours putting on.'

He helped her with her coat.

'You need to follow up with her.'

'Who?'

'The genealogist woman.'

'Mrs Sinclair?'

'The meeting to decide your candidacy is two days away. You know we need the financial and political support of the Bilderberg men. Without it, we have no chance. They are bound to ask about your background. That bloody woman needs to have cleared you by then.'

'And what if she hasn't found anything?'

'Perfect. With nothing to find, they will approve you and we can go ahead. Once you have their backing, nothing can get in your way.'

She reached up to him on tiptoes and kissed him lightly on the lips without smudging her carefully applied gloss. 'I'm sleeping with the next President of the United States. You don't know how excited it makes me feel.'

He reached for her to pull her closer.

She looked at the time. 'We're late. Has the car come round?'

He smiled. 'Of course.'

The press were waiting for them when they came out of the lobby of their townhouse.

'Are you standing for President, Mr Jackson?'

'Is your candidacy going to be announced next week?'

'Is it true you're going to be running as an independent?'

He held his hands up and the reporters stopped shouting. 'I can't say anything at the moment, fellas, but off the record, I strongly believe it's time for a new era in American politics – a new deal, if you like. And if I say anything more, my wife will kill me. Thank you for your time, fellas.'

He helped his wife into the car and followed her in.

The reporters clustered around the door, shouting further questions as the car drove away.

'A new deal. Is that a yes on the candidacy?'

'You're not going to be a Democrat?'

'Have you spoken to President Trump?'

'When are you going to announce, Mr Jackson?'

The shouts gradually faded as the car accelerated away from the kerb.

Inside, Catherine leant in to Dan Jackson.

'Perfectly done, dear. Enough of a tease to get the slimy members of the press excited without giving to much away. Now, we just have to find out what that genealogy woman is up to.'

Chapter Fifty-Eight

June 13, 1944
Hildesheim, Germany

They had gathered around the radio to listen to the evening broadcast from Berlin. Thomas didn't know why most of them came that evening to the canteen. Usually, they were in Hildesheim town seeing their girlfriends or doing what they did best – drinking until they couldn't stand up.

But this evening was different. Most of them were here and, even stranger, most of them were sober.

They were all wearing their SS uniforms, which had been issued on the Führer's birthday, proudly proclaiming they were members of the British Free Corps.

It was McArdle who switched on the set. The rumours had been floating around the camp for a few days, no doubt fuelled by gossip enjoyed in those intimate times after sex and before they had to be back in camp for lights out.

The music was one of those annoying Bavarian folk tunes, played by an accordionist with a perpetually inane grin and a fat tuba player wearing lederhosen that were too short and too tight. Luckily for Thomas and the rest of the British Free Corps, the oompah band was just finishing.

A new piece of music began – Wagner, he thought, heralding the beginning of the news.

'Can you translate, Tom? Your German is best,' shouted McArdle in his Scouse accent. An annoying prick, McArdle wavered between unyielding support for National Socialism and unstinting praise of Winston Churchill.

The female newsreader's voice came through loud and clear. Her voice sounded like a dog with a sore throat and together with a staccato script, she managed to do a passable impression of a female Führer.

Thomas listened carefully. 'She's announcing that tank production has exceeded estimates for the month of May. She is congratulating the workers at the Mittelfeld Werke in Kassel for beating their production quota by 137 per cent.'

Courlander walked in. 'What's going on? Why is everyone—?'

He was silenced by a loud shush from Maton and a waved instruction to sit down.

Thomas listened but he had missed the beginning of the sentence. 'She's talking about the Eastern Front. More army successes against the Russians on the Belorussian Front. Apparently, the Romanians have been fighting like their heroic ancestors on the Iasi Chisinau Front.'

'Nothing about the invasion?' This was from Berry, the youngest of the group, who was captured when he was fourteen on board a cargo ship in the Mediterranean.

Again, a loud shush from Maton, followed by a kick to Berry's shin.

'She's talking about an attack on the British now. The Panzers are throwing them back into the sea at a place called Villers-Bocage.'

'Where the fuck is that?'

'Shhhhhhhh…'

'It's in Normandy. She's just said Normandy.'

The group around the radio went silent. McArdle was playing with the Union Jack badge on his sleeve. Maton was puffing on his pipe, staring out of the window. Only Berry looked excited.

'But Normandy is in France. Went there once, to St Malo. Lovely place, I liked Normandy.'

Maton took his pipe out of his mouth. 'Shut the fuck up, Berry.'

Thomas had been listening carefully to the female announcer. 'She's saying there are other attacks going on at Carentan and Saint-Aubin-sur-Mer, but she's not saying which side is attacking.'

The female announcer's voice was becoming even more strident.

'She's promising that the forces of the Wehrmacht, the Kriegsmarine and the Luftwaffe are united in their goal of pushing the enemy back into the sea from where they came. She's quoting the Führer now. "Those who want to live, let them fight, and those who do not want to fight in this world of eternal struggle do not deserve to live".'

'Jesus H. Christ,' said Maton. 'He don't take no prisoners, do he?'

The radio played the same martial music before a male announcer began to recite the programme for the evening. It consisted of Wagner and more Wagner.

'We're fecked,' announced McArdle in his Scouse accent.

Of course, Berry misunderstood. 'Is it going to be another Dunkirk, with tiny boats sailing out to pick up the Tommies as they wade out from the shore?'

'No, you stupid wee tosser. We're fecked. Us.'

'Why? I don't understand.'

'Because it's the invasion of Europe. It means Britain and America have been able to land an army on the Mainland.' Courlander spoke quietly.

'But the Wehrmacht will throw them off, won't they? Like 1940?'

Thomas nodded his head at Maton and they both walked casually to the door, leaving the rest still arguing around the radio.

Outside the canteen, the air was still and heavy, like the time immediately before a heavy rainstorm. Off to the left an eagle owl hooted after capturing some prey, before flying off to feed the poor mouse to its young.

Maton spoke first. 'What do you think, Tom?'

'I think I've been a bloody fool.'

They both walked down the neatly groomed path leading to the barracks. 'What do you mean?'

Thomas shook his head. 'I should've known it couldn't continue; too good to be true. It would all fall apart one day.'

'So the army won't throw them back?'

'Not a chance, Frank. It's been at least six days since they landed and with air superiority, the Allies will consolidate before advancing inland.'

'The army will fight though...'

'And they'll be slaughtered.'

'Won't the Allies realise Germany is on their side, that the real enemy is Russia?'

'I wouldn't count on it.'

Maton stopped. 'What are we going to do, Tom?'

Thomas shrugged his shoulders, the three lions and the SS symbol on his collar catching the light. 'We carry on, Frank, but we look after number one.' He jabbed himself in the chest.

'What's Roepke going to do?'

'He's a good German, he'll do as he's told. They all do as they're told.'

'I'm going on another recruiting trip around the POW camps. Waste of bloody time, if you ask me.'

'Do it and smile. Me, I'm going to make sure I get out of this alive.'

CHAPTER FIFTY-NINE

Thursday, April 20, 2017
Somewhere beneath the streets of London

He was rehearsing in his head what he would say in the meeting. How to break the news that he had kidnapped the old man and contacted Jayne Sinclair. To give this development the most positive spin. In his mind, it was the correct action to take to ensure the genealogist's compliance, but the Führer might take a different view.

The summons to the emergency meeting was not a good sign. Unless something else had occurred of which he was unaware. He doubted it, though – the most important programme now was the preparations for the meeting with the Bilderberg billionaires.

He picked up his green tea and sipped the warm liquid. It was more bitter than usual; perhaps the leaves had become tainted or his tastebuds were affected by stress.

Whatever. He would change the blend tomorrow.

He stood up from the workstation and pulled the key from around his neck.

Time to face them once again, he couldn't put it off any longer.

He took the elevator down to the lowest floor, opening the door to the room that didn't exist.

The logos on the televisions were already illuminated. Had they begun the meeting without him?

The Führer was seated at his desk. 'Come in, Ostransky, take your normal seat.'

Something was wrong. Every cell in his body was telling him to run, to get out of there. Instead he found himself obeying the voice and sitting down in the black leather chair.

'Ostransky, we have not been particularly pleased with your performance over the last few days. Your instructions were clear; monitor the genealogist's research and remove any documents that could be compromising for our candidate.'

'I can explain—'

A hand came up and he stopped speaking. 'No need. Personally, I would have given you another day, but Argentina has been checking with your team and apparently you have been lying to us.'

'There were no lies—'

Once again, the hand came up and he stopped speaking. 'It's too late, Ostransky. You have lost control of the operation as well as losing track of the genealogist. The kidnapping of the father was unnecessary, if you had been more efficient.' The Führer brushed a small piece of lint from his immaculately tailored jacket. 'I would like to thank you for your sterling service to the cause…'

As the Führer spoke, the door opened and Blake stood in the doorway, a key in his hand. What was he doing here? How did he get a key?

'However, we will no longer be requiring your services.'

Blake stepped into the light. Ostransky could see the livid scar running down the side of the man's face. Then his vision began to fade. Blake's scar doubled and tripled. He shook his head. The Führer was still speaking.

'Blake will be taking over from you as Director of Operations. Your employment has been terminated.'

One by one the screens began to darken and go black. Ostransky shook his head once more. His throat was tightening, the collar around his neck too tight. He tried to undo his shirt button but couldn't; his hands lay on his lap, unmoving.

He couldn't breathe.

A gob of liquid welled up in his mouth with a strong metallic taste.

Blood. His mouth was full of blood.

He felt himself falling forward.

He saw the tiled floor come up to meet his head and strike it.

He felt nothing.

Blake's black silhouette came between himself and the light. He wanted to see the light.

A disembodied voice. 'You are in charge now, Blake.'

'I won't let you down, Führer.'

A slight pause. 'I'm sure you will not.'

Ostransky's throat and chest tightened further. He could not breathe. There was no air in his lungs and the harder he tried to inhale, the less his body responded.

Why couldn't he breathe?

And then he remembered the bitter taste of the green tea.

It was to be the last memory Felix Ostransky enjoyed before he died.

Chapter Sixty

May 2, 1945
Near Schwerin, Germany

He would survive.

He had to survive.

He looked around the barracks for the last time. His SS papers were a smouldering heap of ash in the fireplace. His SS uniform, with its Oberscharführer badges, was hanging from the end of the bed. His boots that had marched up and down Poland and Germany were polished and stood proudly on the pillow.

He had managed to cobble together a British combat jacket and an American pair of trousers from one of the Germans. He was wearing them now as he prepared his escape.

Strange to be wearing the uniform of the Allies after so many years, but the only option for him was to blend in with the fleeing POWs and surrender to the oncoming Americans.

Only Maton, Bennett, a crazy Australian called Broughton, and Cooper were left of the initial group that had been formed.

After training the Free Corps in Hildesheim, Thomas had been transferred out of the unit to a police operation at a train station near Hamburg. Six months of checking passengers' identity cards and travel documents had been fine by him. At least he was out of harm's way.

The transfer had happened after a long and persistent whispering campaign against him by the other British members of the Free Corps. Some of them simply didn't like him. Others thought he was a traitor to the cause of National Socialism. Still others

266

thought they should be ordered around by a real British officer, not some jumped-up clerk from Manchester.

He didn't care.

The bastards were in the frontline now, not in some training camp outside Hanover.

See if they liked it.

None of them did, of course. As soon as he had been sent back to the unit, they were on his case asking him to talk to Steiner, the commanding officer of the Nordland SS troops. They wanted out of the frontline before any actual fighting took place against the Russians.

As one of them said to him, 'I didn't join the Free Corps to fight, just to get away from the Stalags. Fighting wasn't part of the deal I signed up to.'

Luckily for them, he wanted no part of any fighting either. So, with a bit of gentle persuasion of Steiner, and the realisation by the commanding officer that the British would be a liability rather than an asset during any battle, he and the few remaining members of the Free Corps were transferred to a transport unit in the rear.

It was this transfer that had made up his mind to escape.

Germany was dying.

Ferrying men and materials around had opened his eyes. Buildings were bombed out. Food was scarce. Women were selling themselves openly on the streets for a few cigarettes. People were committing suicide rather than surrender. Soldiers everywhere were throwing off their uniforms and blending into the local population, hiding in plain sight. Those who could fled westwards into the arms of the welcoming Americans and away from the embrace of the crazed Russians.

And nothing from Berlin or the Führer. What had happened to him? Was he dead or alive? Rumours abounded of him fleeing to the mountains of Bavaria or escaping on a plane to Japan.

The very fabric of the Fatherland had been destroyed. And Thomas had seen it all.

The only question that remained was how the hell was he going to get out of here before the Russians arrived?

It was Steiner who convinced him. An hour ago, the commanding officer ordered his men to flee to the West.

Thomas wasn't going to wait for a second chance. He'd selected a few trucks, filled them with what food was left, the members of the BFC who remained and a few German stragglers for protection.

After two days on the road, they formed a laager at a camp on the Criwitz-Schwerin road.

They had just settled down for the night when a military police patrol surrounded them.

'Where's your movement orders?'

'We don't have any,' Thomas answered.

'I'm British,' interrupted Maton.

'Shut the fuck up.'

A machine pistol was waved in his face. 'You have no papers, and this man says he's British. You will be shot.'

Thomas put his hands up. 'No, no, no… Take us to General Steiner's HQ. He'll vouch for us.'

'Why should we bother? Easier to shoot you.'

Thomas forced himself to think. Think like a German. 'I wouldn't do that, if I were you. We are the British Free Corps, created by the Führer himself. You would be committing a grave error if you killed us without checking first. You do have a family, don't you?'

He could see the indecision in the man's eyes.

'You have nothing to lose. If General Steiner doesn't protect us, you can shoot us then. If he does, well, you've just protected one of the Führer's favourite units.'

The machine pistol lowered slightly. 'You and one other will drive us to HQ. My men will stay here to guard the rest.'

Of course, Steiner wasn't at the HQ, but luckily another officer, Obersturmführer von Bulow, was able to issue the necessary documentation for the military police.

The right documents always work to placate any bureaucracy.

Now, he was back at the camp ready to leave. He could hear the American artillery in the distance. One of the German drivers had woken him to say the forward American units were just six kilometres away.

Time to go.

He took one last look at his uniform. The yellow ribbon from the young girl was still in the top pocket. He took it out and undid the clasp of the badge given to him so long ago by Baldur von Schirach.

He was tempted to put both of them in his pocket as keepsakes of his war, but he didn't.

He placed the ribbon on what was left of the smouldering documents. Almost immediately, it started to turn brown from the heat.

The image of the young girl, her hands grasping the skirts of her mother as she walked past him, flashed into his mind. His pistol to her head, the flash of flame, the hand and the ribbon, the dead fingers still holding on as he wrenched it from her grasp.

He snatched the thing from the flames before it was consumed by the fires of hell.

This one he would remember. Only this one.

He walked over to the open window and threw the badge as far as he could into the scrub of the surrounding forest.

At least a part of him would remain forever in Germany.

Chapter Sixty-One

Thursday, April 20, 2017
Hackney, London

The elderly woman was putting her key into the Yale lock when Jayne and David approached her.

'Excellent, you're on time. Come on in, hurry along. I only have a minute before the alarm goes off and the poor bloody police will come racing here, truncheons drawn. I do hate to disappoint them again.'

'Here' was a three-storey building on Mare Street with a large sign above the door declaring it was the Hackney Free Clinic. At one time, the building must have been the height of Victorian elegance but now it was run down and dilapidated, in an area that had seen better days. Much better days.

Dressed in their new clothes and with her hair now a warm brunette, they had travelled down from Manchester on the first train, arriving in London at 7.30 a.m.

On leaving the train they had buried themselves deep within the hordes of commuters hurrying to the city from their brick boxes in the suburbs.

Jayne had spent the night and the journey down worrying about her father. What had happened to him? Was he okay? Had they hurt him? Each time she thought of his predicament, she felt her jaw and fists clench. If he were injured in any way, she would track them down one by one.

But at least the journey had allowed her to recover her composure. She felt back in control now, slightly embarrassed at having revealed her weakness to David.

The elderly woman slammed the door shut and strode off to a box on the wall, inserting another key and turning it twice.

'There. It shouldn't go off now. Had to install this when the local junkies took a liking to the Diazepam and the Valium. It was costing me more to repair the windows than to buy the drugs. I would've given them out for nothing if they'd just asked me politely.'

She picked up the large leather briefcase at her feet and bustled into the surgery, taking off her coat as she did so. Jayne and David were left standing in the waiting room.

'Well, come on, I haven't got all day. The coughs, colds and other assorted viruses will start banging on the door at ten o'clock so we only have fifteen minutes. What was it you wanted to talk about? My father, wasn't it?'

Jayne moved into the surgery. The woman was now sitting at her desk, booting up her computer. She was grey-haired and tall, with green eyes and the bushiest eyebrows Jayne had ever seen on a woman. Her body was an amorphous mass, like a sack of potatoes hidden in a green sack. Beside the computer mouse, Jayne noticed a pack of opened Embassy cigarettes.

'Sit down, won't you? You're cluttering up the place.'

Jayne took a seat opposite her. She felt like one of the woman's patients, waiting to be examined. 'You are Mrs Conway?'

'Actually, it's Ms Conway, but I prefer to be called Dr Conway. I worked bloody hard for the degree and I give up the title with reluctance.'

'Sorry, Doctor Conway. We rang you yesterday...'

'You wanted to know about my father, why is that?'

'I'm a genealogist and I'm looking into the family history of a client.'

'And him?' She nodded at David.

'His name is David Mercer.'

'Tell him to sit down. I can't stand people wandering around my surgery.'

David looked for somewhere to sit, finally choosing an examining table covered in white tracing paper.

'So, you're a genealogist. I thought you said gynaecologist for a moment. No point in examining my father, he's been dead for thirty years. And he was most definitely male.'

Jayne took the health certificate of Daniel Jackson's grandfather and placed it in front of the doctor. She scanned it quickly with a professional eye.

'It's a health certificate.'

Jayne reached forward and pointed to a signature. 'Signed by your father in 1946.'

'So?'

'The person named on the certificate died in 1922. Your father couldn't have seen this man and couldn't have passed him as healthy.'

The older woman stared into mid-air, not blinking.

'I'm sorry, Doctor Conway, did you hear what I said?'

She continued to stare at the wall, answering in a monotone. 'I thought this would happen one day. My father created all this, you know.' She indicated the building and the surgery. 'I followed in his footsteps. He was an idealist – a dreamer, my father, not a man for the concrete or the pragmatic. When he graduated in the thirties, it was a time of mass poverty, starvation, extremes of wealth and deprivation. He thought he'd found the answers. He hadn't, though, and eventually he saw the mistakes he had made and opened this. His way of atoning, I suppose.'

Jayne glanced at David. 'I don't understand.'

The woman took a large breath. 'My father was a fascist, Mrs Sinclair. A card-carrying, Mosley-loving, Jew-hating fascist. Is that clear enough for you?'

Jayne could see the pain in the woman's eyes. 'I'm sorry to bring these memories up.'

'It's in the past. But it still reaches to us in the present. Why do you think I am still here?'

Jayne let the silence sit between them before saying, 'But he repented, your father, didn't he?'

'He did. This clinic was his atonement. He worked with immigrant communities until the day he died of a heart attack in 1982. He died here, in this room, still working, still writing.'

Jayne heard something in the woman's voice, a hint of something. 'Still writing?'

'My father kept diaries throughout his life. He wrote down what he did, what he thought and why he was doing it all.'

'Are there diaries for 1946?'

'There are diaries for every year of his life, from the time he went up to Oxford at the age of eighteen. Seven fat volumes full of his memories. And unlike most doctors, his writing was actually legible.'

'Could we see them, Doctor? They might be able to help us clear up the mystery of this man's identity.' Jayne pointed towards the health certificate lying between them.

The doctor paused, her hand reaching for the cigarettes and then stopping, as if she realised she couldn't smoke now. She glanced at the clock on the wall. It was approaching ten.

'Please, Doctor Conway, they may be able to help.'

The doctor nodded and stood up. 'They're in the store room. Follow me.'

She strode out of the surgery. Three patients were already waiting for her and the receptionist was carrying a stack of files. 'Won't be a minute. Put the files on my desk, Julia.'

She carried on down a corridor and up a flight of stairs at the end, Jayne and David trailing in her wake. From the bunch of keys in her pocket she selected one, and unlocked the door. Inside were metal shelves filled with boxes of tissues, plastic gloves, wooden spatulas, paper towels, adult diapers and freshly laundered white uniforms.

'You'll find them in the corner, I think. I need to work now. Let me know when you leave.'

She bustled past Jayne and David and hustled down the stairs.

Jayne switched on the light. A single bulb hung from a flex in the ceiling. They found the books stacked in the corner between some plastic gloves and a box of enemas. The doctor was correct: there were seven thick black volumes. Jayne opened the top one in the middle. David leant close to her, reading over her shoulder.

The ink was brown with age and the paper had yellowed slightly, but the writing was surprisingly fluent and easy to read. An old-fashioned hand with curls and curlicues for each of the letters. This was a plain volume with no printed dates on the cover. Instead, the doctor had written the date and the time he had written it above each entry.

Jayne had once kept a diary herself, until Dave Gilmour died, and then she couldn't bear to keep it any longer. Like all diarists, she had enjoyed experiencing everything she did three times; when it happened, when she wrote it down and when she read it later, reliving it all. But after his death, there was no point. Why relive bad times?

Looking at the thickness of the doctor's diaries, it was not a sentiment he supported.

She felt a nudge in her back. 'What does it say? Read it.'

Jayne looked at the entry and began reading.

'March thirteenth, 1933. Finally graduated and found a post already; in London at Barts starting in July. Gives me time to go to Germany to see the progress Herr Hitler has made since his appointment as Chancellor. Have booked passage already with Thomas Cook's, leave on Friday.'

Jayne turned the page.

'That date is too early, we don't have time to read every single entry,' said David impatiently.

Jayne picked up the second volume, opening it again at random. She began to read:

'October fourth, 1938. Jim McArdle came to me late this evening, blood pouring from his face. The Reds had attacked the meeting in Hackney as it was dispersing. They had come in force this time, after the debacle of their last attempt. McArdle wasn't ready for them and they gave him a beating. He will survive, no broken bones, but he's going to be sore for a few days. How many times have I told them to be prepared at all times? Why keep the baseball bats when they are not prepared to use them? We must make the Reds scared of us, so scared they will never attempt to attack.

'I have ordered a raid on the Sandys Row Synagogue. We must show the Reds we are not afraid, and there will always be reprisals if they dare to attack us. The police will stay out of it this time.

'Better news from Chamberlain. It looks like war between the Aryan races has been rightfully averted. Chamberlain has come back from Munich waving his piece of paper in the air with a peculiarly smug smile carved into his face. What an idiot the man is! Does he not realise that he cannot stop the expansion of the Aryan peoples across Europe? Herr Hitler will take back the Sudetenland, and Danzig, as they have recovered Austria. It's all in his great book, *Mein Kampf*. Can the idiots not read? I can't wait for the day when England wakes up and aligns with Germany to crush the red menace.'

Jayne finished reading and let out a long sigh. 'This man's a believer, isn't he?'

'What's in the next volume?'

Jayne placed the second volume down and picked up the next one on the shelf, again opening it at random.

She began reading:

'August twenty-second, 1940. War has started now,' she said over her shoulder to David.

'I do know my history, Jayne. We Americans do have a modicum of intelligence, you know.'

'Sorry.'

'Read it anyway.'

Jayne took a deep breath.

'August twenty-second, 1940. Well, I have escaped arrest under Article 18b, so it looks like I'm not going to be sent to the Isle of Man after all. The Special Branch and some strange man dressed in a chalk-striped suit and bowler hat visited me in the hospital. They took me into one of the side rooms and interrogated me for an hour. Apparently, the Deputy Assistant Commissioner has put in a good word for me. Great news, but I may have to be more circumspect in my politics. Can't risk imprisonment. But I will not give up my beliefs, whatever they say. Now, I wait for Herr Hitler to win and a treaty to be signed between the Aryan nations. It will happen. It must happen.'

'He's hoping that Britain would lose the war. Not a pleasant man,' David said.

Jayne flicked through the volume to the back. There were pages and pages of his writing, all in the same faded brown-tinged ink.

'The books seem to be in order, David. What was the date of the health certificate?'

'January third, 1946.'

Jayne picked up the fourth volume, blowing dust off the cover. She opened it to the first page. February 7, 1943. She flicked through the pages, checking the dates as she went along. March 12, 1944. September 4, 1944. May 7, 1945. December 12, 1945.

Now she slowed down, turning over the pages slowly until she came to the right date.

She began reading.

'The Nuremberg Trials have started. I've been following them daily through the news reports. The descriptions of atrocities committed in Hitler's and the other leaders' names are frightening. How could they have done such things? Did Herr Hitler know? The answer seems to be yes. How had such a perfect ideal of National Socialism been so perverted? Or was it always in there anyway? The hatred of Jews inbred through centuries of fear and misunderstanding. I've been working more in the East End recently. I can't believe how wrong I was in the past. They are people like any other. They bleed, they get sick, they give birth, they die, just like every other people in every other country down through the years.

'Johnnie Hawley came to see me today about rejoining the movement. I told him exactly how I felt. How it was perverted and cruel and barbarous. He threatened me as they always do. But he forgets, I once ran the thugs, I know what they can and can't do. Then he pleaded with me for one last favour. They needed health certificates for two men who fought in the British Free Corps, Robert Bennett and Thomas Green, and have given them new identities.

278

To get rid of him, I signed them. Anything to get out of their hands. I'm free now. Free to do what I want. It took me years to recognise it, wasted years. What was it Voltaire wrote? *"Il faut cultiver notre jardin."* That's what I'm going to do. Look after my garden, look after my people. Do what I should have done years ago. Cure people, not attempt to change them.'

Jayne finished speaking and checked the top of the page. 'The date is correct, so Jackson must be one of these two people.'

'But which one?'

Jayne closed the book. 'I think I know how to find out.'

Chapter Sixty-Two

Thursday, April 20, 2017
Hackney, London

'Come on, this way. It's not far.'

Jayne and David hurried down Mare Street, dodging between the shoppers looking for the local supermarkets or some Vietnamese Cha Gio. By the time they had finished reading through the diaries and taking notes, it was 11.30. They had then said goodbye to the doctor, who was already on her second pack of cigarettes.

'Where are we going?'

'The National Archives.'

Jayne picked up the pace, and David tried to match her, but his ankle still ached. As they came to an open area outside Hackney Town Hall and the Hackney Empire, he finally grabbed her arm. 'Hold on, why are we going there?'

Jayne checked her watch. 'Look, if there are any documents about POWs, that's where they will be.' She started to run but he grabbed her arm again.

'But you don't know, right? It could all be a wild-goose chase?'

'It could, but it's the only lead we have. If Thomas Green and Robert Bennett were interviewed by the police after the war, the documents will be in the National Archives.'

'And if they weren't?'

She shrugged her shoulders. 'We will have to think of something else. And then, of course, the documents may be there and not available.'

'Why not?'

'Official Secrets Act. Or people were mentioned who are still alive. Or even the document might prove embarrassing. Lots of reasons why stuff stays secret, most of them illogical.'

David looked up to find a CCTV camera mounted above the street, looking down on the busy traffic as it stopped and started on its way past the Hackney Empire. 'And what about *them*? I thought you said we had to stay off the streets.'

Jayne checked out the camera. 'What's the point of hiding any more? They have my father, they know I'm going to do exactly what they want. I have no choice any more. We have to report tomorrow afternoon. Before then, we have to explore every possibility, however remote. This is our last throw of the dice.'

'So we're going there on the off chance that the man we're looking for was interviewed at the end of the war, the document is available and the National Archives will let us look at it?'

'That's about it. Even worse, the National Archives is only open until five. It's going to take us over an hour to get there, at my guess, but it could be longer given the state of the rail system.' She checked her watch. 'So that means we have only a few hours to check the documents.'

'If they exist…'

'If they exist.'

'And if they are available…'

'If they're available.'

'What are we waiting for?'

They both rushed towards Hackney Central Station, David shuffling along, trying to put as little weight on his injured ankle as possible.

Chapter Sixty-Three

Thursday, April 20, 2017
National Archives, Kew, London

The overground train took them to Kew Gardens station and from there it was only a short walk to the National Archives, hurrying past the fountain to enter the main door. After passing through security, Jayne immediately began taking off her coat.

'What are you doing?'

'They won't let you in with any bags or coats. We have to leave them in the cloakroom. Did you bring a pencil?'

'No, just this.' David held up his Montblanc pen.

'Not allowed. Luckily, I bought a pack at the station, plus a notebook.'

She placed her coat into the locker and took out a clear folder. 'Give me the pen and I'll put it in here.'

David handed over his Montblanc. 'Where to now?'

She pointed to a row of computer terminals with a big 'Start Here' sign hanging above them. 'Let's check if the documents exist before we waste any more time.'

She sat down behind one of the terminals and typed 'British Free Corps' into the Discovery section of the catalogue.

77 hits.

'Damn, I was hoping there wouldn't be so many. What are the two names we're looking for?'

'Thomas Green and Robert Bennett.'

She added the first name to the search and had six hits. 'There it is. There's a security service file on him. She wrote down the number: KV 2/257. She added the second name and found another security service file: KV 2/264.

'The documents exist?' David asked.

She nodded. 'One of these two men is Daniel Jackson's grandfather. But which one?'

'We can get to see the files today?'

'I'm just ordering them.' She brought up another form and reserved a seat in the Document Room. Then she entered the document numbers from her notepad. A timer showed the documents would be available in twenty minutes.

'We're done, but you'll need a reader's ticket first.'

'Huh?'

'You can't enter the document room without one. You remembered to bring your passport and driving licence?'

David nodded. 'English bureaucracy beats anywhere else I've ever been to.'

Jayne brought up the correct page on the terminal. 'We need to register online first.'

'It's getting worse. You have to register online here and then go and pick up a ticket? Why can't you simply fill in a form and hand it over?'

'I don't know and I don't care. You're wasting time, David. Or would you prefer I checked the documents alone?'

'No, I get it. Let's just do it.'

After registering, they collected David's reader's card and went up to the second floor to find the document room.

Jayne sat down at Desk 3a and was joined by David. She stared at a row of lockers in the far wall.

'What are we waiting for?'

She checked her watch. 'Two more minutes.'

'And then?'

'And then I get up, walk over to the locker and we find out who Daniel Jackson's grandfather was… I hope.'

'You hope? I thought you said this had to be him?'

'It all depends if the doctor's diary was accurate. What if he wrote or spelt the name incorrectly? What if he didn't write the truth in his diaries? In research, David, it's never over until there is a proven, documented link.'

'And what would that "proven" link be?'

'Something that would tell us exactly who he was and why he went to America.'

'A smoking gun?'

'An unfortunate phrase, but correct.' She checked her watch again. 'Time's up.'

She strode over to the locker. Inside was a large brown box file and a smaller folder. She carried both back to their desk.

'Let's start with the box.'

Cautiously, she lifted the cover and saw a photograph of a man wearing Nazi uniform, chatting with two other soldiers.

'It's him. It's Thomas Jackson.'

A loud shush came from the man on the next table.

David lowered his voice. 'It *is* him.'

'All we can say is it looks like him.' Jayne turned the photograph over. Beneath it was a typed document: 27 pages of tightly packed sentences all held together by a slightly rusting paperclip. At the top, the first line read:

Statement of Thomas Stefan Green:-

Each paragraph was then numbered.

1. I have been cautioned that I am not obliged to say anything, but anything I do say may be given in evidence.

2. I was born...

Chapter Sixty-Four

May 23, 1945
British Military Prison, Brussels, Belgium

'Good to see you, Green. Stand easy.'

Captain Michael Hand pulled his notes from his briefcase and sat down at the table. He placed his cigarettes and lighter next to the ashtray.

'Do sit down, man. We've a lot of questions to go through today and I'm going to have a crick in my neck if I have to look up at you for the next two hours.'

'You heard the hofficer, sit.' The redcap sergeant tapped the back of the chair with his cane.

'Thank you, sir,' said the prisoner, taking his seat.

Captain Hand lit a cigarette and opened his notes.

'Your name is Thomas Stefan Green, is that correct?'

'Answer the hofficer.'

'There's no need to pass on my questions, Sergeant Ramsden. I'm sure the man has a pair of ears.'

'Yes, sir.'

'Well, are you or are you not Thomas Green?'

The eyes of the prisoner darted left and right.

'It's an easy question, man.'

'I am, sir. Thomas Green.'

'Finally, we have an answer. Let's be quicker in the future, Green, otherwise I will be here until hell freezes over.'

'Yes, sir.'

Captain Hand turned a page in his notes, umming and aahing as he did. 'Now, when you were found by our American cousins you claimed that you were a POW, is that correct?'

'Yes, sir.'

'A POW who just happened to be a secret agent working for a man called General Fortune.'

'That's correct, sir.'

'A secret agent who just happened to know the whereabouts of Obergruppenführer Steiner's HQ and the whereabouts of some of Himmler's staff.'

'I was just trying to help, sir. Capture the enemy and all that.'

Captain Hand lit one of his cigarettes, blowing smoke up into the light above their heads where it hung around the bare bulb like a cloud of gas. 'The problem is, I work for the First GHQ Liaison Regiment. We're rather wittily called the 'Phantom' Regiment because we haven't a ghost of a clue what's happening.' He smiled at his own joke.

Thomas just stared at the notes on the table in front of him. He didn't smile.

'My problem, and yours, is that we've been aware of your activities for a long time, Green. Shall I give you the list? Member of the Hitler Youth, private in the Leibstandarte Adolf Hitler, sergeant in the Waffen SS, posted to Poland, injured while on duty, seconded to the British Free Corps... Shall I go on? We even have transcripts of your talks in the POW camps. You will have to improve your speaking style in the future. You can't bore people into becoming fascists.'

Thomas's hand shook. 'I think you are mistaken, sir.'

'I think not. You are Thomas Stefan Green of Ardwick, Manchester?'

Thomas's head went down. He nodded.

'Your sister sends her love. I'm afraid your mother died last year.' Captain Hand stubbed out the cigarette in the ashtray. 'Now, what I need from you, Green, is a complete written confession of everything that happened to you since your arrival in Germany in 1938.'

He shoved the notepad and a pen across the table.

Thomas stared at it, not moving.

Captain Hand lit another cigarette. 'You either write the confession, telling us exactly what you did and when you did it, or else…'

'Will it help me, sir?'

Captain Hand blew a stream of smoke towards Thomas. 'It can't hinder your case. If you were to tell us exactly who all the members of the British Free Corps were, and their roles in the organisation, I'm sure that would help you. Show that you want to make a clean break with the past and all that.'

Thomas picked up the pen. 'Just one thing, sir. When I was in Poland, all I ever did was guard the offices and barracks. I was never on active duty.'

Captain Hand pointed to the pad. 'Write it down.'

'And I was forced to join the British Free Corps because I was English. You can ask the others. I was sent away to be a policeman because I worked to ensure the BFC was a failure.'

'Write down who the others were. Tell us all you can remember of them.'

Thomas picked up the fountain pen.

'Before you start, can you number each new paragraph? It makes my secretary's life so much easier when she comes to type it.'

Chapter Sixty-Five

Thursday, April 20, 2017
National Archives, Kew, London

They both finished reading Thomas Green's witness statement.

'Jesus, he was a traitor, fighting for the Germans. He admits it here.'

A loud 'hush' came from the nearby table, where a senior professor was bent over a decaying parchment, reading the writing with the aid of a large loupe.

David held up his hands in apology. 'He was a member of the Waffen SS, for God's sake,' he whispered.

'But we can't prove it.'

David prodded the papers. 'It's here in black and white.'

'No, it isn't. We have a picture that looks like Thomas Jackson. We don't have solid proof linking the two men.'

'And the doctor's diary?'

'Again, not solid proof. Just a supposition. Two men were named, remember?'

David's voice became louder. 'Oh, come on, Jayne.'

There was another loud 'shush' from their neighbour, followed by a long stare through the loupe. The professor's eye appeared three times larger than it should have been.

'Let's carry on. There are still some more papers here.'

She turned over another paper in the box. It was a yellowed form handed out to POWs in Germany.

Fellow Countrymen,

We of the British Free Corps are fighting for YOU!
We are fighting with the best of Europe's youth to preserve our European civilisation and our common cultural heritage from the menace of Jewish communism!

Jayne skipped through the rest of the pamphlet. 'It's pretty savage stuff. They were quite mad, all of them.'

David remained silent. He handed her the next sheet of paper. It was a movement order for Thomas Green to be flown to London and be imprisoned at Wandsworth Jail on the 20th October, 1945.

'At least we know he's back in London now,' said David.

Jayne picked up the following two sheets, which were tied together. They were headed 'Metropolitan Police' and beneath were a few stamps and the words 'Special Branch'.

2nd November 1945

With reference to M.I.5 letter X/2103/F 3 a, regarding Green.

The subject of the enquiry has been identified as Thomas Stefan Green, born at Ardwick Green, Manchester on September 27, 1919. His parents were Arthur Green, a British subject born in Hereford on 23 March 1881, and Greta Annemarie Green, nee Schnaubl, born in Stuttgart, Germany on 7 September, 1886. The mother became a British subject upon her marriage in 1918. The couple separated shortly after Green's

birth. There is a sister, Trudi Elizabeth Green, now Mrs Trudi Esterhazy, born on 13 July 1926. This sister has a different father than the subject. Father unknown.

'It's him, it's definitely him!' David shouted.

The professor looked up from his parchment. 'I will not tell you again, young man, to be silent. This is a reading room, not a football match.'

Another loud 'shush' came from a table across the room. The attendant looked up from his computer.

The professor whispered in a loud voice, 'Be quiet, or I will report you.'

David held his hands up and mouthed, 'Sorry'

Jayne carried on reading the note from Special Branch.

Thomas Green was educated at Holy Cross School, Ardwick Green. Whilst there, he was an altar boy at St Columba's Church, Ardwick Green. He left school in February 1936 and commenced employment as a clerk in the accounts department of Messrs Hawley and Sons, Ardwick Green, Manchester, until he left in May 1938. Enquiries show that before leaving his employment, Green obtained British passport number 220115, ostensibly to 'visit relatives', and it appears he went directly to Germany.

During the time he was at the company, Green does not appear to have come under notice in any way, but it is said he spoke German quite well. Further discreet inquiries reveal that he was a vain young man, taking part openly in political activities with the British Union of Fascists. My informant tells me he was strongly pro-German and very proud of his German family

connection. Following this lead, it was discovered he was charged with affray after the Cable Street riots of 1936, but was found not guilty after no evidence was presented.

I have not identified any of his contacts at this time because it was said he was very much a loner. He had a girlfriend, a Miss Turner, but she refuses to talk about him as she never heard anything from him when he went to Germany. She married in 1940 but is now widowed, having lost her husband at El Alamein.

His description when last seen in Manchester was: tall, 6 feet 1 inch, cropped hair, very slim build, pale complexion, high cheek bones. Attached is a copy of the passport photograph submitted with his application in 1938...

Jayne looked for the photograph but it was not in the file.

Before leaving this country, Green lived with his mother and sister at 27, Foulsham Close, Ardwick Green, Manchester. Other than his one charge in 1936, I can find no further evidence of any convictions or charges in the criminal and other records both here in this office and in Manchester.

The father, Arthur Green, worked as a painter and decorator in Gloucester until 1939 when he died from Cirrhosis of the Liver brought about by alcoholism. There seems to have been no contact between father and son from 1922.

The mother remained in England at the address in Ardwick Green until 1944, when she died of ovarian cancer. The sister, Trudi Green, married a Jewish businessman, Alfred Esterhazy, moving to 27, Wellington Road, Battersea, and taking her husband's name.

The father was well known in Gloucester until his death. But none of his associates knew of any son called Thomas. On the other hand, the mother retained strong German sympathies until her death. Her internment was considered in 1940 but it was thought at the time she posed no threat to national security. She does not seem to have been aware of the activities of her son.

Signed

Sidney Baines
Inspector

'It's definitely him,' whispered David.

'Perhaps it is. There's still three more notes to look at.'

The first note was short and to the point. Again, it was from Special Branch:

The suspect, Thomas Green, was released on bail into the custody of his sister, Trudi Elizabeth Esterhazy, on 23 December 1945. His whereabouts and movements will be monitored until the date of his trial in February, 1946.

Signed

J Lowndes
Superintendent

'How has he been released? The man's a war criminal, but they've let him out on bail,' said Jayne. 'He should have been kept in Wandsworth until the trial.'

Chapter Sixty-Six

December 22, 1945
Wandsworth Prison, London

'Stand here, 1276843.'

The warder unlocked the door in front of him. Thomas Green trooped into the lime-green interview room at Wandsworth. A captain, from the pips on his shoulder, was facing away from him, reading the notices and posters that had been hastily taped to the wall. 'Careless Talk Costs Lives', 'Prisoners will not be left alone at any time' and 'We're all in this together' shouted their nonsense at him.

Thomas had been marched from his cell that morning without being told what was going on or what was going to happen. He had to obey a series of curt commands.

'Get up, 1276843.'

'Stop there, 1276843.'

'Raise your arms.'

He was searched and then marched to the room.

The captain turned towards him slowly, removing his hat and running his fingers through his hair.

It was Johnnie Hawley. He was here. It had been so long since they had seen each other. In fact, it was nearly eight years since the day they had said goodbye at the camp in Baden Baden.

Johnnie signalled with his eyes not to show any sign of recognition, pointing to a chair next to a table. 'Sit down, Green,' he said roughly.

Thomas sat down at the table in the middle of the room. The warder took his place by the door.

The captain sat down opposite him, taking out a file from his briefcase. 'Now, Green. My name is Captain Hawley. I'm attached to the Intelligence

Corps. I'm here today to clear up some of the misunderstandings and comments you made in your witness statement, given to Captain Hand on the twenty-third of May, 1945.'

All the time he was speaking, the captain was scribbling on his pad making sure the warder couldn't see what he was doing. He showed the note to Thomas: *Just answer my questions.*

'How can I help, sir?' Thomas said slowly.

Captain Hawley looked at the warder standing beside the door. 'You can leave us alone, Warder…?'

'It's Suggs. I'm not supposed to, sir, the governor's instructions.'

The following instruction was phrased as a statement but was actually a command. 'Don't worry, this man isn't going anywhere. Leave us.' And then the charm. 'Get a cup of tea and come back in half an hour. I'll look after him.'

The warder looked at his watch. 'I'm not supposed to, sir.'

'Leave us, Warder Suggs. I'm going to ask this man questions regarding national security. I don't want you or anybody else to hear his answers. If you need to, go and clear it with your governor. If not, have a cup of tea and come back in half an hour.'

The warder looked at his watch again. 'Half an hour, sir?'

'Thirty minutes precisely, Mr Suggs.'

The warder took a final look at his watch before nodding his head. 'I'll be back at eleven, sir.'

Captain Johnnie Hawley ignored his departure. Instead, he reached into his pocket and pulled out a full packet of Woodbines, laying them on the table. 'How did you get in this mess, Tom?'

Thomas eyed the cigarettes lying between them, before reaching over and opening the packet. He took one out and lit it, blowing the smoke up to the tanned ceiling. 'It's a long story, Johnnie.'

Captain Hawley took a folder from the briefcase. 'Don't I know it. I've read all about your adventures here. It makes fascinating reading.'

There it was again – that languid, lazy voice Thomas remembered so well. A voice saying so little but hinting at so much. 'And what about you, how was your war?'

Johnnie laughed. 'Quiet, generally. I was at the Ministry in London for most of it, seconded to Intelligence. Never actually saw any fighting of the guns and bombs and bullets kind at all. Should have done, of course, but I could never bring myself to actually volunteer for anything remotely dangerous. Daddy did well out of it, though. Switched to making uniforms. A lot of uniforms.'

Johnnie took a cigarette out of the packet and lit it, languidly blowing the smoke up to the ceiling.

'But you're in a frightful pickle. Looks like they are going to throw the book at you, index and all.'

'I was just doing what we all believed in before the war, Johnnie.'

'I know. Unfortunately old chap, as it turned out, Germany rather than the bloody Soviets were the enemy.'

'In my place, you would have done exactly the same.'

'Probably.' He blew another long stream of smoke out of his mouth. 'But knowing me, probably not. Luckily, I wasn't in your place.'

'I only went to Germany because you and Mr Mosley sent me.'

'But you stayed, Tom, you were a naughty boy and didn't come back to the party. Sir Oswald was most displeased that you didn't return … still is.'

And then those last words seemed to break Thomas's coolness. He reached over the table. 'You've got to help me, Johnnie, you owe it to me.'

His old friend pulled his arm back. 'We owe you nothing, Tom, remember that.' He took another long tug at his cigarette before stabbing it out in the full ashtray in front of him. 'However, there is a certain group in the government who believe an investigation into an Englishman fighting in the Waffen SS during the war would be frightfully embarrassing. A blot on our copybook, as it were. And now, with the Soviets being *persona non grata* in the West, this sentiment is becoming stronger with each passing day. And there is, of course, a group who shares your beliefs and will help you.'

Thomas eyed him doubtfully. 'What does that mean?'

'It means, me old Waffen SS cock, you will be allowed to wander off and reinvent yourself. Thomas Green is to be no more.' He checked his watch.

'But what about my family, my sister?'

'You can say goodbye to her. And then Thomas Green will no longer exist.'

'How?'

'Look, there are thousands of ex-SS men who would not reveal what they did in the war. There are people that can help, furnish you with a new identity, a new passport and the means to get out of dear old Blighty.'

'And what do I have to do?'

'In return, you have to keep your mouth shut and be available whenever they call on you.'

'What happens if I decide to take my chances and stay in England?'

'Well, Mr Pierrepoint, is always looking for new necks to stretch. A traitor's is as good as any.'

Thomas Green thought for a moment. 'You can guarantee that I will escape all punishment?'

'Nothing is guaranteed, old cock, but the Organisation has already helped thousands. One more should be a doddle.' Johnnie took two cigarettes from the packet, handing one to Thomas. 'The world has changed, but it stays the same. The enemy is not you or the Germans any more, but a certain Mr Stalin in the Kremlin. We've always needed enemies, it helps keep us together. The fear of the bad, herding the sheep together like a well-trained dog.'

He lit both cigarettes. 'Did you kill any Jews?'

Thomas leant backwards. 'Is this where you get me to incriminate myself?' He checked under the table. 'You get me to tell you everything because you're a friend. I gush it all out and suddenly, I'm up before some Jewish beak with an axe to grind on the back of my neck.'

Beneath the table was bare, unpainted wood.

Johnnie held his hands up in mock surrender. 'You are a suspicious soul, aren't you? I suppose living under Hitler does that for you.' He inhaled smoke from his cigarette. 'So, did you?'

'Did I what?'

'Kill any Jews?'

Pausing for a moment to consider his answer, Thomas said, 'I may have done.'

'Well, did you or didn't you?'

Thomas simply nodded slowly without saying a word.

There was a rap on the door, followed by the heavy boots of the warder entering the room.

'Thank you, Warder Suggs. I have one more request for you, Mr Green. Please roll up your sleeve and show me the tattoo?'

'My SS tattoo?'

The captain nodded.

In full view of the warder, Thomas rolled up the rough cloth of his prison shirt to show the round circle with the 'O' in its centre, in dark blue ink on his left arm.

'O is your blood group, is it not?'

Thomas nodded.

'That is sufficient proof you were in the Waffen SS.'

The captain stood up and placed his folder back in the briefcase. 'That will be all, Mr Green. Thank you for your co-operation.'

'When will I hear?'

'About your court case? Soon, I expect. Your solicitor has made an application for bail pending your trial. It's rarely given in treason cases, but because you have been co-operative, the rules may be relaxed this time.' He snapped his briefcase shut. 'Thank you, Warder Suggs, I'm done with this man. I don't think I need to see him again.'

Suggs marched over to Thomas. 'Come on, let's be having you, back to the cells.'

'Johnnie…'

Johnnie smiled. 'I'm sure you mean Captain Hawley, don't you, Mr Green?' He tossed the pack of cigarettes to Thomas. 'Keep your nose clean. We wouldn't like anything to happen to you.'

With those last words, he turned and knocked on the door leading to the outside world.

Thomas felt the hairy hand of the warder on his shoulder.

'Come on, Green, back to the cell.'

Chapter Sixty-Seven

January 7, 1946
Battersea, London

He placed the small case on the step and knocked on the door of the well-kept house. The day was cold, with heavy grey skies louring over London, threatening rain.

His sister opened the door almost immediately. 'Thomas…' Her hand rose to her mouth. Was she crying?

She looked older than he imagined, but that was to be expected. The last time he had seen her was in 1938, when she was just twelve years old. She had been a lanky young girl then, all freckles and pigtails.

Now a young woman stood in front of him. A young woman married to a Jew.

He held out his hand. She knocked it aside and threw her arms around his neck. 'I've missed you so much.'

He tried to hug her back, but he couldn't. He felt nothing at all for this woman. She was just another stranger like so many others he had met over the years.

Like so many he had killed.

She stepped back, realising he was not responding to her warmth.

She gave an embarrassed smile, smoothed down her apron and said, 'Don't stand there on the step, you'd better come in out of the cold.'

'Is he here?'

'Who? Alfred?'

Thomas nodded.

'No, he's at work. Won't be back till after six.'

'I'll come in then.'

He entered the house and took off his hat and coat, keeping the small case. The hallway was warm and inviting, decorated in the latest wallpaper with a heavy walnut cabinet along one wall.

'I'll brew a pot of tea. Come in and sit down.'

He followed her into the sitting room. Again, this was bright and warm. Trudi had created a beautiful home for herself and her Jew husband.

After a few moments, she returned with a tray. 'I've made some salmon paste sandwiches just in case you're feeling peckish. I remember you liked them so much.'

She poured the tea and placed a few of the sandwiches on a separate Doulton plate. The tea was hot and milky, just how he liked it. Had she remembered?

'I can make it a bit stronger if you like.'

'No, it's fine.'

She sat down opposite him. For a moment, there was that awkward silence as both of them wondered what to say next. It was Trudi who spoke first.

'We missed you, Mum and I, when you went to Germany.'

'I sent you cards.'

She smiled. 'Mum loved those. Reminded her of when she was young.' Again a moment of silence before Trudi continued. 'She died two years ago, you know.'

'I heard.'

'Ovarian cancer. It was very painful for her in the end. She had to go into a hospice. Her last words were about you. She loved you so much.'

Thomas didn't say anything, but simply drank his tea. The china cup was too small in his hand; he was used to the tin mugs of prison or the Billy cans of the SS.

'Your court case is in February, isn't it?'

'Yes.'

'Do you want me to go?'

'Why?'

'To support you, a friendly face and all that…'

'No.'

'I could go, Alfred is at work during the day.'

'I won't be there.'

'I don't understand.'

'It's simple. I won't be there. I'm leaving for America, the Organisation has arranged it all.'

'Organisation?'

'You don't need to know.' He pushed the small case he had been carrying towards her with his foot. 'I need you to keep these things for me. I'll come back for them when I'm settled.'

Trudi looked flustered. 'But you can't leave, you're on bail. They'll come after you.'

'They'll never find me, the Organisation will see to that. And I've no desire to spend the rest of my life in some poxy English prison simply for doing what I knew was right.'

'But they say you fought against us…'

Thomas slammed his cup and saucer on to the table. 'That's not true. I fought for Germany against the mongrels of the East.' His tone softened. 'They gave us no choice. We had to kill them before they killed us.'

'But the pictures of the gas chambers – Belsen, Auschwitz…'

'Don't you see, Trudi? It had to be done. They were polluting the blood of the German nation, feeding on us, profiting from our work, our sweat.'

She stared at him for a long time before softly saying, 'Alfred is a Jew.'

He shook his head. 'How could you, Trudi? How could you betray me like that?'

302

She put her cup and saucer on to the table. 'He's a good man, Thomas – a gentle man, and I love him. His parents and sister were arrested in France in 1942. He doesn't know where they are.'

For a moment, the image of the young girl holding the skirts of her mother flashed into his mind. The look on her face as she passed him, as if she knew she were going to die and pitied him for killing her. What right did she have to pity him?

He stood up. 'They're dead, Trudi, like all the rest. It had to be done. I'm proud of what I did.'

He strode out into the hallway to collect his hat and coat.

Trudi came running after him. 'When will I see you again?'

He struggled with his coat. 'When I feel safe, then I'll come back.'

She went to hug him, but he pushed her away. 'Goodbye, Trudi.'

He opened the door and strode out into the smog-laden air of a frozen London.

He didn't look back.

303

Chapter Sixty-Eight

Jayne checked the clock. 16.40. Only twenty minutes before the National Archives closed. 'Let's quickly check the last two documents.'

The first was from Superintendent Lowndes again:

The subject, Thomas Stefan Green, has absconded whilst on police bail despite being under surveillance by Special Branch. His sister claims she has no idea where he has gone. An APB has been issued for his immediate arrest and detention.

Signed

**J Lowndes
Superintendent.**

'That's a bit like closing the stable door after the horse has bolted,' she whispered to David.

Jayne turned over the last document. It was from the office of the Department of Public Prosecutions, Devonshire House, Mayfair Place, Piccadilly, dated 28 July 1948, and addressed to Superintendent Lowndes.

Dear Lowndes,
In view of the continued absence of the suspect, Thomas Stefan Green, the department has decided not to proceed with the prosecution of the said subject as there is little to be gained from pursuing this matter any further. The At-

torney General is in complete agreement with this decision, feeling further prosecution would only serve to embarrass the Ministry and the Government.Please return all your outstanding files on this case to me, as soon as possible. Given the secrecy attached to this matter, it is felt these files should be closed until further notice.

Yours sincerely,

Theobald Rensevair

'They're closing the case. He got away with it,' David said loudly.

'This is intolerable.' The professor had gone red in the face. 'I'm going to report you to the archivist.'

Jayne stood up. 'Please don't bother, we're leaving now.'

'Good riddance. And do take the annoying American with you.'

Now David pushed back his chair. 'Look, you pompous old fool—'

Jayne grabbed his arm. 'David, we have fifteen minutes to get copies of these documents.'

He sat down again, whilst Jayne arranged for the printing using her reader's card. As the clock approached 17.00, the copies were finally ready.

They left the document room at the same time as the professor, both staring at each other.

'Let's grab a coffee in the cafe.'

'Do we need a reader's card and a form in triplicate for that too?'

'Probably, but we're going there anyway. We have a lot to talk about.'

After David had carried the coffee to the table, Jayne took a deep breath. 'We're not there yet.'

'What do you mean? We have a picture matching the one on the American visa. We have him being born in the same place in Manchester. We even have him being an altar boy in the same church.'

'It's strong, but it's not rock-solid proof.' She took another deep breath. 'It's a photograph, so identification is not certain. The man here could just look like him. The church and the birth in Manchester could be coincidental. We have nothing to say that this man, Thomas Green, took the name Thomas Jackson when he arrived in the States. And that Thomas Green is the grandfather of a presidential candidate.'

'It could stand up in a court of law.'

'But would it stand up in the court of public opinion? Remember, Obama had to produce his long-form birth certificate to show he was born in Hawaii. And still forty per cent of Americans didn't believe him. We have to link Thomas Green with Thomas Jackson using incontrovertible proof.'

'Like what?'

'Like a witness who saw him before he went to the States.'

'But we don't have one of those. Plus, even if they were still alive, would they still remember him?'

Jayne smiled. 'His sister would.'

David stared at her.

'We need a computer, quick.'

'Why?'

'The White Pages online. Luckily, his sister's name is not common: Trudi Esterhazy.'

On a nearby table, a young woman was tapping away at her laptop. David leant over and asked, 'Hi there, sorry to bother you.' She looked up. 'But I wonder if we could check something on White Pages? Unfortunately we've forgotten our laptop.' He followed the request with a rather winsome, lost puppy grin.

The girl pushed her glasses back on to the bridge of her nose. 'No, you can't.' The puppy-like grin disappeared. 'But if you give me the name, I will look it up for you.'

Jayne wrote it on a piece of paper for her. 'The surname is Esterhazy and the Christian name is Trudi.'

'Just a moment.' The girl brought up the website and typed in the name. She turned the laptop around. 'You're in luck. There's only one Trudi Esterhazy and she lives not far from here in Battersea.'

Jayne tugged David's sleeve. 'What was the address on the document? Wasn't the address in Battersea?'

David sorted through their photocopies. 'Here it is.'

Jayne looked at it. 'It's the same address. She hasn't moved in seventy years. She must be in her late eighties now.'

The girl held out her hand to David. 'That's two quid, I had to use one of my credits.'

'Pay the woman, David, while I make the call.'

Jayne used her burner phone. The call rang down the line for what seemed like an age and a half. Finally, a woman's voice answered.

'Hello, who is it?'

The voice wasn't weak or feeble as she expected from such an elderly woman. On the contrary, it radiated a quiet strength and confidence.

'Hello there, am I speaking to Mrs Esterhazy?'

'You are. And what do you want with her? If you want to sell her something, she's not interested. Never has been, never will be. Clear?'

'As sunlight, Mrs Esterhazy. Your Christian names are Trudi Elizabeth, am I correct?'

'You are. But who is this calling and what do you want?'

'My name is Jayne Sinclair. I'm a genealogist. That's a person who—'

'I do know what a genealogist is. I'm old, not stupid.'

'Sorry, Mrs Esterhazy. I'm researching the family of a Thomas Green. Are you his sister, by any chance?'

There was a long silence at the end of the phone, before the woman's voice finally answered, less strongly this time. 'What happened to Tom?'

'Mrs Esterhazy, could we come to see you? I know it could be a problem, but we won't take up too much of your time, we promise.'

'And you'll tell me what happened to Tom?'

'We think we know who he is, Mrs Esterhazy, but we're not sure. Perhaps you could help us.'

The voice was abrupt. 'Come tomorrow at eleven to my house. I'll be waiting for you.'

'I know this is an imposition, but could we come earlier?'

'No.'

Then the phone went dead.

'I heard what she said. But we have a meeting with Dan Jackson at one p.m.'

'We'll make it, David. We have to make it.'

Chapter Sixty-Nine

Thursday, April 20, 2017
Somewhere beneath the streets of London

'Sir, the web tracker just reported that an individual with the name David Mercer has applied for a reader's ticket at the National Archives in Kew.'

Got the bitch. She is a persistent woman. He should have been allowed to kill her when he had the chance at Manchester Square. Well, no matter. He would enjoy the moment even more when it finally came on Friday. 'Send a team to the National Archives now. Maintain a watching brief. Do not, I repeat, do not interfere with either suspect. Follow them only.'

'But Mr Blake, Ostransky—'

'Convey the orders, Whitaker.'

'Yes, sir.'

The operative spoke into his headset.

Everything was finally under control. Mrs Sinclair had led them a merry dance. He must congratulate her before he killed her. It would only be polite. 'Our prisoner is in the cells?'

'He is, sir. Stevens reports the man initially had breathing difficulties, a reaction to the drug, but the doctor has seen him and he's now stable.'

'NOTHING IS TO HAPPEN TO HIM,' he screamed. The scar on Blake's face glowed a bright red. He took a deep breath. 'Maintain a twenty-four-hour watch. He is to remain alive, is that clear?'

'Yes, sir.'

Not long now. The real games would begin once the Bilderberg meeting had endorsed Daniel Jackson as the candidate to be President. Blake was ready to implement Project Fear as soon as he was ordered.

They had waited so long for this day.

Too long.

His mouth watered at the prospect of finally achieving what his grandfather had set out to do all those years ago. The man would now be able to rest in peace in his grave at Bit burg cemetery.

The Fourth Reich was within their grasp.

Chapter Seventy

Thursday, April 20, 2017
Near Victoria Station, London

Jayne and David checked into a seedy hotel around Victoria. It was the sort of place where no questions were asked and fewer answers were given.

They paid for three nights, cash in advance. When they counted out the notes in front of him, the Romanian receptionist's eyes visibly widened. Jayne wondered if the owners would ever see the money. Probably not. He hadn't even asked them to sign the hotel register. As far as the hotel's owners were concerned, the room was empty for the night.

Exactly how Jayne wanted it. The less imprint they made, the better.

They entered a dingy room with an old television hogging the corner, and a double bed which had obviously seen better days.

David went to switch on the solitary neon light on the ceiling. Jayne stopped him, walked to the window and looked outside. She'd had a vague feeling they were being followed on the way here. She had looked behind her several times, but nobody was there. Once she had even used the trick of pretending to window shop and looking at the reflection in the glass. But still she saw no one.

She closed the curtains and slumped into an old armchair.

David sat down on the bed. The springs groaned aloud in protest at his weight. 'Still worried about your father?'

She nodded. 'He's not well; high blood pressure. I hope those bastards are giving him his tablets.' For a moment, the image of her father, lost and disori-

311

ented, flashed into her mind. 'If anything happens to him…' She left the sentence unfinished.

David got up from the bed and knelt down in front of her. 'I'm here to help, Jayne. You can't carry the burden on your shoulders all the time.'

She looked down, nodding as she did so.

David lifted her chin gently with the tips of his fingers, leant forward and kissed the edge of her lips. His body moved closer to hers and he kissed her again, harder this time, more urgent. She felt the tension flood from her as she responded to his embrace, throwing herself into the moment.

Gently, he lifted her up off the armchair, wrapped his arm around her shoulders and led her to the bed.

After they made love, Jayne had stayed awake while David slept the sleep of the Gods, his head resting on her chest.

Perhaps this wasn't such a good idea. She understood why it had happened but blamed herself for allowing it. She should have stayed focused on saving her father, not become distracted by a man.

She forced herself to concentrate on the problem. How were they going to get out of this alive? She didn't believe a word of the man's promise to release her father after she had reported her findings. How could they? He had seen his kidnappers. They could no more release him than they could allow her and David to live after they presented the report.

It wasn't until the first rays of dawn fought their way through the smog of London that she had worked out a plan. It was complex, fraught with problems. Many things could go wrong, but it was a chance. The only chance David, herself and her father had of coming out of this alive.

When David woke up, there had been a moment of awkwardness between them which had soon vanished as they went over their notes and prepared for the meeting with Dan Jackson. It was as if nothing had happened. The moment of intimacy between them was a dream that existed only in her imagination.

Perhaps there was more to David Mercer than she suspected; a sensitivity unusual in such a man.

She banished those thoughts from her mind. There was only one thing that mattered now.

Rescuing her father.

While David took a shower, she began to put her plan into action.

Chapter Seventy-One

Friday, April 21, 2017
Battersea, London

They walked to the woman's house from Battersea Park station. On the right was the famous cats and dogs home, with the disused splendour of the power station beyond. The trip from Victoria had taken them less than five minutes once they started but, of course, Southern Rail was late again. Problems with points in Clapham, according to them.

Still, they were early as they turned into a street with a long row of Edwardian terraces on one side and the red brick of elegant apartments on the other.

After David had finished showering, Jayne had been tempted to tell him about the plan but eventually decided to keep it to herself. The element of surprise was too important. Without it, her plan could fail.

'It's just along here, I think.' David interrupted her thoughts. 'Number twenty-seven.'

They stood outside an Edwardian terrace which had obviously seen better days. The concrete steps leading up from the street were dirty and unloved, the paint on the black and white door was peeling in lumps across the surface and the balustrade above the door was in dire need of repair, whilst yellowing lace curtains covered the windows facing the street – to stop people looking in or looking out, Jayne wasn't certain.

They walked up the steps carefully and knocked on the door. There was no bell, only a single, unpolished brass knocker.

No answer.

They knocked again.

Immediately the door opened and a tabby cat slithered out through the small gap. 'Do stop her. She's off down to number forty-three again, and I can't be dealing with more kittens, not any more.'

Jayne hooked the runaway cat expertly under the chest, handing it back to its owner. 'My cat's a tom, I'm afraid. One of the bad boys.'

'Oh, they're easy to handle, just let them out to sow their wild oats and they always come back. But this one...' The older woman nuzzled her face into the tabby's fur. The cat miaowed loudly. 'This one does like to be pregnant. Forever coming back after a night of dreary passion.'

'Why don't you have her neutered?'

'Oh, I couldn't do that. Wouldn't be right, would it?' The elderly woman lifted her glasses and looked Jayne up and down. 'Are you the Sinclair woman who called me?'

'I am.'

'Well, come on in and bring your fancy man with you. He looks like one of those who prowls the town looking for naughty little friends, doesn't he, Tabby?' She nuzzled the cat again, turning away to walk down the hall of the house.

'Actually, my name's David.'

'This one's an American cat. We should be careful of him, shouldn't we, Lady Tabby?' she said to the cat once more.

She vanished into the back room before quickly popping her head around the door. 'Well, don't just stand there, come on in before Lady Tabby escapes again.'

Jayne ushered David across the threshold. The smell of cat pee assaulted their nostrils. The wood of the hall was painted in a dark shade of brown, while the walls sported tan wallpaper that had been popular in the 1930s. On the left, a large dresser in a heavy dark wood stood guard.

Jayne took off her coat and hung it on the stand. 'I hope we're not intruding,' she said as she walked into the back room.

'You are. Intruding, I mean, but it's only to be expected. I thought you would have come sooner.'

A gas fire was burning in an ornate Edwardian fireplace, the only concession to modernity in the whole room. The table was covered in a lacy table-cloth that was yellowing with age. On it were an array of tea cups and a teapot, sugar bowl and milk jug. A vintage television set from the sixties stood forlornly in the corner, protected by another piece of lace. Four pottery ducks flew up the wall, looking for a place to nest. The mantelpiece was covered in bric-a-brac with a sepia-tinted photograph of a round-faced man in place of honour at the centre.

The elderly woman sat down in a chair by the fire, knocking off four skeins of knitting wool from the seat on to the floor.

Jayne took a seat on the small couch opposite. David joined her and the couch immediately sagged beneath their weight. Jayne readjusted her position, sitting on the edge. 'Why do you think we should have come sooner?'

'Well, you said you wanted to talk to me about my brother, didn't you?'

The woman's eyes were a bright eggshell blue. There was a strength here Jayne recognised. This woman had lived through a lot and somehow man-aged to survive. 'We did, Mrs Esterhazy. I should ex-plain. I am a genealogical investigator looking into the family tree of one of my clients.'

'He's an American, is he?'

'Why do you ask that?'

She pointed at David. 'He's a bit of a giveaway.'

316

Jayne smiled. 'I suppose he is.'

'And my brother went to America in 1946. Simples. As they say on the television adverts.'

Despite being in her late eighties, this woman was as smart as a row of guardsmen. *She's playing with us*, thought Jayne. 'My client is American. He believes his grandfather went to America in 1946, using a different name than the—'

'The one he was born with.' The woman finished Jayne's sentence. 'And you want to know why?'

Jayne nodded.

'Why?'

Jayne nodded again.

'I meant, why should I tell you?'

Jayne paused for a moment. Only the truth would work with this woman. 'My client is a potential candidate for the Presidency of the United States. He needs to know where he came from.'

'What's it to me? I have nothing to do with America or their elections. I haven't even voted in a British election since' – she thought for a moment – 'since that chap Wilson was elected in 1964. Couldn't stand Douglas-Home. The man had no top lip.' The cat on her lap purred in agreement.

David interrupted, trying to use his charm. 'Mrs Esterhazy – can I call you Trudi?'

'No, young man, you may not.'

David went quiet, his lips flapping like a fish out of water.

Jayne tried a different tack. 'My client is possibly your great-nephew. Doesn't that mean anything? You could meet a close relative; your brother's only grandson.'

A small smile appeared on the woman's lips. 'If – and it's a big if – the man you are looking for was my brother, then I haven't heard a sound or peep out of

317

him or his family since they left England. Why would I want to meet them now? For me, they have never existed. Why should they trouble my existence now?'

Jayne noted a hint of bitterness creeping into the woman's voice. She was angry. A restrained anger, kept under tight control, but it was there. 'The lack of contact was nothing to do with your great-nephew. Both his father and grandfather were difficult, uncommunicative men. He is different, though. He wants to discover his family. A family from whom, through no fault of his own, he has been separated for far too long.'

Jayne watched as the woman considered this, before finally rejecting it. 'I'm getting on now. What do I need with new relatives? I have lived alone since my husband died in 1963. Where were these relatives when he passed away from cancer? Nursed him, I did, night and day, on my own. They were nowhere to be found.'

Jayne breathed out. 'I know how you feel. My own father has early onset Alzheimer's. Sometimes he becomes confused and angry when he can't remember things or when he can't express what he wants to say. But despite this, he's found himself a new woman. A kind, thoughtful woman, who will help him live life to the fullest, despite his illness. Somebody to spend the rest of his days on earth with.'

'What do I need with a man at my age?'

'You need nobody, Mrs Esterhazy.' Jayne pointed to the room and the house. 'You've managed by yourself for so long.' Here she paused, finally saying, 'But people need you. My client needs you. My father needs you.' Jayne took a deep breath. 'I need you.'

The woman stared into mid-air. And then she started to speak as if someone was standing close to her. 'I've kept the secret too long, Rolf, it's time they knew.'

Then she cocked her head as if listening to an answer.

She nodded and started to rise from the chair. Jayne rushed forward to help her up. 'Thank you, Mrs Sinclair. You have to help me up the stairs, I have something to show you. He can stay here, though. I don't like him; shifty eyes.'

David opened his mouth to speak and then closed it once again.

'This way, Mrs Sinclair. It's in a chest upstairs. I've kept it ever since the night he left all those years ago.'

Chapter Seventy-Two

Friday, April 21, 2017
Battersea, London

It was already 12.43 when Jayne finally descended the stairs, a deep frown creasing her forehead. 'Come on, we've got no time to lose.'

David was waiting for her in the hallway, checking his watch constantly. 'Did you get the proof?'

She nodded.

'What is it?'

Jayne brushed past him to get her bag from the back room. She placed the object that the old lady had given her into it. Then she walked over to the chair beside the fireplace and began searching it, as if she had left something there before they both went upstairs.

'Where is she?'

'Sleeping. She's tired.' Jayne continued to search, eventually finding what she was looking for hidden amongst the detritus on the mantelpiece. She put it in the bag without David seeing.

'Does it link Thomas Green with Thomas Jackson?'

'I think it does. But there's no time to explain.' She pointed to the clock above the mantelpiece. It chimed 12.45 with a single ring.

'Shit. Shit. Shit.'

'Now do you want me to waste the next hour telling you, or would you prefer to hear about it when I tell Dan Jackson?'

David looked at his watch. 12.47 now. The clock was running late. 'Let's go, we have to find a taxi. Can you at least tell me a short version on the journey?'

She bustled past him. 'I'll try, but I will tell you one thing…'

'What's that?' he said, following her.

'It's not a story you're going to want to hear.'

Chapter Seventy-Three

Friday, April 21, 2017
Hilton on the Park, London

They had rushed across London in their black taxi, fighting with the traffic all the way. Luckily, the cabbie was a seasoned warrior, weaving in and out of the long lines of cars and buses with all the grace and power of a knight of the road.

Jayne told David the basics of what Mrs Esterhazy had shown her. Afterwards, they had both sat in silence as the driver worked his way through the traffic.

Had she got it right? Were there any mistakes in her logic? Had she covered all her bases? Was there a flaw in her research?

Doubts assailed her with every swerve of the cab as it thrust and parried its way through the streets of London.

How was she going to rescue her father? The answer was… she didn't know. She had made all the arrangements, the rest was left to chance. It was a risk, she knew, but a risk she had to take. He was going to die unless she made the right calls.

She took a deep breath, hearing the brakes of the cab squeal as it charged up to the entrance of the hotel.

They ran through the lobby to the lift, David pressing the buttons continually in a vain attempt to make it arrive more quickly.

It didn't.

Jayne looked up at the numbers slowly counting down in the lights above the lift. Why were lifts always synchronised when you were in a hurry, descending together as if holding hands?

322

The doors opened eventually, people streamed out and Jayne and David rushed in, pressing the button for the Jackson's suite on the 28th floor. The doors closed and the lift rose imperceptibly, the numbers slowly lighting up one at a time.

Had she got it right? Had they brought her father? Were her guesses correct? Would she survive this meeting? Or would the man with the scar be there too?

The numbers lit up one after the other: 12. 13. 14. 15.

David spoke. 'Good luck, Jayne.'

What a strange thing to say. She had assessed the risks, analysed the evidence, checked the research. She must have the right answer.

If she wasn't right, then she, her father and David would be dead in thirty minutes, the man with the scar standing over their inert bodies.

The lift doors opened.

They stepped out into a short corridor with a door at either end. A small sign above the one on the left indicated it was the Presidential Suite. They walked towards it and David rang the bell.

Jayne took one more deep breath.

The door was opened by a butler dressed in the traditional black uniform. 'Mr and Mrs Jackson have been expecting you.'

After checking out the living area of the suite, Jayne sat down on a couch on the right. The Presidential Suite was large, the sitting room bigger than her whole house in Manchester. Two four-seater sofas faced each other with an expansive coffee table in between.

The hazy afternoon sunlight streamed in through two large picture windows. The views were of Hyde Park and a panorama of London beyond. On another day and at another time, Jayne would have loved to have stayed here, to enjoy sitting in front of the windows watching the theatre of London play out beneath her feet.

But this was not the day, nor the time.

David paced up and down in front of her. The butler who had let them in stood to one side, waiting for instructions.

The door on the left opened.

Chapter Seventy-Four

Friday, April 21, 2017
Hilton on the Park, London

'You look surprised, David.'

'I… you… You're dead…'

'I can assure you I am very much alive.' Jack Wayne pinched his skin. 'See, flesh and blood.' He turned to Jayne. 'You, however, Mrs Sinclair, do not look surprised at all.'

'I'm happy to see you again, Mr Wayne. And no, I'm not surprised by your resurrection. Only three people other than Dan Jackson knew the exact location of the meeting in the restaurant. Myself, David and you. If I didn't reveal it, and David didn't reveal it, then the only person who could have done so was you.'

'When did you first know, Mrs Sinclair?'

'I first suspected when I was washing my hands of your blood in the church. The texture was wrong, too sticky, and the smell was most definitely wrong.'

'Yes, you weren't supposed to act so quickly.' He touched his chest. 'I performed the act of being dead quite well, though. Doing nothing is far more difficult than I thought.'

'An Oscar-winning performance, Mr Wayne,' said Dan Jackson as he entered the room. 'You can leave us, Hordern.'

'Yes, sir.' The butler departed as silently as a ghost.

Dan Jackson held his arms out wide. 'We are so sorry for the little piece of theatre, Mrs Sinclair. My wife felt you needed to be encouraged to work quickly. That you would leave no stone unturned if you felt somebody had died protecting you.'

Catherine Jackson coughed. 'We read your file, Mrs Sinclair. Your partner who died gave me the idea. I do apologise.'

'But that means, all the shots... the running through London...' spluttered David.

'All a charade. Devised to keep us guessing, keep us working for them,' Jayne confirmed.

'Speed was of the essence,' said Dan Jackson, smiling his practiced politician's smile.

'But one thing bothers me, Mr Jackson. Why kidnap my father? I was already working on the case, finding your answer. There was no need.'

Dan Jackson's mouth opened. 'I... I don't know what you mean, Mrs Sinclair. I didn't order anything of the sort.' He looked to his wife.

She laid her hand on her husband's arm but looked at Jayne as she spoke. 'Unfortunately, one of our operatives was a little too zealous in the performance of his duties. But once the action was taken, we realised the positive aspects. It gave us extra insurance, if you like, to ensure there would be no...' she searched for the word, 'no recalcitrance on your part when presenting the research. We couldn't risk you going to the press with your findings before we had seen them.'

Jayne's tone changed. 'Where is he?'

'Nearby. As soon as you have told us what you found out, he will be brought here.'

'If you have hurt one hair on his head, you will pay, Mrs Jackson. I will kill you, do I make myself clear?'

Dan Jackson turned to his wife. 'What's going on, dear? What father? Who has been kidnapped?'

'Don't you worry, dear. Myself and Mrs Sinclair are simply discovering who holds all the cards in this game. I do believe I've just trumped her.' She stared at Jayne. 'He will be brought here when you have revealed what you discovered, Mrs Sinclair. I suggest you start now.' She checked the clock on the wall. 'It is one fifteen. I want to be finished by two p.m. so we can meet the Bilderberg group at four. A few selected journalists have been flown in from the States; we want to make the announcement of my husband's candidacy at six p.m. this evening. As you can imagine, we are working to a rather tight deadline.'

'If you want to see your father again, Mrs Sinclair, it's time to begin,' the once-dead Jack Wayne said softly.

Chapter Seventy-Five

Friday, April 21, 2017
Hilton on the Park, London

Jayne looked at the clock herself. 'I will begin at the beginning, Mr Jackson. Your grandfather was a murderer. A man who took pleasure in pain and torture. A man who betrayed his nation during a time of war. A man who murdered Jews in the Krakow ghetto. A man who led death squads, murdering Jews in the villages of Poland.'

'What? It can't be. My grandfather was an elderly man, a quiet man who kept himself to himself and wouldn't hurt a flea.'

'Your proof, Mrs Sinclair?' said Catherine Jackson.

'Your grandfather's real name was Thomas Stefan Green. He was born to a German mother and a British father in 1919 in Manchester, England. He probably joined the British Union of Fascists in the mid-1930s, but he was definitely living in Germany by 1938.'

Dan Jackson interrupted her telling of the story. 'How do you know all this?'

'He gave an interview to the British Army in the time after he was arrested in 1945, admitting almost everything.'

She brought out the photocopies from the transcript of the interview. 'He joined the Waffen SS, fought in Poland, then he was injured before joining the British Free Corps.'

'British Free Corps?' asked Dan Jackson.

'A group of mainly British Prisoners of War whom the Germans managed to con into joining their army and becoming part of the SS.'

'That's impossible, no British people fought for the Nazis.'

'Oh, but they did, Mr Jackson.'

'Let her finish, dear.'

Jayne could see the bright red nails of Catherine Jackson's fingers dig into her husband's arm. He went quiet.

From her bag, Jayne produced the picture of Thomas Green in his Waffen SS uniform with the British flag prominently displayed on the sleeve. 'This is your grandfather as a member of the British Free Corps.'

Dan Jackson stared at the photograph.

His wife reached across and picked it up. 'There is a startling resemblance, as you say. But where is the proof that this man, this Thomas Green, is actually my husband's grandfather?'

Jayne reached into her bag once again and produced the picture given to her in the restaurant of a young Thomas Green, dressed in shirt and shorts, smiling happily. 'If you compare the two, the faces are similar.' She turned the picture over. 'You were puzzled why the initials were HJ and not TJ written on the back.'

Dan Jackson frowned. 'Why would they get my grandfather's initial wrong?'

'They didn't. HJ stands for *Hitler Jugend*. Your grandfather was a member of the Hitler Youth, Mr Jackson.'

Dan Jackson picked up the picture as if seeing it for the first time. 'It can't be… He can't be.'

Catherine Jackson looked over his shoulder. 'There is a similarity between the two pictures, Mrs Sinclair, but nothing more. These could be two different people. And my husband will deny the man in either photograph is his grandfather. "More fake news", I believe the headline will read.'

Jayne breathed out. 'There is more.' She reached into her bag for the third time and pulled out a black book. 'David and I visited your great-aunt this morning.'

'What?'

'You grandfather had a sister, Mr Jackson. She is still alive and living in London.'

'A sister? He didn't tell me about any relatives. He said they all died in the war.'

'He left this album with her. You told me your grandfather was proud of what he did in the war. This album shows what he was proud of.' She handed over the black leather album.

'That's what Mrs Esterhazy gave you,' said David.

Dan Jackson opened it. A faded yellow ribbon with brown scorch marks streaked across the surface slipped out of the pages and fell to the floor. He picked it up, looked at it for a second and then threw it into the waste bin beside the coffee table.

The first two pages were pictures of street scenes in Germany, captioned 'Baden Baden' and 'Stuttgart'. The next three pages showed a young, pretty blonde girl with long braids down her back. She smiled shyly at the camera, the freckles across her nose looking like dark spots. There was only one word beneath each photo: 'Ilse'.

The following photo showed a young man in uniform. It was the same young man as in the Hitler Youth picture, but his shoulders were broader and he was more muscular, the hair cropped short in a military crew cut.

'It is the next picture you should look at.'

Dan Jackson turned the page. The picture was darker and more blurred. A group of men and women were lined up, a German officer inspecting them. The men were aged and afraid, all wearing cloth caps and mufflers. On the page after, the men

330

and women had been separated into two smaller groups. Three German soldiers were watching and smiling.

'It goes on.'

The next picture showed a line of younger men against a wall. Some were looking down, others staring defiantly into the camera.

'I don't want to look,' said Dan Jackson. His wife reached over and turned the page of the album for him.

The picture stuck inside showed the same group of men and the same wall. But they were spread across the ground now, their bodies twisted into unnatural shapes. One arm pointed towards the sky, a dirty finger extended upwards.

Dan Jackson looked away.

'This album was given by Thomas Green to his sister the night before he left for America. She never heard from him again. She kept the album, hoping one day he would come back to collect it. He never did. Thomas Green left London for America the same day as your grandfather.'

Dan Jackson said nothing, staring at the picture of the dead men lying against the wall.

A throaty laugh came from Mrs Jackson. 'Well done, Mrs Sinclair. I thought I had produced a piece of theatre with my friend Jack Wayne, but you have excelled.'

She clapped her hands slowly, mimicking applause. 'There is one thing I am missing, though, in all this…' She indicated the pictures and album lying on the table. 'Where is the proof? How do we know for certain that this man, Thomas Stefan Green, is my husband's grandfather? They may have simply sailed on the same ship together when they went to America. To my knowledge, that is not a crime in my country.'

'You are forgetting, Mrs Jackson, that your husband's grandfather used a false name and a false identity to enter the United States.'

'An honest mistake on the part of the immigration officer, nothing more.'

'And the pictures?'

Catherine Jackson picked one up. 'A vague similarity, but again, nothing more. They could be of anybody.'

Jayne checked the clock. 'And the album?'

Catherine Jackson sighed. 'Don't you know, Mrs Sinclair, that over eight thousand SS men were allowed into the States after the war? I believe an additional three thousand were allowed to settle in the United Kingdom. This album could have come from any of them. In fact, it could have come from your own grandfather. What did he do in the war, Mrs Sinclair?'

'I don't know. He never talked about it.'

'See what I mean? Neither did my husband's grandfather. He was a kind, quiet man, who never talked about the war or what he did in it.'

Dan Jackson's eyes lit up. 'That's him, that's how I remember him.'

Jayne checked the clock once again. 'There is one piece of proof you won't be able to refute, Mrs Jackson.'

Catherine Jackson laughed. 'And what is that, Mrs Sinclair, more pictures?'

'No. This.' Jayne reached once more into her bag and produced a well-used tortoiseshell hairbrush, clogged with long strands of grey hair, which she placed carefully on the table close to the photo album.

Catherine Jackson started to laugh loudly, followed by her husband and Jack Wayne. 'Mrs Sinclair, you call this proof?'

Jayne spoke quietly and directly to Dan Jackson. 'I took this from the mantelpiece of Mrs Trudi Esterhazy this morning. She was your grandfather's sister.'

Catherine Jackson interrupted. 'This has nothing to do with my husband.'

Her husband raised his arm to stop her speaking. 'Go on.'

'A simple DNA test on the hair on the brush will show she is your great-aunt, Mr Jackson. And that your grandfather, her brother, was a murderer.'

Chapter Seventy-Six

Friday, April 21, 2017
Hilton on the Park, London

Jayne heard another slow handclap.

'You have surprised me, Mrs Sinclair. Far more enterprising and determined than your file indicated.' Catherine Jackson swept all the pictures, the documents and the hairbrush off the table.

'Shame you won't be able to take credit for a brilliant piece of research. An even greater shame you have now condemned yourself, your father and David to a rather ignominious death.' A smug smile spread across Jack Wayne's face as he finished the sentence.

David got up from the sofa. 'Hey, this has nothing to with me. I only tagged along. Jack, you know me, I'm just a young guy who got caught up in something he doesn't understand.'

'Too late, I'm afraid, David.'

'But you and my father—'

'I'm sorry. I'll make it up to him. I'll tell him you died bravely, his name your last words. He'll love it, and you, even more.'

Dan Jackson finally woke up from his dream. He leant over and picked up the brush from the floor. 'Catherine, what's going on? What are you saying? You want to kill these people?'

Again, the hand touched his arm. 'It can't be helped, dear.'

He shook his head. 'I don't understand... I can't let you do this.'

'Dan, you've listened to me and obeyed me your whole life, why act differently now? It's for the best. I know what I'm doing.' 'But this is murder...I...I can't allow you to murder somebody.'

Her voice changed, becoming harder and more commanding. 'Dan, don't spoil it. My advice has made you the man, the success you are. Who told you to create the company and buy the communication patent? Who told you to invest in Facebook? Who wiped your nose when you screwed up? Who got rid of the idiots who were destroying your company? Who cleared up the mess after your little secretary killed herself? Who put you in the position where you could be the next President of the United States? Don't screw it up now. Just do as you're told. Always do as you're told.'

Dan Jackson went quiet, staring at the hairbrush in his hand. He sat still for a moment, before slowly rising and walking towards the door.

'Stop,' Catherine ordered. 'You'd better stay here and watch this. I want you to be complicit in what I'm about to do. Nothing is going to stop us now.' She nodded at Jack Wayne.

He got up and opened the door to the bedroom. Jayne's father was standing in the doorway, tape covering his mouth and the man with the scar holding a gun next to his head.

'Dad,' Jayne shouted, getting up from her seat and advancing towards him.

'I wouldn't go any further if I were you, Mrs Sinclair.'

The barrel of the revolver pressed closer to her father's temple and shoved his head sideways.

Jayne stopped dead, raising her hands.

'It's over, Mrs Sinclair. Return to your seat if you please.'

'Dad, are you okay?'

Her father nodded, eyes staring at her, his body trembling.

'Return to your seat.'

Jayne did as she was told.

'As you can see, not a white hair on your father's head has been touched. Unfortunately, this will no longer continue. Blake here will arrange an accident for all three of you. A terrible car crash. The bodies incinerated in the accident, slowing down the identification.'

'Catherine, you can't—'

'I told you not to speak, Daniel. You are to listen and be complicit, understand?'

Her husband looked down at the ground.

'And this trash,' she pointed to the documents and pictures on the ground, 'only the photographs give us a minor problem. They will be removed from the National Archives today. As for my husband's great-aunt...' She thought for a moment. 'A burglary, Blake. An elderly woman battered to death by a heartless intruder, the place ransacked in the search for valuables. The *Evening Standard* will love it.'

'Why didn't you remove all the evidence earlier?' asked Jayne.

Catherine Jackson shrugged her elegant shoulders. 'Why does stuff not get done? Incompetence? Slackness? The belief nobody will ever find out? But you did all the work for us, Mrs Sinclair. Now we can remove all the evidence before my husband begins his campaign. Thank you for your help.'

Jayne looked across at Dan Jackson, standing there, the hairbrush still in his hand. 'Is he still going to run?'

As she spoke, the noise of a police siren drifted into the room from the road beside Hyde Park.

Catherine Jackson listened for a moment, then ignored it.

'My husband will do what he is told, as he always has done. And now he is complicit in your murder, Mrs Sinclair. I think that is even greater encouragement to obey orders, don't you?'

336

For a moment, Dan Jackson looked up and stared at his wife, before slowly lowering his head.

She checked her watch and stood up. 'Time is running out, we must prepare for the meeting. Daniel, come with me.'

He hesitated for a moment before turning to follow her.

Catherine Jackson smiled indulgently at him. 'You will make a great President.' She reached out to touch his cheek. 'And I will make an even better one. Blake, make the arrangements.'

'Yes, madam.' The man with the scar spoke for the first time.

'And keep the Führer informed. His plan was successful, as we always knew it would be.'

Outside, the sound of more police sirens, the slamming of doors, voices shouting.

'One last question…' Jayne raised her voice.

Catherine Jackson stopped and stared at her.

'Why? Why are you doing all this?'

'I would have thought it was obvious, Mrs Sinclair. Power.' She glanced at the clock. 'We have been working for this day for the last seventy years. My father brought Thomas Green and thousands of his kind to America. We had to shelter them from the communists and those who would have their revenge for the work they had been doing. Righteous work.'

'Killing Jews, murdering homosexuals, plunging Europe into chaos?'

'As I said, righteous work. Unfortunately, the first Führer left the work undone. The conditions are ripe now for it to be finished. It's time to get rid of the Reds and the Jews, and when we do, the world will rejoice. We will see a new age – the Fourth Reich, the age of Aquarius, where the world will be ruled by competent men and women. Democracy is such an inefficient system of government, Mrs Sinclair. It

337

allows the poor and the stupid and the sheep to elect our leaders. When those who are best able to lead are left by the wayside, looking on as the world goes to ruin – the bankers and the Jews ravaging it for their own private profit.'

'But what if—'

'I'm so sorry, Mrs Sinclair, I would love to explain it all to you but we do not have time. Please understand there is a plan, there has always been a plan. Make the arrangements, Blake.'

Catherine turned to go, and as she did Dan Jackson straightened, pulled back his shoulders and clenched his jaw. 'I'm not going anywhere, Catherine,' he shouted before flinging the hairbrush in his hand directly at Blake's good eye. The revolver in the man's hand lifted slightly and a loud shot echoed around the room.

Jayne's father fell to the floor.

Dan Jackson charged into Blake like a linebacker taking out a quarterback, catching him square in the chest with his swinging right arm. Both collapsed in a heap on the floor.

David swung the hard edge of his hand at the spot on Jack Wayne's neck below the ear, where his jawline joined the neck. The man lost consciousness before he had time to reach for the gun in the holster in his jacket.

Jayne ran to her father. There was the stench of cordite all around. Blood poured from the top of his head and dripped down his face.

'Dad, Dad.' She cradled him in her arms, lifting him off the floor. He looked dazed, confused. She checked the wound. Black gunshot residue covered his white hair and mixed with the flowing blood.

He opened his eyes. 'Can see your lips move, lass, but can't hear a thing except ringing.' He spoke loudly, almost shouting.

David had moved round to help Dan Jackson, kicking Blake twice to the side of the head in quick succession.

Jayne looked back at Catherine Jackson, who was searching through her bag, looking for her gun. A wave of anger shook her body. She laid her father's head back on the ground and roared.

Catherine Jackson's eyes flashed up to Jayne whilst her hands kept searching in the bag.

Outside, the sound of heavy boots on the carpeted corridor, more shouts, commands and then the wood around the door began splintering.

Jayne launched herself at Catherine Jackson just as her hand was raised out of the bag, holding something metal.

Another loud noise, a strong smell of cordite and Jayne's body crashed into something softer, something female.

They both went down. Jayne's arm came up and the point of her elbow struck down across Catherine Jackson's nose. The shockwave thrilled up her arm as she struck the bone between Catherine's eyes.

She leveraged her body against the woman beneath her, leaning away and striking down again with the point of her elbow.

Her police instructor had told her long ago, 'In a fight, use everything you have, but especially use your anger.'

She leant back once more and struck down again, this time with her fist. The knuckles struck the point of Catherine Jackson's jaw and Jayne heard a snap. The body beneath her went limp. She struck down again. And again.

Within seconds, she found herself lifted from the inert body. She struck out again, catching whoever was holding her across the head. Two strong arms encircled her and lifted her off the floor.

A voice, David's voice, spoke in her ear. 'It's okay, Jayne, it's over. '

She stopped struggling. Around her an army of men in blue, wearing stab vests with the reflective letters for POLICE on the front and back, were surrounding Blake, Wayne and Dan Jackson.

Another policeman was helping her father to his feet, holding a white bandage to the flesh wound on his head. Her father was shouting: 'You'll have to speak louder. Can't hear a thing. Gunshot near my ear.'

The policeman was nodding and pointing to the chair, indicating her father should sit down.

Jayne found her feet being placed on the floor, David's arms no longer wrapped around her.

More police came into the suite, escorting three other men. 'We found these men in the lobby. All armed, sir.'

The lead officer had his back to her. 'Take them through to the bedroom and hold them there until we can get these thugs down the nick.'

The officer turned back to her and took off his soft cap. A smiling Harry Rimmer brushed his fingers through his chestnut hair and winked at Jayne.

'You took your time coming.'

Harry looked around the Presidential Suite of the hotel. 'Well, Jayne, you've really managed to stir the shit this time, haven't you?'

'If you had arrived on time, this would have been a lot easier.

'Better late than never Jayne.'

'But better never late,' her father shouted. 'I can hear again.'

At her feet, Catherine Jackson let out a loud groan. Jayne gave her a sharp kick in the groin. 'Quiet, bitch.'

340

Chapter Seventy-Seven

Tuesday, April 25, 2017
Heathrow Airport, London

He relaxed back in his business-class seat. The air marshal had given him the once-over as soon as he boarded the plane, the bulge beneath his jacket shouting, 'I'm the security on the plane, look at me.'

He had been surprised that there was a second one in economy too. They were taking security seriously these days.

Offering him a glass of champagne, the stewardess smiled as he said, '*Toda raba.*'

God, it was good to speak Hebrew again after all these years in America. Buying new clothes on his last day in London had been an experience too. Gone were the preppie ties and Brooks Brothers jackets with their starched shirts. Now it was something far more comfortable and relaxed. A safari jacket and jeans. It felt wonderful.

The engines roared as the El-Al plane taxied away from the boarding gate. It had been so long since he had gone home. All those years he had been in America, placed with a family and brought up the American way. If he never saw another hamburger in his life, he would be happy.

He regretted telling Jayne his little white lie. He had always known he was adopted; the American family had been honest with him from the beginning.

When he was eighteen he had returned to Israel to meet his real mother. It was on this trip that he had been recruited by Mossad. After only a few weeks training in tradecraft and martial arts, they had given him the job of infiltrating a Nazi cell in America. He was glad the mission was finally completed.

They had been stopped for now, but they would come back.

It had been hard not to blow his cover with Jayne. He had enjoyed working with her. For a moment, his mind danced back to the night they had spent together in the dingy hotel near Victoria. A smile crossed his face. She was a very special woman. He loved her intensity and passion and, if he were honest, it also frightened him a little.

One day, he would see her again – perhaps in the future, when the work was finished.

He pulled back the sleeve of his jacket to reveal the blue number tattooed on his arm. His grandfather's number from Auschwitz, etched there so he would never forget.

He finished his champagne and smiled at the stewardess as she topped up his glass. The air marshal glared at him.

He was sure he would meet his genealogist again. Perhaps he would let her know the truth.

One day, but not today.

Today, he was going home and that was all that mattered.

Chapter Seventy-Eight

Tuesday, April 25, 2017
Euston Station, London

Jayne and her father relaxed in their seats as the 10.20 train left for Manchester.

'I've never taken First Class before, lass. I could get used to this very easily.'

'For once let's treat ourselves, Dad. After what you went through, it's the least you deserve. How's the hearing?'

He cupped his hand around his ear, 'What?'

'How's the—?'

A large smile appeared on his face. 'Just kidding, lass. It's fine. Doctor says it will gradually come back.' A look of panic flashed into his eyes as he looked around him. 'Where's the present?'

'Calm down. I put it on the rack.' Jayne pointed upwards.

'Vera would kill me if I lost it.'

'I'd kill you if you lost it. What are you doing about the wedding?'

'Vera talked to the vicar and we're moving it back a week. The reception is at the home, so Matron's okay. Looks like you're going to have to be best man.'

'I thought I was giving you away.'

'That too. You've got an awful lot to do on our wedding day.'

'Has Vera forgiven me for lying to her?'

'Of course she has. She knows you were just doing it for me. When that copper—'

'Harry Rimmer?'

'That's him. When he rang her from London to ask about the policemen, well, she knew then I was in trouble.' He took her hand. 'No more excitement, lass. Not for a while, at least. I don't think I can handle it any more.'

'No more excitement, Dad, promise. I'll just live a boring old life from now on.'

'That Harry Rimmer, he said you did very well. Didn't think he could do it himself.'

Jayne stared out of the window as the beauty of England whizzed by at one hundred miles an hour. She had done well, hadn't she? For a short moment, the burden of Dave Gilmour's death was lifted from her shoulders. They had all said it wasn't her fault, but she hadn't believed them. Now, she knew that she would have prevented it if she could. Sometimes, stupid stuff happens through nobody's fault except the criminal's. Her plan had worked: calling the police that morning hadn't been easy, and convincing Harry was difficult. But the kidnap of her father had been crucial. The police could not ignore such a crime.

'Let's forget about it, Dad. It's over now.' She patted his hand. 'And I've got a new case. A TV presenter.'

'Is he famous?'

'It's a she, and she is.' Jayne leant over and whispered the name in his ear.

'Ooh, I like her. Vera will be very happy. She watches her whenever she comes on, proper funny she is.'

'But I'm not starting it until after the wedding, it's time you two were hitched.'

'Thank you, lass. Now, that begs the question, what are you going to do?'

'About?'

'About Paul?'

She took a deep breath. 'It's over, Dad. We'll go our separate ways.'

'Whatever's right for you, lass, you know that's what I've always wanted.'

'I know.' It was her turn to take his hand. 'Dad, did you know my real father?'

He nodded. 'I did, lass. He wasn't a happy man. Your mother and him just didn't get on.'

'I often wonder what happened, why he left.'

'You could find out.'

'You wouldn't be upset?'

'Of course not, lass, it's your family, you have to know where you came from.'

'Perhaps I will look for him. But not yet. I've got to get you married off first.'

Her father tilted his head and stared at her, a mile crossing his lips,'One last important thing, lass.'

'What's that, dad?'

'I think I prefer you as a blonde. Brunette's definitely not your colour.'

If you enjoyed reading this Jayne Sinclair genealogical mystery, please consider leaving a short review on Amazon. It will help other readers know how much you enjoyed the book.

Other books in the Jayne Sinclair Series

The Irish Inheritance

When an adopted American businessman dying with cancer asks her to investigate his background, it opens up a world of intrigue and forgotten secrets for Jayne Sinclair, genealogical investigator.

She only has two clues: a book and an old photograph. Can she find out the truth before he dies?

The Somme Legacy

Who is the real heir to the Lappiter millions? This is the problem facing genealogical investigator, Jayne Sinclair.

Her quest leads to a secret buried in the trenches of World War One for over 100 years. And a race against time to discover the truth of the Somme Legacy.